WAS I EVER FREE

NAOMI LOUD

CONTENT WARNING

This is a dark romance and may contain triggering situations such as drug addiction, needles, forced drug use, murder, maiming, torture, gore, waterboarding, parental abuse, physical abuse, childhood neglect, incest (off page), rape (off page), religious trauma, pet play, anal play, blood play, breeding kink, voyeurism, nightmares, and explicit sexual situations for 18+.

AUTHOR'S NOTE

Lucy's speech pattern fluctuates with her emotional well-being. The more flustered or distressed she is the more she reverts back to her old pattern of speech. This is completely intentional and not an editing issue.

For my readers; look how far we've come.

PROLOGUE

BASTIAN

Past

I was in mid-conversation with you, in my thirties, standing in the small kitchen of the house I built for us when I blinked and I was back here. Back to being eighteen and so doped up that I can't even make out who I am or if I'm dead or alive.

I crack an eyelid.

Alive it seems.

Where did all this time go?

The now familiar throb in my thigh where the Narcan was jabbed in a muscle can only mean one thing.

I was overdosing.

Wasn't my first. Third in less than a year, to be precise. May not be my last either. Not when heroin is like unfiltered freedom in a needle. Some say it's better than an orgasm. But that doesn't even begin to describe it. It's more like a rolling wave of warmth, starting at the tip of your toes all the way to the top of your head. The feeling is so euphoric that it releases you from all your problems. It unshackles you from the weight of life itself. The French call orgasms—*la petite mort*—the little death. Whoever came up with that name never shot up a day in their life, or else they'd be waxing poetic to the gods of opioids.

Even with the help of Narcan, a medication that reverses the effects of opiates, I'm still foggy—just not dying. Exhaustion is a heavy weight trying to pull me back under. I could let it take me. Maybe I should.

It's too loud in here.

I crack the other eyelid.

My vision is unfocused. Still, I recognize my friend Damien hovering over me, shaking my shoulders and yelling something I can't be bothered to understand. I swat him away.

"I'm fine," I rasp.

I pull myself up from the ratty couch I was sprawled on and situate myself. The scent of unwashed bodies lingers in the air. I'm still in Damien's basement. Old brown vinyl walls, yellowing posters hanging on for dear life, an orange shaggy carpet—most likely three decades old—and smoke so thick I could chew on it. Some of our friends are scattered around—most of them too lost to their own highs to have noticed my own plight.

"Dude, I almost called an ambulance this time, your lips were turning blue," he says, chewing on his own bloodied and cracked lip, pupils so wide I can barely see the brown of his eyes. Luckily, this idiot is into stimulants and was wide awake when I began to overdose. Most likely for days now.

Shooting him a look of disdain, I try to stand up but my body isn't cooperating, so I slump back onto the couch and rest my head behind me, closing my eyes.

He tries to speak again but I don't let him.

"Fuck off, Damien."

He falls silent. I can feel him linger for a few seconds, then I hear his soft footfalls move across the carpet. The music grows louder. He must have turned up the volume on the old stereo he stole from his aunt. Him settling on the couch beside me is the last thing I remember before I'm swept up on the wings of oblivion, disappearing for a little while longer.

I'M STANDING at the corner of Chesterfield and King, in the heart of Noxport's less desirable neighborhood, having left Damien's a few hours ago. The California sun burns my eyes, making me squint. To my right, and down the road, is my dealer's house—my last crumpled twenty burning a hole in my pocket, next to an equally crumpled piece of paper with a phone number—and to my left is a family-run hardware store. I wipe the sweat from my forehead with the back of my hand and try to think through the haze. For once, my mind seems to have quieted.

My feet make the decision for me.

I don't question it.

I turn left and walk into the store, the bell chiming above my head. A teenage girl with a low ponytail and caked-on mascara greets me from behind the counter. I ignore her. At least there's AC in here. The place is disorganized, the aisles so narrow, it feels like the walls are closing in on me, but I eventually find what I'm looking for.

Dropping the padlock on the counter beside the cash register, I barely glance up while she rings it up for me.

"Your total is $19.22," she sing-songs with a too-wide smile, the twinkle in her eyes making me cringe.

I fish the twenty out of my pocket and hand it to her before I can convince myself otherwise.

"Would you like a bag?"

"No."

I stare her down, and her smile wavers. She hands me my change, and I grab my purchase, heading out. Back in the sweltering heat, I don't know who to call. Or more accurately, who would bother to pick up. I could call Connor, my older cousin, but decide against it. He barely knows the extent of my drug use. I'd rather keep it that way.

Glancing over, I notice a payphone and walk over. I take out the piece of paper and use one of my last quarters to call the one person who, I think, could be willing to do what I'm about to ask. The phone rings, and my grip on the receiver tightens.

"Yeah?" Kenzie answers, seeming distracted.

"It's Bastian," I say, my voice flat as always.

He scoffs. "I don't know what you're about to ask me, but the answer is no." His Scottish accent still thick even after years of living in the States.

"It's different this time." I can't hide the impatience in my tone, but I can't blame him either. There's no one less reliable than a junkie. "I just need a place to get clean."

He falls silent over the phone. For a second I think he's hung up. Then finally I hear a long sigh. "I'm busy right now. But you can come to the ranch later tonight."

The relief is so sudden that I smile. I drop it as soon as it forms and clear my throat.

"I'll be there."

"You owe me," he says.

I'm sure if we'd been face to face he'd be rolling his eyes.

"I know," I mutter and hang up.

I wipe my clammy palms on my jeans, unsure if the cause is stress, heat, or the withdrawals already starting to take effect, but I ignore it, heading home to pack a bag and get myself ready.

"HOW'D YOU GET HERE?" Kenzie asks while he closes the front door behind him.

"Cab."

I've known him for a little over two years now. He lived in Scotland most of his life until his mother died a few years back. He ended up across seas with his uncle, who happened to be the president of the Black Plague MC, based in Pueblo Quieto. It's also where his family ranch is located, about two hours away inland from Noxport. With my cousin Connor now at the lead of the Sin Eaters, the most influential crime syndicate in Noxport, let's just say we run in the same circles.

Even at his ranch, away from the MC compound, Kenzie wears his leather cut faithfully. While we walk, his rusty brown shoulder-length hair falls into his face, his build far bulkier than mine. Despite all his time spent in the sun and on the back of a bike, his skin is as pale and white as mine. He leads us down a narrow dirt path to the back of the main house. He glances at me from over his shoulder, blue eyes narrowing in the waning evening light.

"That's an expensive cab ride."

I shrug. "Stole some cash from Connor before I left."

He grunts in response but says nothing more, boots crunching over dry dirt.

"Here we are," he says. We stop in front of what looks like a large, rustic shack. "You can stay in here while you do… whatever you got to do."

I adjust the strap of my cross-body bag higher up my stiff shoulder and nod. He opens the door, flipping the light switch. From the inside, the room looks less like a shack and more like a bare room with a bed, a place where the ranch workers sometimes rest when desperate. There's a mattress on the floor in the far corner near the only window in here, a small TV placed atop a milk crate, a fan, and not much else. Luckily, there's a connecting bathroom. It's dirty, with dust coating the sink and toilet, but beggars can't be choosers.

Before dropping my bag on the floor, I find the padlock I bought earlier and hand it over to Kenzie, then fix him with a determined stare. "Lock me in."

His eyebrows knit in worry but still, he takes the lock from my hand. "What if you bang on the door, screaming to get out?"

"I won't."

He takes a heavy inhale and shakes his head, turning for the exit. "Good luck, pal," he says before disappearing behind the closing door.

The slide of the lock echoes in the now heavy silence of the small, stuffy room.

Luck will have nothing to do with it.

I've lost track of time. My body is shaking so hard, I can't lie still. I'm burning up and in the next breath, I'm freezing.

I can't sleep. I can't rest. The TV is broken, so I'm left with my own thoughts and I think I might be dying.

My time in the room has bled into one long, torturous haze of existence. My sweat has soaked through the sheets, but I turned off the fan long ago, the air feeling like needles on my over-sensitive skin. The only thing keeping me half-sane is the intermittent visits from the other side of the door. Food and water are brought to me. I think it's Kenzie. Could be anyone else. I wouldn't know. Then I'm locked back in and barely touch the food, nausea a continuous malignant pulse inside of me.

Give up, give up, give up.

When the hallucinations arrive, I let them in. Like being haunted by ghosts past, my father sits at the edge of the bed, flickering in and out.

"I'm sorry," I tell him.

But he doesn't listen. He's never listened.

TEN DAYS.

Ten miserable fucking days.

The lock is finally removed and I'm allowed to leave the room. Someone comes and cleans my sheets, airing out the room as I sit on the rocking chair outside, smoking a much needed cigarette. I thank them and they nod. I've lost so much weight, I can barely keep my jeans up.

Taking my black leather-bound notebook out of my bag, I rest it on the armchair beside me. I've been jotting things down in here ever since the overdose. It doesn't seem to mean much—just a nonsensical stream of consciousness —but it doesn't stop me from writing it down nonetheless. If I would allow myself to be honest, I'd admit that whatever I'm writing down, seems like it's attached to a feeling… a feeling evoking a sense of arrival, like finally reaching my destination, and being exactly where I was meant to be all along.

It feels warm—loving even.

Whatever the fuck that means.

"You look like shit," Kenzie says with a small grin while walking up to where I'm sitting and taking one of the smokes from my pack.

"Feel like it too," I answer quietly, closing the notebook with the pen tucked inside.

I watch his eyes close for half a second on a long inhale, his rusty brown hair glinting in the afternoon sun. "Does anyone know you're here?" His Scottish lilt curving around every letter.

I let the silence stretch before answering. "Not necessarily."

His gaze slides to mine and he chuckles. "Not necessarily," he repeats, shaking his head. He then falls serious, studying me while he takes another drag. "I hope this time it sticks."

Looking down, I flick my cigarette to the ground and crush it with the heel of my boot.

"It will."

Not quite a promise. How can I keep that promise when addiction has no expiration date? It just stays dormant, waiting for the day I raise it from the dead. But going cold turkey is a hell of a deterrent. I'd rather stay away from that shit if only to avoid ever feeling like this again.

"I'm holding you to it," he says.

I shoot him the smallest of grins. "I know."

1

BASTIAN

Fourteen years later

"Lucy is going on a cross-country road trip and you're going with her."

I'm in Connor's study, sitting across from him, wondering if I heard him right. But he doesn't add anything more, trying to intimidate me in his thousand-dollar suit and a glare that would make most people fold. Good thing I'm not most people. When I realize he's not joking, I stand up and turn to leave.

"Wait!" Lenix yelps. She swats Connor on the shoulder, standing up from the arm of his chair she was resting on. She's my cousin's wife and Lucy's sister. "Why did you have to say it like that?" she scolds, rounding the desk and approaching me. "Look, Bastian." She wrings her hands, looking nervous. "I know this is way below your pay grade, and, well—"

"I'm not a glorified bodyguard," I say with my usual bored tone.

She sighs in defeat. "I *know* that," she says with a slight eye roll, tucking her black chin-length hair behind her ear. "But I don't trust anyone with my sister, other than you three."

Three as in me, my cousin Connor, and Byzantine. The latter happens to be her best friend's boyfriend and Connor's second-in-command.

"Lucy needs this. Even *you* know that. She's been out of the commune for over a year now and—and she's ready to explore a little." She rolls her eyes again and sighs. "For whatever reason, her mind is set on a road trip across the country," she says with a snark.

Both she and Lucy were raised inside Sacro Nuntio, a fucked up religious cult a few hours away from Noxport. Lenix ran away when she was sixteen, but Lucy only managed to escape thirteen years later with the help of her sister and the Sin Eaters, Connor's organization. He inherited it sixteen years ago when he was only twenty-one after his father died during a shoot-out. We've been running Noxport ever since.

Lenix raises her hands in exasperation and shrugs. "What am I going to do? Just leave her to go alone?"

"Then you should go with her." I try to make my exit again.

"I can't just up and leave for a month," she says with a huff.

Turning back around, I glare at her. "And I can?"

"I thought one of the selling points of being a tech genius is that you can do your job anywhere," Connor drawls with a raised eyebrow.

I glance at him, keeping my expression blank.

He settles back in his leather chair, his hand smoothing over his mustache. "I'll give you two hundred grand."

Fucker thinks he can tell me to jump and I'll ask how high. Irritation roils in my gut while I pick at the hangnail on my thumb. As much as I want to tell him to go to hell, I know I won't be leaving this room the victor. While Connor is *technically* my boss, he lets me undermine him on occasion. He's still at the helm of the Sin Eaters—I'm just the resident hacker—and unfortunately, he's right, I can do my job from anywhere. Saying no will be fruitless.

Annoyed I won't win this, I decide to aggravate him further just for the sake of it. "Half a million." I don't need his money, but it feels good to fuck with him.

Connor scoffs, steepling his hands over his open suit jacket. But whatever he was about to say dies a quick death when Lenix shoots him a look, and his mouth falls closed, lips slightly pinched.

She glances back at me and smiles. "Deal. You leave next week."

I wade through the thick pool of dread, swallowing hard, and slowly nod, face vacant but inside I'm raging. I can't fucking believe I'm being roped into accompanying Lucy on this ridiculous road trip. It's not that I don't like Lucy—she's nice, maybe a little too kind, too soft, too… everything I'm not. I just don't *like* much of anything. And picturing having to spend long stretches of time in the same car with no other distraction but stilted conversation and music I will most likely despise, is starting to sound worse than the time I got shot in the arm.

This time when I turn away, they don't stop me. I leave without saying another word.

WHEN I GET to my industrial loft, located in an artsy neighborhood near Old Town, I keep the lights turned off. There's enough moonlight streaking through the large windows for me to see. I tread softly over the haphazardly placed oriental rugs, taking up most of the space in the vast room, eventually reaching the kitchen. Opening the fridge, I grab a beer and crack it open. I take a swig while heading to the space I designated as my office.

When I got clean, I stayed away from any kind of substance until I felt stable enough mentally not to have it trigger the *other* craving. It was over a year before I trusted myself with a few drinks here and there. I was never a huge drinker anyway, just something to take the edge off every once in a while.

But the craving never really does go away. Especially during those first few months when all I could think about was my next potential hit. Always at the back of my mind, whispering soft nothings and promising such sweet release.

But I never listen. At least… not yet.

Swiveling the computer chair around, I sit and face the wall of monitors I have set up for work. I move the mouse, waking up one of the main ones. Sitting there for a few minutes, lost in thought, I sip my beer until something makes me reach for the middle drawer of my desk. Hiding under a pile of loose papers, I find the leather-bound notebook I used to carry around when I was younger. I'm not sure why I'm even opening it now, flipping through the crinkled pages arbitrarily, until I fall on a list I made when I was going through my withdrawals.

It must have meant something. I vaguely recall an aching feeling attached to the list itself. But there are too many years separating me from whatever awareness I was experiencing. Maybe it was simply a melancholic side effect of getting clean. The memories are muddy at best now, the trauma of going cold turkey in a shack effectively rationalized and filed away as being dealt with.

Still, I can't help but scan the pages, ignoring the small pinch the words have on my heart. The feeling doesn't even make sense.

It's just a list of objects and things.

US... blue... cowboy hat... flamingo... magnets...

I've tried to find patterns. I'm *good* at finding patterns. But this list has always stayed a mystery. Maybe I'm reading too much into it. A list made by an eighteen-year-old junkie. Why *would* it make sense? I slam it shut and throw it back into the middle drawer. I run my fingers through my hair, exhaling loudly, and stand up. Draining the rest of my beer, I throw the can in the wastebasket beside me. Staring out the windows, the cityscape twinkling awake, my mind circles back to the impending road trip with Lucy. Apprehension squeezes my stomach like a vice.

How the hell did I end up here?

2

"You did *what?*"

I try to keep my voice as calm as possible, but deep down I feel the pinpricks of discomfort—no, more like embarrassment, needling my insides. Lenix sits across from me on the couch in my condo. It is in a highrise downtown and used to be my sister's before she moved in with Connor last year.

Her brown eyes are wide like she has been caught doing something she was not supposed to. "You said you really wanted to go on this road trip…" she says quietly, voice trailing off.

"I can go on my own, I am an adult you know? I cannot believe your solution was to tell Bastian to babysit me as if I was a child." My tone is bitter and Lenix winces. She is only five years older than me but acts like my mother most of the time, and still carries the guilt of us being apart for thirteen years heavy on her shoulders.

"Lucy… I know you're not a child, but—but in a lot of ways you're still very inexperienced. You've only been out

14

for like—" She waves her perfectly manicured hand limply in a circle, eyes raised to the ceiling as if trying to count, her gaze then finding mine again. "Fourteen months. That's nothing."

I press my lips together and take a deep breath.

I know she is right. It does not make the words sting less.

At twenty-five, I still barely know anything about the outside world. Sacro Nuntio was cut off from everything else surrounding us, tucked and hidden beside the Redwood forest, a few hours away from Noxport. There was electricity, but nothing connected us to the outside. I grew up believing my father's word was holy. That his presence alone was healing—when in reality it was anything but. When he died my brother Frederick took his place and continued in his egregious footsteps. It took me a lot of time and therapy to process my life in Sacro Nuntio and it is far from over yet. But I have faith that one day I will get there.

Even if I try my best to assimilate, I am still marked as an outsider. Simple things give me away, like not understanding vernacular or idioms, or rarely using contractions when I speak. I have been consciously trying to incorporate them, but it still feels so foreign, that I forget most of the time—especially when my emotions are heightened. Then there is all the *stuff*. Like the television that I frequently forget to turn on. Or the closet full of clothes Lenix left for me. Most of them are dresses. They sit untouched and unwanted. I was forced to wear dresses my entire life. Now I would rather burn them all. I am not sure I have found my style yet, but for now, jeans and a loose-fitting t-shirt will do. Showing any kind of skin was jarring at first, and I am still not as comfortable as my sister. Maybe I never will be. And that is okay too.

Although Lenix still funds most of my life, I need to prove to myself that I can do this on my own. This road trip feels somehow—necessary. A need more than just a want.

"You could have warned me before you asked him at least," I finally express, a little less aggrieved and more resigned this time.

Lenix's eyes study me as she stays silent, a wealth of words unspoken as if she is too scared to hurt my feelings.

"I'm sorry, Lucy…" she says softly but sternly. "But there was no way I was letting you leave on your own *across* the country. You just got your license. It was this or have Bastian hack your phone and bank account to make sure you wouldn't leave." Her voice slightly teasing. "I just got you back. I'm having a hard enough time simply letting you out of my sight, let alone having you disappear for over a month."

She slides closer to me and takes my hands in hers, squeezing them three times—our secret way to reassure each other. We have been doing it since we were children. We were always the closest of all our sisters and brothers. Polygamy was encouraged, but we were the only two to have the same parents, leading us to share a lot of the same features.

Begrudgingly, I smile. I know she has my best interests in mind, and she has been nothing but supportive, but she has been coddling me. Maybe I needed it at the beginning when life felt insurmountable, my newfound freedom feeling like being given the gift of eyesight, but realizing I still could not see what was right in front of me.

I am better now.

"I need to do this," I say softly.

My sister's eyes glimmer with unshed tears, her

eyebrows dipping low like she is trying to keep it together. "I know," she croaks, sliding even closer. "I'm so proud of you. I hope you know that." Her voice quivers, and I swallow down the knot in my throat that is threatening to turn into the same emotions mirrored in Lenix's expression.

"I know… I love you," I reply with a watery smile.

"Love you more," she says with a small winning grin, and I laugh.

Falling into her arms, we hug tightly and I breathe in her soothing scent of vanilla and jasmine. When we let go, she keeps her hands around my shoulders and straightens her arms to look at me.

"My baby is all grown up," she chirps in a jokingly teary tone.

I swat her away and laugh. "Stop it. You are being embarrassing."

"Good," she replies with a wink. "That's what big sisters are for."

Lenix stands up, adjusting her red pencil skirt, and smoothing her black hair back in place, before grabbing her purse and phone from the coffee table. "I have a meeting in fifteen, but come over for dinner later? We can talk more about the road trip, then we can order in and force Connor to watch reality TV with us," she says mischievously.

I let out a small chuckle and walk her to the door. "That sounds lovely."

She blows me a kiss from the outside hallway and I wave, waiting for her to reach the elevator doors before closing the door behind me.

I lean back on the door and let my head fall with a thud, releasing a long exhale. Now that I am alone with my thoughts, the same embarrassment I felt earlier creeps back up and my face falls into my hands with a groan.

I am going on a month-long road trip with *Bastian Maxwell*.

The man who never speaks, let alone emotes.

I invariably feel awkward around him, Lenix is usually always close by to fill in the deafening silence he carries with him everywhere he goes. He makes me nervous, in a way that Connor and Byzantine never have. His bleached blond hair only makes his dark brows and hardened expression all the more striking. Even though Connor and Byzantine are heavily tattooed and Bastian does not have any—that I know of—he still carries himself with a deadly aura. And now I will be stuck in a car with him, alone for days at a time.

Great. Just great.

I push myself off the door and walk to the oval kitchen table, reaching for the map I left there. I unfold it and smooth it across the hard surface. I could have used a computer to map out my trip, I know that. But technology still does not come naturally to me, and I prefer to do certain things the "old-fashioned way"—as Lenix would put it. What an odd expression.

I trace my finger along the highlighted path I decided I would take months ago. Route 66. California to Chicago. When I found out about the famous highway in an old movie I watched with Lenix, it spoke to me. It was one of the first movies I ever watched, and it tugged at my soul like a tethered thread telling me it was time for an adventure. I am not quite sure why, but it resonated so deeply that I have desired it ever since.

And now, after all these months of planning, it is about to become a reality. Not even the idea of being stuck in a car with Bastian can ruin the thrill lighting up my veins.

3

BASTIAN

The smoke curls around my eyes, momentarily blanketing my vision in white. I inhale deeply and flick the ash from my cigarette with my thumb, letting my hand fall to my side. Lucy's talking animatedly with Lenix outside of her condo building beside the black BMW X3 that I'm assuming we'll be taking for this whimsical fucking trip.

I'm a block away, relishing my last few moments of peace and quiet. I took a cab here—had them drop me off further up the street so I could assess the scene first. Nothing much to see, just two sisters standing beside a parked car. Lucy's wearing a navy tracksuit with sneakers, and a white baseball cap, her brown curls falling to the middle of her back.

I take one last drag, before an unnecessarily long exhale, dropping the cigarette on the sidewalk, grinding it with the tip of my checkered Vans.

I chuck the bags I brought over my shoulder and leave my hideout for the glaring sun and my impending future as a babysitter. As of yesterday, I'm half a million richer, but I'd rather take a papercut to the eyeball right about now than have to suffer through small talk and fun facts about whatever tourist attraction Lucy is bound to drag me to.

Approaching the car, Lenix is the first to notice me.

"Hey, weirdo! Ready to go on a trip of a lifetime?" Lenix's tone feels forced like she's trying to put on a good face for her sister's sake. I let my eyes fall on Lucy, who jumps when she sees me, flashing a nervous smile but quickly busying herself with a suitcase in the trunk. I slide my gaze back to Lenix and shrug. Circling around her, I drop my two bags next to Lucy's five or six and step back, shoving my hands in my faded blue jeans.

Lenix's expression drops, her eyes turning hard. Grabbing my arm, she pulls me toward the front of the car. I yank myself out of her grip but still follow. She glances back, presumably to check if Lucy is out of earshot. "Don't ruin this for her, Bastian," she says in a low hiss.

"Ruin?" I drawl.

"You're going to have to speak more than your allotted five sentences a day if you two plan to survive the month together," she answers heatedly.

I fix her with one of my dead-eye looks I know freaks her out. She bristles but doesn't step down.

"The deal was that I'd go." I wave my hand down my body as if to say *here I am*. But before Lenix has time to over-dramatize the situation, I cut her off. "Look, Connor already went through all this with me last night. I don't need to hear it all over again. I thought you said you trusted me with your sister. Was that a lie?"

Lenix presses her red-painted lips together and drops her shoulders in a small exhale. "No."

"Settled then."

Before I can step away, she flings her arms around my body and hugs me.

Fuck.

I keep my arms stiff to my side and stand still while she has her moment, mumbling a thank you into my shoulder.

When she pulls away, I quickly head for the driver's side, where I find Lucy already opening the door to climb in. Her almond eyes widen and I fight the urge to give this entire ridiculous situation a giant eye roll. Instead, I say, "I'm driving."

Lucy's brown freckled cheeks turn a shade darker as she flusters her way into answering me. "I–um…well, I was going to, ah…"

"She's driving. Don't push it," Lenix interjects while walking up to her sister.

Lucy's gaze hasn't left mine, and I decide to stare her down a little while longer. She's like a startled bird, and all I want is to tighten my grasp to see how much she'll struggle.

"*Bastian,*" Lenix chides.

Suddenly bored with this entire exchange, I turn around and leave them to their teary goodbyes, grabbing my backpack before slamming the trunk shut. Opening the passenger door, I slide into the seat, adjusting it to give me enough leg room to sprawl out and set my laptop on my knees.

The silence is interrupted by a door opening and closing, followed by a small sigh. The subtle notes of mandarin and warm florals fill the air. I haven't looked up from my computer, but a quick rap on my window forces my gaze up. Lenix waves, her smile wide but cheeks tracked with tears. I consider a half-smile but give her a lazy salute instead. She blows kisses to Lucy beside me, and finally, I look over.

Her green eyes are sparkling as if this is truly the adventure of a lifetime for her and fuck, maybe it is... all things considered. I guess it wouldn't kill me to make an effort.

"Ready to Rock 'n' Roll?" I ask her with as little condescension as I can manage, trying not to visibly cringe at what I just said.

She starts the car and answers with a nervous but hopeful smirk. "Ready!" Her tone is forced but still excited. She holds her hand up, folding her two middle fingers down, her index finger and pinky still standing straight. I'm assuming she thinks she's giving me the devil sign but her thumb is still up, so she's actually signing *I love you* instead.

I reciprocate the devil sign—the proper way—and after a beat, she looks at her own raised hand as if noticing I've tucked my fingers under my thumb. She carefully mirrors me and then looks up beaming, the specks of gold in her green eyes shimmering.

I'm slightly stunned by my body's reaction to such an honest and open smile.

Luckily, her attention turns back to the task at hand—driving us out of here—but I let my gaze linger a little while longer, studying her. She gives Lenix one final wave and pulls out onto the street, driving away. I watch her sister grow smaller and smaller in the rearview mirror until she finally disappears. What's left is just me, Lucy, and the uneasiness of two practical strangers on the road together.

4

B eing caged in a vehicle with less than an arm's length separating me from Bastian is harder than I ever expected. He has not said a word since we pulled out of my street twenty minutes ago. I am not surprised, based on the little I know of him. But as much as I would rather sit in silence and let my nerves eat me up from the inside out, I need a co-pilot. I wring my hands around the steering wheel while chewing anxiously on the inside of my cheek, trying to build up the courage to open my mouth and speak.

With my eyes on the road, I try to pop the compartment between us, but with my limited experience driving, I struggle to multitask and end up swerving hard to my left, narrowly missing a parked car, then over-correct and land in the next lane over. Letting out an embarrassing squeak, my hand flies back to the steering wheel and I grip it even harder, my shoulders up to my neck. With no music in the car, the silence is deafening and all I can hear are my shaky breaths as I try to recover from what I just did.

Bastian curses under his breath, but keeps his eyes down on the screen in front of him, the silver chain bracelet on his left wrist clinking against his laptop while he types, looking as unbothered as ever.

My nostrils flare, knuckles white. I am still quite flustered, but try my best to appear calm and address him. "I–I need your help."

I give him a quick sideways glance, as he does the same. If you can call that a glance. More like a small twitch of the eyebrow, and a slow slide of his eyeballs. He stays silent, apparently waiting for me to speak again, so I stutter into my next sentence.

"I need you to tell me where to go." I point to the middle compartment. "Can you open this for me, please?"

For a second I think he will not do it, then I hear him let out a long heavy sigh. He closes his laptop and slides it into his backpack at his feet, finally opening the compartment. Quickly, I dip my hand in and grab the map I placed right at the top.

"Here," I say, handing it over to him.

"What's *that*," he says with a bite of disdain, taking it from me with two fingers and holding it up as if it is contagious.

I try to willfully ignore his reaction, but I answer him nonetheless. "It is a map of the United States."

When he takes too long to reply or *do* anything, I look over. He is staring at the map, now on his knees, as if lost in thought.

"What is wrong?" I ask.

Snapping out of his reverie, he gives his head a small shake. "Nothing," he quickly says, and then, "What do you expect me to do with this relic?"

"I need you to give me directions."

"With this thing?"

"*Yes*," I manage to say with a semblance of authority.

"No." His own dominance slicing mine clean in half. He drops the map back into the compartment and closes it. "First stop?" he asks while pulling his phone out of his pocket.

"Emma Jean's Holland Burger Café." I cannot help the small smile appearing on my lips while I say it.

This is it. I am finally taking the leap, and going on an adventure.

I can feel Bastian staring but ignore it, and wait for him to enter the address into his maps app.

"It's two hours away," he says, as if I am unaware or even care how far away it is.

"I know."

A long pause. Then a scoff.

"Alright then."

THE DINER IS in the middle of nowhere, Southern California. A truck stop more than anything. Pale blue painted bricks adorn the front, the Highway 66 driving sign painted in black and white to the left of the restaurant, with large potted flowers flanking the white double doors of the entrance. Bastian did not say a word the whole way here, the only exception was when he needed to give me directions, which were few and far between. Eventually, he put some music on to dull the awkwardness between us. Good thing, since I had no idea how that car system worked.

I walk into the diner first, Bastian following behind. Although, deep down I know he would have rather stayed in the car. The interior is painted pale yellow, with a wide choice of counter space, and a sign that says *Happiness is Homemade* adding extra charm to the already charming café. With a quick perusal, I choose a table near a large window.

"Hungry?" I ask as he settles into the chair facing me. He shrugs and turns his head to look for a waitress. Gradually, the excitement of having arrived at the first stop of my road trip settles and the realization that I am about to have lunch with Bastian overtakes my thoughts. I have not had a meal alone with a man since… well, since I was still married to Patrick and under the sharp claws of the cult. My husband died in the same fire that took our brother, on the day I escaped. Even then, without having anything to compare it to, I knew they were evil men masquerading as godly. I do not mourn them, never shed a single tear—nor do I have the desire to. Rather, I pretend they never existed.

It does not take long for a waitress to come and drop menus at our table and I unclench my fists from my lap and adopt a very forced casual pose while I try to decide what to eat.

I can barely concentrate.

"How's everyone doing this afternoon?" Our server asks when she comes back with a grin.

Relieved to have a distraction, I return her smile. "Great, thank you."

"Have any questions about the menu, or are you ready to order?" she continues, pen hovering over her notepad.

"I–uh." My eyes land on Bastian. He gives me a quick jerk of the head as if to say *you first*. My gaze lands back on the lady waiting for my order and I smile politely before asking, "What is the most popular item on the menu?" Then before she responds, and without any prompting, I find myself adding, "This is actually our first stop on our road trip across Highway 66. This place was at the top of the list of attractions for the state of California."

I hear Bastian scoff and mumble under his breath. An inexplicable impulse to kick him in the shins overcomes me, but I keep my gaze on the server instead, my casual smile steady.

She lets out a small pleased chuckle and nods. "The only reason why people still come through here," she says and then points to my open menu. "The Brian burger with fries is your best bet, honey."

"Lovely. I will have that and a chocolate shake, please," I respond perkily.

Still smirking, she scribbles down my order. I hand her back my menu and all eyes fall to the brooding man sitting in front of me.

Barely looking up he says, "Bacon cheeseburger, mayo, no ketchup, and fries."

"Anything to drink?"

"Water," he mutters, crossing his arms and leaning into the back of the chair, effectively ending the conversation.

Grabbing his menu from the table, our waitress simply nods, tells us it will be right up, and leaves. With the only distraction now over, my attention is forced back onto Bastian as I gently place my clasped hands on the vinyl tabletop. His bleached, almost white, blond hair looks slightly disheveled, a few straight strands falling over his prominent dark brows. Somehow, it leaves me slightly uneasy. Like finding a marble statue in a state of disarray.

"Something on your mind?" he says.

I startle.

Get it together, Lucy.

"Nothing." I force my gaze away and pretend to be

interested in anything else but dissecting the enigma staring at me.

Is he staring?

I peek a glance.

He is.

I swallow hard, and force myself to look directly at him. Needing to keep my hands busy, I pull my baseball cap off my head and discard it beside me on the table. Bastian's dark brown eyes slowly track my movements, following my hand and then back up again as I fluff my curls at the roots into something better than a flat triangle. He has not moved an inch while he unabashedly continues to study me from his seat, casually clinking his silver thumb ring against the table. With his pale white skin paired with his equally white t-shirt, he looks more like an apparition than human.

After approximately ten minutes of this, I am about to bolt to the bathroom just to escape his gaze when the server finally comes back with our order. I let loose a relieved sigh, eager for another interruption, however small it is. I dig in, humming delightfully after taking a bite of my burger. Before last year, I knew nothing about fast food. We grew all our own food in Sacro Nuntio. In the outside world, at first, everything tasted too salty or just too *much*, the flavors harsh on my palette. Now, I have become insatiable. Eager to try anything and everything.

I prop my food back on my plate and take a small sip of the milkshake. My eyes fall expectedly back on Bastian and the image in front of me is as startling as his disheveled hair. I cannot remember if I have ever seen him do such a normal thing as eating. His eyes are pinned to mine as he bites into his burger in a slow, deliberate manner, as if even this, chewing his food, is bothersome for him. His chiseled jaw flexes, silver nose ring glinting with the motion. My gaze slides to the side of his mouth when his tongue peeks out, licking an errant crumb, while he reaches for his water. From over his glass, he watches me. Holding up a napkin, my hand has stopped midway to my mouth and is now hovering in the air, the action abandoned for watching Bastian eat a burger.

"Have you ever dipped your fries in your milkshake?" he asks.

"Excuse me?" I croak, winding back to life, breaking eye contact, lifting the discarded napkin to my lips. I heard him, but the question just slipped out as a nervous reflex.

Instead of repeating himself, Bastian leans over and steals a fry off my plate, his own sitting uneaten in front of him. With his stare still cold and assessing, he dunks the fry in my chocolate shake with an unhurried flick of his wrist.

He then reaches forward, holding it close to my mouth and I think I have stopped breathing.

My heart slams in my chest, but I force myself to hold his gaze while my lips part and Bastian carefully feeds me the chocolate-dipped fry.

The taste explodes on my tongue. It is incredible. Sweet. Salty. Hot. Cold. I focus on the flavors blending together, while I chew and pretend not to be monumentally distracted by Bastian leaning back in his chair, licking his fingers, his dark brown eyes still watching me.

Trying to snap myself out of whatever is happening between us, I bring my hand to my mouth while I finish swallowing. Not knowing what to say I just mumble, "Wonderful combination. Thank you."

He gives me the smallest of nods, his expression sliding back into existential boredom while his attention shifts down to his food.

We finish our meal in silence.

When the waitress hands us our bill, I try to take it, but the look he gives me has my hand snapping back as if I have been burned. He pays, and we leave as I wave goodbye to the staff.

Back in the car, Bastian fishes his phone out of his pocket.

"Where to next?" he mutters.

I smile, starting the car.

"A forest made of glass."

5

BASTIAN

I'm standing in the middle of rows and rows of what is essentially garbage. Dusty and derelict glass bottles hoarded over time, all of them faded, all of them unnecessarily *here*. A glass forest—according to everyone else but me. The multi-colored bottles hang, like branches, off large rusted metal pipes, over six feet high, and staked in dirt.

I can't believe this place is called an attraction. We're in the middle of the Californian desert, the sun is beating down on my shoulders, the heat causing sweat to prickle across my forehead and down my back. My hands are stuffed in the pockets of my jeans and if the owner of this place looks at me one more time with that bright open smile of his, I'll jam one of these bottles down his throat.

Lucy is a few rows down, busy talking to another tourist with the same zeal as hers—as if they were visiting one of the seven wonders of the world. I'd rather be shot in the head. Finding a small pocket of shade, I take my phone out to catch up on work. I'm barely getting a signal and that alone is enough to make me go nuclear. My head falls on the fence behind me, eyes closed. I take a deep breath, frustration biting at my skin, and I flex my hand open and closed, trying not to snap.

Hearing gravel under tentative footsteps nearing me, I keep my eyes closed, knowing Lucy is approaching. I can almost hear the flutter of her heart, a little bird braving the wolf.

"Done?" I say without looking at her.

"Yes," she murmurs.

I push off the fence and let my gaze fall on her face. I'm stopped short by the sight of her. Hues of red, blue, and green bouncing off her warm brown skin, shimmers of refracting light akin to glass mosaics in a place of worship. She smiles, and I can almost imagine a hallowed light surrounding her loose curls.

The impression of her like this only lasts long enough for me to blink, but it traps my heart in a tight squeeze all the same. Her smile fades the more I stare and I do nothing to stop it. Without adding to the already stilted conversation, I lead her out of this fucking hellscape and back to the car.

When we've both settled in, I quirk a brow, phone in hand. *Next stop?* I say without a word ever leaving my mouth.

Lucy drums her fingers on the steering wheel, biting her lip. "It is getting a little late. I was thinking of simply finding a place to sleep for the night?"

"You have a place in mind?"

"Not really," she answers with a small huffed laugh.

"All this planning and you didn't think of researching motels?" I say unimpressed.

A flash of irritation travels across her face, but she quickly hides it behind one of her beatific smiles before looking directly at me.

"I, um… I just thought finding places to sleep last minute would be part of the charm of being on the road…" she trails off, looking like she thinks she's getting into trouble.

I study her for a beat longer and then shrug. "Sure."

WE END up at a motel a few miles away, Highway 66 memorabilia decorates the walls of the reception and I fight an eye roll or two. The place seems deserted. I ring the bell on the counter while Lucy stands a healthy distance away from me still acting like I'll shank her at any given moment. The clerk, a short middle-aged man with bifocal glasses and a cowlick, ambles up to the desk and greets us.

"We need a room with two beds for the night," I say.

Lucy squeaks beside me and gives me a quick tap on the shoulder. I tilt my head to look at her and the deer-in-the-headlights expression she's currently sporting.

"We are not—I am not, ah," she stutters while her eyes get wider and wider. "Separate rooms," she finally manages to croak out.

I slowly turn my body to face hers, my palm leaning on the counter beside me.

"Your sister wouldn't be all too pleased to know I've let you out of my sight for an entire night alone. We're in the middle of nowhere and I don't trust anyone, especially this guy," I say, pointing a thumb at the man behind the desk. He seems smart enough not to say anything in protest.

She huffs. Her upturned nose scrunches, her mouth opening and closing as if trying to find the right words for a counter-argument.

"I am an adult," she finally says sternly.

"An adult who doesn't know anything about anything," I mutter unimpressed.

Her eyebrows knit and she crosses her arms, staying silent for a beat before saying, "If I cannot even have the little independence of having my own room... well, then—that does not make you any better than *them*."

The bite in her tone surprises me but I keep my face blank. Them. As in the men from Sacro Nuntio, including her now-dead husband, who controlled her all of her life and forced her into a constant state of submission. I clench my jaw, grinding my teeth at the thought. I was there the day we got her out, and the Lucy I met then was a ghost compared to the person standing up to me now. She's come a long way in a year.

I slide my gaze to the clerk.

"Do you have rooms with a connecting door?"

"Yes, we do," he says, nodding agreeably.

I turn back to Lucy. "Two separate rooms but you keep the connecting door open. Deal?"

I can tell she's still dissatisfied, but shit, I'm being paid to watch over her. Connor would have my head if anything happened to her while under my care. He'd probably suffocate me under the weight of all the money he paid me to even be here in the first place.

Her nostrils flare, chest rising but finally, she nods. "Fine."

With that settled, we check in and get the keys. I walk away while the clerk is still droning on about motel policies and check-out times, pulling out my bag from the car and letting Lucy do the same. She stays silent all the way to our rooms, located on the ground floor at the back of the parking lot. I hand her a key and she mumbles a thank you as we go our separate ways, into our respective rooms.

One day down. However many to go.

6

I close the door behind me, breathing in deeply, then
wrinkle my nose.

Smells like mold in here.

From my vantage point, I do a quick perusal of the
room. It is small. A queen size bed draped with a floral
print duvet takes up most of the space. Even to my
untrained eye, the television looks outdated. That, paired
with the yellowing paint, the room has seen better days.

I grin.

It is perfect.

Almost immediately, I hear a rap on the door
connecting my room to Bastian's. Dropping my smile, I roll
my eyes and push myself off the wall. I ball my hands into
fists and walk around in a tight circle trying to let out some
frustration. To not even be allowed a room all to myself is
triggering a rage I can barely describe. It burns hot in my
chest, but I quickly repress it. As easy as muscle memory,
and just as unconscious.

Stomping over to the door, I unlock it and yank it wide

open. Bastian appears on the other side, arms folded over his white t-shirt.

"Happy?" I say rather petulantly and I regret it immediately.

His upper lip twitches while a lazy gaze sweeps over my body. It feels clinical more than anything—as if he is making sure I have not lost a limb from the front door to here. Without saying a word, he walks into my room as if checking if everything is safe and sound, doing the same in the bathroom, then flipping the deadbolt on my door. Turning around, he struts back into his room, takes off his t-shirt, and disappears into his bathroom.

I stand there long enough to hear the shower turn on. The sound snaps me out of the small daze I drifted into.

Well, then.

I should do the same.

After a quick rinse, I change into fresh clothes, my hair still in a top bun to keep it from getting wet in the shower. I slip into a pair of jeans shorts and one of Lenix's old t-shirts I stole months ago. It is from a band I do not know. An easy feat when I have only had a year to catch up. I try to not let those things get to me, but sometimes I let the sting burn just to remind myself that I have survived. That I have made it out.

Eventually, I end up standing in the middle of the room, not sure what to do next. I worry my lip while I cycle through my options and finally make a choice. Reaching into the suitcase I brought in with me, I find the small bottle of vodka I packed for the trip. I do not really drink, alcohol was prohibited in Sacro Nuntio, but I figured if there was ever a time for a celebratory drink, it would be now. I find two plastic cups in the bathroom, taking them with me as I tentatively take a peek into Bastian's room.

His front door is open, and I can smell the faint aroma of tobacco wafting from outside. My heart crawls up my throat, but I swallow it back down. Closing my eyes, I take a deep breath and try not to chastise myself for the uncontrollable nerves I have when around him.

So what if he is intimidating and barely speaks? He is only human—and I know he would not hurt me. I also do not take it personally, he is like this with everyone, even Connor and his long-time friend Byzantine.

Squaring my shoulders, and giving myself a small nod of encouragement, I take a steady step across the length of his room towards the open front door.

The sun has set, navy blue hues painting the sky a darker shade, and I find him sitting in a plastic chair, arms draped over the sides, a cigarette hanging loosely from long fingers. With his eyes closed and head resting on the cement wall behind him, I think he has not noticed me. But then an eyelid pops open and I startle. Clearing my throat, I hold up the cups and bottle of vodka, flashing him what I hope is an inviting smile.

"Where'd you get that?" he asks, his eyelid falling back closed.

Refusing to take his lack of interaction as anything but Bastian being Bastian, I perch on the chair beside him and answer, "My suitcase."

Silence lingers in the space between us. I can hear the hoot of an owl echoing faintly in the distance before he bothers to speak again.

"Oh?"

I could almost detect amusement in his tone.

I do not bother waiting for his approval and uncap the bottle, pouring a few inches' worth into each cup. Bastian is poised in such a way that I can tell he is paying attention to every little sound and movement I make like a dog perking its ears. When I lean over and hand him his drink, he finally opens his eyes and straightens up in his chair, taking a long drag of his cigarette, eyes fixed on me.

I force a smile and tilt my cup toward him as if to say *cheers*. Holding it up to my lips, I take a large sip. The burn is so sudden and intense down my throat that I choke and start coughing. I wave my hand near my mouth as I gasp through catching my breath while the mortification settles in, my cheeks burning.

"Harsh," I manage to croak out as an explanation.

Bastian grins. It is sudden and gone nearly as quickly that I almost convince myself that I made it all up.

"First time drinking vodka?"

"No," I say far too swiftly.

He does not even have to do his usual stare-down for me to concede.

"Yes." I look down at my drink. "I am not sure I like it."

He lets out a small hum while draining the cup. "Next time try it with soda. And some ice."

Nodding in agreement, I watch him. My hands are wrapped tightly around the flimsy plastic cup as his gaze slowly drags down to my chest and then up again.

"Nice shirt," he drawls.

I look down as a reflex, knowing exactly what piece of clothing I am wearing and mutter, "Thanks, it belonged to Lenix."

"Connor's," he replies.

"What?" I ask, slightly confused.

"It was Connor's."

I give him a questioning look.

"I used to be in a punk band in high school. We were called Wannabes." He takes another drag, smoke spilling out of his mouth and into the dark night before continuing, "That's my band you're wearing."

I shoot up from my chair, pulling on the hem of the shirt. Then realizing my overreaction, I sit back down.

"Oh." I let out a small awkward laugh and I immediately want to fade into the ether at the sound. "I did not know."

Bastian reaches for the vodka bottle and pours himself another drink, giving me a bored shrug. "Now you do." He takes a slow sip, eyeing me intently. "Suits you."

Warmth spills in over my chest and I convince myself that it must be the vodka as I take another sip, suppressing a cough when it burns my throat once again.

We fall into what can almost be described as companionable silence, the starry night sky twinkling over us. The stars are so much brighter here than in Noxport.

It reminds me of home.

The thought feels harmless, but it is equally as jarring.

Because I meant the commune.

That place is not home... I am not sure it ever was.

And I am not so sure Noxport feels like home either.

7

BASTIAN

Lucy's laying sideways, fully clothed, on her unmade bed. Watching her from the doorway, I can hear her soft slumbering breaths while I chew on my inner cheek, lost in thought. I could tell that one pour of vodka would do her in. She's out like a light.

I turn back into my own room, pacing across the faded gray carpet.

I shouldn't leave her alone. But the thought of just lying here wide awake for hours—most likely till dawn—tightens my throat. The urge to pull out all my hair is starting to sound really good right about now. I could work, which is what I do most of the time when the insomnia takes hold and doesn't let up.

Not now. I'm not sure what makes tonight different. Or if it has anything to do with the girl sleeping in the next room. I just know that I need to get out of here. I just need some air.

First, I need to know that Lucy will be safe here. I

already have her phone tracked but she barely uses the damn thing. I contemplate quickly installing a surveillance camera in her room—but that's more Connor's thing. This stir-crazy feeling isn't letting up, only growing worse with my lack of decision.

Fuck it.

It'll just be a couple of hours, she'll be fine for tonight. I make sure her front door is triple locked before heading out and locking mine from the outside. Now that it's night, there's a chill to the air, but I welcome it. It manages to subdue the craving. Just a little. Like a dull knife instead of a sharpened tip. But right now, it refuses to leave.

Tonight the dark angel of temptation has taken up residence on my right shoulder, trying to seduce me with wistful ballads filled with stories of irresistible escape. I ignore it.

Not tonight.

Or the next.

Or the next.

I look up to the inky sky as I walk up the street. I take a large inhale, still chewing on my inner cheek, my hand stuffed into my jeans pockets. I spot Saturn right away, it shines brighter than the stars surrounding it. All planets do. The promise of a universe so much bigger than me is the only thing keeping me half-sane right now. How could my issues—whatever they fucking are—matter when I'm so insignificant compared to everything else. A lone grain in the sand. Somehow, it brings comfort, no matter how existential it is. And maybe a little nihilistic too.

Finally, I spot a blinking neon sign at the corner. Opening the nondescript door, I walk into what will most likely be a hole-in-a-wall dive bar.

It is.

The bar is busier than expected for a—actually, I don't even know what day of the week it is. I don't blame them. There doesn't seem to be a lot to do around here but to drown your boredom into a pint or five.

I do a quick sweep of the place. Bar to my right. Pool table to the far left. Brown decor. And a few wooden tables in desperate need of a wipe peppered about. I walk up to the corner of the bar and sit on a barstool, signaling the bartender. Long brown plaited hair, pink painted lips. She saunters up with a twinkle in her eyes and tits up to her neck.

"Pilsner," I order before she even speaks. I pull out my wallet and hand her two crisp hundred-dollar bills. "And this is for you to leave me the fuck alone. Just keep my pint full."

She drops her smile and pops a hip, snatching the money out of my hand. "You got it."

An hour later, I'm on my third drink and my usual uncontrollable thoughts have slowed into a tolerable hum. Doesn't take long before my mind slowly meanders to the leather-bound notebook and its contents.

An old map of the United States.

I give my head a small shake, finishing my beer. How common is a *map* in the first place? But when Lucy handed me that old thing this morning, I was struck with the feeling that I had seen it before. Touched it. Opened it. Smelled the scent of aging paper on my fingertips.

Fucking driveling nonsense.

Just a coincidence.

Standing up, I head for the men's bathroom in the back. There are saloon doors instead of normal ones—fucking stupid and kitschy like everything else on this road trip. Biting back a groan, I swing them open. I notice two younger-looking guys near the sink having a heated conversation, but ignore them while I head for the urinals.

By the time I take a piss, these two jokers have launched themselves into a fist fight and I barely have time to zip my dick back into my jeans before I get punched in the ear. It only takes one quick blink for the angel on my shoulder to turn into a snarling jackal.

Slowly, I turn around and find them now scuffling on the dirty bathroom floor. I can't be sure who landed the punch so I simply reach for the closest one.

I pull him off the other guy by his back collar and launch him into the sinks beside us. His head slams into porcelain and like a discarded doll, he falls to the ground. He's unconscious now. Bummer. I was hoping for more of a fight. I turn my attention to the one currently trying to stand up. Maybe he'll put up more of a challenge.

"Hey man," he blubbers while trying to scamper to his feet but failing. "Chill the fuck out."

I snatch his shirt in my fist and slam the other into his face. His head snaps backward, his nose already pouring blood, gargling a protest. Somehow, he manages to clock me in the left eye before my fist finds purchase again and again. After a few more swift punches, his eyes roll to the back of his head, and I release him. I spit in his face before he falls like dead weight to the floor.

I notice his phone beside him and crack the screen with my heel just for the hell of it before stalking out of the bathroom. Walking past the kitchen, I slip out the back door and head down the street toward the motel with bloody knuckles, now calmer than ever.

Back in the room, I find Lucy in the same position as before and I fight the grin trying to form on my lips. I wash the blood off my hands, strip down to my boxers and fall into bed.

For once, I sleep until morning.

8

I t is too loud here. Noxport. I never knew a city this big even existed. Sitting on the edge of the couch, I wring my hands while my eyes slice to the open window in the therapist's office. The sounds physically hurt, my nerves raw even though I have been out of the commune for over two months now. Imogene, my therapist, waits for me to speak but today, I feel empty.

"How are you feeling?" she asks. Her tone is warm and inviting, but it is having the opposite effect on me. How can I tell her that I feel as trapped here as I did back in Sacro Nuntio? How do I tell her that my faith has started to waver? The only thing that kept me from giving up, is now the reason nothing is making sense.

She patiently waits for me to answer. I take a large breath in and then out.

"Lost," I mutter with barely any emotions.

"How so?"

I close my eyes, trying not to burst into tears, but my lower lip trembles, and I can feel myself cracking like a porcelain doll in malevolent hands.

"Lucy, you're safe here," she says while sitting closer to the edge of *her chair. "You don't need to keep everything inside when it's just us two."*

Looking down at my hands, I nod but say nothing until I am positive that my voice will not crack. "I do not know if I will ever be free," I say quietly, avoiding Imogene's supportive gaze.

"Free from what?" she says softly.

"Them."

WAKING UP WITH A START, I crack an eyelid. I am laying on my stomach and I push myself up with the help of my forearms. Feeling a little groggy, it takes me a few seconds to situate myself.

Motel.

I hear a rustle from the adjoining room and let out a large sigh.

With Bastian.

Realizing I fell asleep fully dressed, I stand up and pointedly avoid peeking into the other room, while I head for my bathroom to freshen up. It is still early in the morning, but I call Lenix anyway. She picks up on the first ring and I spend the next fifteen minutes trying to convince her that I am *fine*. Eventually, I hear Connor bark in the background, most likely telling her to stop being so dramatic and we hang up after she sniffs an emotional goodbye.

Changing into some fresh clothes and fixing my hair into two braids, I pop my baseball cap on and work up the courage to just stroll into Bastian's room.

It is empty.

Instead, I find him reading a book on the rusty table just outside his door.

He peers up from his sunglasses. I clear my throat and smile, standing near him awkwardly.

"What are you reading?" I ask, solely because I have nothing better to say.

"Parable of the Sower," he says while looking down at the open pages.

"Oh." I clasp my hands in front of me, putting my weight on the balls of my feet and then back on my heels. "I am not familiar with that book."

He hums in response, one long finger resting on his temple, his thumb cradled under his chin. I notice his knuckles look raw, but do not question it as I peruse him further. His white blonde hair looks damp from the shower, a silver chain necklace rests against a gray t-shirt, and blue jeans. I let my eyes wander down and then quickly snap them back up when I realize I am staring at his bare feet. I gaze into the distance, trying to act casual, pretending I did not just react like I saw him naked.

"Where are we heading today?" he says so low I can barely catch the words before they fade into the morning breeze.

"Amboy crater?"

"Is that a question?" he replies, slowly looking up at me.

I smile tensely. "Amboy crater," I repeat with a determined nod this time.

"Better," he mutters before standing up and disappearing into the room.

AFTER A QUICK BITE at the diner close by, I slide into the driver's seat and watch Bastian climb in beside me. With my hands already on the steering wheel, I smile wide and say, "Let us stomp the road."

The faintest dimple appears on Bastian's cheek but it disappears by the time he looks at me.

"Hit," he says.

"What?"

"It's *hit* the road."

Maybe it really is amusement in his tone that I keep hearing.

"Oh." I force a laugh, still full of nerves as usual. "Right."

Pulling out of the motel parking lot, we fall into a, now expected, silence and I wait for his directions while he also busies himself on his laptop. Eventually, I glance over and notice Bastian has taken his sunglasses off. I do a double take, my hands gripping the wheel to steady myself when I realize his left eye is bruised.

I must have made a sound. He tilts his head my way and raises his dark brow, acting like he did not acquire a black eye from the time I left his room last night to now. Now his knuckles are looking a lot more suspicious.

But instead of saying anything, I choose to play nonchalant.

"Thought I saw something," I say pointing to the road.

He blinks and then looks back down, effectively ending our conversation—if you can call it that.

When we arrive at our destination, I change into hiking boots, and Bastian keeps his sneakers on. I do not bother telling him otherwise.

The trail to the crater cuts through the Mojave desert and since it is early spring the wildflowers are in full bloom, a field of yellow accompanying us up the trail.

I cannot seem to stop smiling.

Two hours later, we finally reach the wide rim of the crater. I am sweaty and exhausted but somewhat exhilarated. An unfamiliar sense of accomplishment overcomes me when I take in the vastness of the desert before me.

I have never been this high up before.

I look over to Bastian, who has been wearing my backpack for the last hour. For once, he looks like anyone else who spent their morning hiking in the sun. Slightly winded, shirt sticking to his chest with sweat, cheeks red.

The sight of him like this makes me want to burst into a full belly laugh.

It must be the endorphins.

Sliding the bag off his shoulders, he digs into it and hands me a water bottle. I take it and slink down onto the dirt with a large contented exhale. I take a long drink of water and hand it back to Bastian who is still standing. My gaze lingers on his lips—and how they are on the same bottle where my own lips just were. My stomach flips, and I suddenly feel twice as hot as before.

Startled by my body's reaction, I tear my eyes from the alluring sight and slowly admire the landscape instead. The highway is so far away from here that the cars look like miniature toys from this distance. I could almost pluck them up from here if I tried. It is breathtaking.

"It is hard not to find the beauty of God in places like these." The words just slip out, surprising me. I wrinkle my brows, biting my lip while I silently chastise myself. For once, a part of me hopes Bastian ignores me.

But finally, after a long stretch of silence, he sits beside me, arms wrapped around bent knees. "Why does it have to be God's beauty? And not ours?" he inquires in an even tone.

I keep my eyes fixed on the horizon. "Whose?"

"Us." I can feel his stare burning the side of my face but I do not meet his gaze. "Our co-existence with the world around us. Nature. Earth. Whatever you want to call it."

I mull over his words for a while, a soft breeze cooling my heated skin. "You do not believe that God created life on earth?" I probe tentatively, finally looking his way.

He studies me, and I match his gaze. "Do you?" he says while bringing a flame to the cigarette between his lips. I watch the smoke roll out of his mouth, his throat bobbing with a swallow, the blue turning almost purple under his left eye, and I am suddenly hit by the powerful beauty of the man sitting beside me. Like he could create a crater of his own with just a flick of his cigarette.

I turn my attention back to the desert. "I do not know what I believe in anymore," I finally whisper.

Bastian lets out a quiet chuckle and I nearly startle at the sound. He takes a long drag before saying, "Welcome to being human, Lucy."

9

BASTIAN

"Can you take a picture of me?" Lucy asks, handing me her phone.

We're standing in the middle of the desert, yet again. This time in Santa Claus, Arizona. The place is a ghost town. The remaining buildings are heavily vandalized and in a dilapidated state. Nonetheless, Lucy is standing under an old faded sign that says *This is it! Santa's land*, wearing denim overalls with a blue t-shirt underneath, beaming like she just found a hidden treasure under a rock.

We've been on the road for a few days now. The more time spent together, the less jumpy she seems to get like she's gotten used to being around me. Not sure if I like that idea or not.

I squint against the bright sun and take her phone out of her grasp, doing as she says.

"Did you know I was not aware that Christmas even existed a year ago?" She talks through her smile, still trying to pose for the picture.

"Yeah? So why did you even want to come here?"

I guess the tone of my question had a bit too much bite because Lucy's smile drops as soon as she takes her phone back, pocketing it without even looking at the photo I took.

"I do not need to justify everything I do on this trip to you," she says in a clipped tone, walking away.

"Fair enough," I mutter while I put my shades back on, squinting up at the clear blue sky.

Now standing a few feet ahead, peering into the hole in the ground, she says, "The well looks dry."

I saunter closer. "I think it used to be a wishing well."

She gives a small pout, freckled nose scrunching. "A wishing well? What is that?"

The innocence in her question makes my chest tight, but I ignore it.

"You whisper your wish into the well and then throw a coin in. Supposed to make your wishes come true."

Her face morphs into a wide-open smile, green eyes twinkling like I just told her she won the lottery. "How fun!" Then her eyebrows knit together. "Wait, what if the well is dry?" she asks with all the seriousness in the world.

I stay silent for a few seconds as I think.

"Stay here," I finally say, walking back to the car.

"Where are you going?" she says half-heartedly but I don't answer.

Finding what I'm looking for in the middle console, I return with a water bottle and uncap it. I empty the water in the well while Lucy watches studiously.

"There," I say, meeting her curious gaze. "Now it's not dry."

Her warm smile makes the side of her eyes crinkle. I pretend none of it is affecting me, my face carefully blank when I hand her a dime I fished out of my pocket.

"Thank you," she says in earnest.

I shrug, looking away. Deciding I can't bear another fucking second of this wholesome exchange, I turn and say over my shoulder, "I'll wait in the car."

Back on the highway heading to another sad-looking motel for the night, I'm busy working on my laptop when Lucy breaks the silence.

"Let's play two truths and a lie," she says excitedly.

She can't be serious.

I slowly turn my head toward her and the delighted expression on her face confirms it. She's being serious.

"No."

My attention returns to the screen in front of me, hoping she'll drop it.

She doesn't.

"Oh come on," she replies, a slight whine in her tone while she lowers the music. "I am bored, and you are always on your computer. What do you do on there anyway?"

"Work."

"But what do you *do*?"

I close my laptop in defeat and slide it back into my backpack, letting out a long sigh. "Given your history, I don't think you'd understand even if I explained it."

"Try me," she says while straightening in her seat as if preparing for the world's best gossip. Holding back another sigh, I decide to start simply.

"Do you know what the dark web is?"

"Like a Google?"

I bite back a grin.

"Yeah like Google," I say while looking out the window at the passing landscape. "But for criminals."

"What do you do on there?"

"Top secret shit."

A small huff falls from her full lips. "You are not going to tell me are you?"

I look back at her. "No."

She falls silent for a beat, eyes on the road.

"So can we play that game then?" she says hopefully.

"No."

She lets out a disgruntled noise. "Please?"

"How do you know about that game anyway?"

She turns to me for a quick second before saying, "I researched 'fun things to do on a road trip' and it came up."

"Savvy," I say, crossing my arms and staring into the distance.

"Look Bastian, we are going to be spending a few more weeks together. Might as well get to know each other," she says sternly.

I would rather saw off my left foot with a butter knife than play two truths and a lie. But I roll my eyes and find myself conceding anyway. There's just something about Lucy that makes me not want to deny her, maybe it's knowing how dire her life was before we got her out... maybe it's something else entirely.

"Fine, you start," I concede.

Her smile sends a warm trickle down my spine.

It irks me.

I would rather stay cold.

She falls into a concentrated silence before she finally speaks again.

"Okay, ready?" she asks, as if I need some major preparation time in order to play this dumb game. I nod. "I once had a dog named Molly, I am a Sagittarius, and I have a fear of frogs."

"I'm surprised you know about astrology," I say instead of guessing the lie.

"Lenix is really into it."

"Should have known," I mumble.

"Now guess," she says much too animatedly.

I slide my gaze toward the driver's seat, studying her.

"You don't have a fear of frogs," I finally say.

She barks out a laugh. "I do, actually. It is called ranidaphobia," she says with a side grin. "I looked it up."

I swipe my hand over my face, trying to hide the small smirk appearing on my lips. "Why frogs?"

"Their wet skin unnerves me." She shivers in mock disgust. "My brother used to trap them when we were young and he would run after—" Her voice dies down, her face turning serious. Her expression feels conflicted as if she caught herself remembering a sweet memory that has now turned sour.

After a beat, I say, "You mean your brother Frederick?" The religious freak who became the leader of Sacro Nuntio when their father died.

I seem to snap her out of her reverie, and she gives me a quick look before staring straight ahead, forcing a grin on her lips.

"Anyway, I never owned a dog," she says, ignoring my question. "Okay, now your turn."

I don't press her, and think through what I'll say, instead. I can practically feel Lucy's anticipated glee beside me.

"I've been shot five times, my middle name is Jared, and I hate this game."

Her laugh is bright, but she ignores my not-so-subtle dig.

"You have not been shot five times," she says with too much assurance.

"I have."

"Really?" A surprised look paints her face.

I shrug. "Part of the gig."

"That is so dangerous," she says quietly. "I do not understand why you all do what you do."

"Yeah? And what does your God say about the company you keep since you've been out of that cult?" I didn't mean it to sound harsh, but it does, and I regret the words as soon as they're out of my mouth. Especially when she falls silent, her face suddenly serious.

I don't bother filling the silence and wait for her to speak.

"I have encountered much bigger evil than you Bastian. *Or* the Sin Eaters."

The words hurt to hear, a spike of anger slicing through my chest at the implication. I want to tell her that I'd kill her brother if he wasn't already dead. Even if I only have a vague idea of what happened to her inside that insidious cult. It doesn't matter. I'd still dig him up and desecrate his corpse just to stop Lucy from ever saying shit like that again.

Instead, I say nothing. I barely acknowledge that I heard her.

We stay silent for a long stretch of time, the low hum of music covering up the sound of our breathing.

"My middle name is Malcolm," I finally utter, avoiding her gaze.

"Hmm?" she says distractedly.

"That was the lie. My middle name isn't Jared, it's Malcolm."

Her smile is genuine when she glances over. "Bastian Malcolm Maxwell," she says slowly, her smile widening. "I know so much about you now."

I let out one single chuckle. "Don't let it go to your head."

10

B astian and I have been on the road for over a week now. We have settled into a routine. It mostly consists of me dragging him to roadside attractions and him hating every second of it.

Today is no different. While I explore, Bastian is near the entrance, ignoring everything—and everyone—around him.

One foot up on the cement wall, black t-shirt and usual blue jeans, his head rests behind him while he smokes a cigarette. His white blonde hair falls into his eyes and suddenly, the need to capture him like this—unbothered, but his presence still so... *bold*—makes me pull out my phone from my pants pocket. Making sure his attention is elsewhere, I take the photo.

My heart rate triples when I stare at the screen. The picture feels illicit, and an indescribable warmth trickles through my veins. I must have been studying my phone for longer than expected, jumping when I hear Bastian's voice close to me.

"Ready?"

I quickly shut off my screen along with the incriminating picture and shove it back into my pocket, hoping I do not look guilty.

"Locked and loaded," I say, slightly flustered.

A faint dimple appears on his left cheek while he puts his sunglasses on.

"That's inaccurate," he drawls.

"What is?"

"The—never mind. Let's go," he replies.

And this time I *know* that it is amusement I hear in the low tenor of his voice.

AN HOUR LATER, we are sitting across from each other in a diner as I watch Bastian take a bite of his burger. After sharing most meals together for the past ten days, the novelty of seeing him perform something so domestic should have worn off by now.

And yet, my eyes have not quite gotten the memo, because I cannot seem to look away.

"What?" he says after swallowing his bite.

My gaze lands back on my plate, taking a huge bite of creamy pasta. I try to act like I have no idea what he is talking about, but the icy glare he sends my way makes me shiver.

Waiting until my mouth is not full of food, I answer, "You always eat the same thing."

With a deliberate slowness to his movements, he picks up his water and takes a sip.

"And?" he says with his casual boredom I have now gotten used to navigating.

60

"Just curious," I answer with a shrug, knowing he is more likely to continue the conversation the less interested I seem.

He lets a long drag of silence curl around us before saying anything else. "I don't like surprises." He takes another bite of his burger, now his turn to observe me.

I am aware he has not asked me a leading question but I fill the silence anyway.

"I have eaten too much of the same thing for far too long. Now I want to taste new foods as much as possible. How else am I supposed to find out what is my favorite, if I have not even experienced it?"

Bastian's dark eyes roam over my face, expression blank but seemingly lost in thought.

"Is it this?" he says with a small jerk of his chin toward my plate.

I look down at the now-congealed pasta in front of me and laugh. "No, definitely not this."

He wipes his mouth with a napkin and stands up.

"Noted," he replies before walking up to the counter and settling our bill.

It is early evening. The sun is dipping low behind the desert landscape when the car suddenly starts sputtering and I barely have time to pull over on the side of the road before it stutters to a stop.

I look over toward Bastian, wide-eyed and concerned.

"What the heck just happened?" I manage to say through the worry clogging up my throat.

He eyes me suspiciously. "Didn't you just fill the tank?"

"Yes…"

"Pop the hood," he orders while opening the car door.

I give him a dead stare, my mind completely blank. Not bothering to explain further, he leans over. While he finds the necessary button, his shoulder grazes my chest and my breath catches in my throat at the sensation and proximity. Then he is out of the car and I let out a shaky exhale. Eventually, I climb out myself, needing some fresh air on my heated skin, as well as being too anxious to sit alone and wait.

I stand near and watch, but I have no clue what he is even trying to do. After a few minutes of Bastian tinkering at the engine, he finally closes the hood and wipes his hands on his jeans.

"We're going to have to walk to the nearest gas station, we haven't had proper phone service for miles."

I gape at him. "But we do not even know how far that is."

"Better start walking then," he sighs while reaching for his backpack and then the flashlight in the glove box.

"But what is wrong with the car?"

"Not sure."

"We are just—just gonna leave all our things here?"

"You'd rather we drag everything with us?" he says, walking away.

For a few seconds, I am frozen between wanting to stay with our belongings and following Bastian. Eventually, I let out a small groan, balling my fists in frustration. Grabbing my own backpack, I scurry behind him.

"Why are you acting like this is simply a minor inconvenience?" I say, trying to catch up.

"How would you rather I react?" he mutters, keeping his gaze straight ahead.

"I do not know, just—just act like you care about something for once." My tone is clipped, and my words hang heavy between us. Focusing on the sound of our steady steps on gravel, I wait for him to reply.

I am about to apologize when he finally speaks. "Would it help?"

It is my turn not to immediately answer. I wrap my arms around my chest, a slight chill to the air. Then finally, I whisper, "No. I guess it would not."

"Here," he says while pulling his black crew neck over his head. A small sliver of skin near his hips appears and then disappears with the t-shirt rising underneath. "It's getting cold."

I stumble over my step and laugh nervously. "No, that is fine. I am fine," I say quickly, focusing on putting one foot in front of the other.

"It's not a suggestion," he says flatly.

A twinge of irritation flares inside me, but I say nothing and snatch the sweater out of his hand.

"Thank you," I grumble while slipping it on.

I am struck with the scent of him; eucalyptus, fresh laundry, and tobacco. His body heat still lingers between every thread. This time the shiver traveling down my spine stems from a different physical reaction entirely. I barely recognize it and effectively pay it no mind while we continue to walk under the darkening sky. All I know is that when I think about the fact that I am wearing his clothes, I get that feeling again.

Forty-five minutes later, like a mirage in the Arizona desert, we finally reach a gas station. Bastian tells me to sit on a bench while he heads inside to speak to the clerk. I heed his command—only because my feet are tired and I was going to sit and wait anyhow.

I have time to grow bored before he reappears.

"They'll have someone tow the car to the garage up the road," he says, meeting my gaze, hands on his hips. I notice black grease still staining his fingers. "It'll have to wait 'till morning though. Guy says there's a motel ten minutes away." He studies me for a beat. "You okay to walk?"

I stand up and dust off. "Sure. But what about our bags?"

"We'll just have to manage," he says, looking into the distance then back at me with the first crack of the closest thing to a smile I have seen from him. "Part of the adventure, Luce."

WHEN WE FINALLY REACH THE motel, I am bone tired.

That is until the receptionist informs us that they only have one room available.

Then I am wide awake.

"We're in the middle of nowhere, how is that even possible?" Bastian says dismissively.

She shrugs. "The circus is in town," she answers flatly as if that explains everything.

"The fucking circus?" he says in a slow deliberate fashion that would typically intimidate most people —not her.

She gives Bastian a slow blink before repeating herself. "The circus."

I touch him on the shoulder and his head snaps to my hand, then up to my face. I do not let my fingers linger, absentmindedly wondering if that was the first time I have ever touched him deliberately.

"It is fine. We will figure it out. Just get the room," I tell him in a quiet voice.

After handing her some cash, she gives us the key and we walk up the outdoor stairway to the second floor, where we find our room at the end of the walkway.

The room has a similar smell to every other motel we have frequented; stale with a hint of cleaning products mixed in. The one king-size bed looms in my periphery, taunting me to acknowledge its presence. It is Bastian that mentions it first.

"I'll sleep on the floor," he says somewhat stoically.

"No, you will not," I say it so quickly that I even surprise myself and cringe internally. "I—I just mean, we—we are two adults. We can share a bed without making it weird. I used to share a bed with Lenix all the time." I let out a nervous chuckle. "Not that you are like a sister, but… uh." I snap my mouth shut, hoping it will help with my rambling. When I notice that I am clinging to the straps of my backpack just like Lenix did in the video of when she went skydiving, I let go and try to shift my stance into something a little more casual.

I *am* making it weird.

Either, Bastian does not notice or does not care—could be both—because the next thing I know he is pulling his grease-stained t-shirt over his head, heading to the bathroom.

I stare at the now-closed door, then down at my feet. They feel rooted to the faded gray carpet. My mind latched on to the image of Bastian's naked back walking away from me. I listen to the pipes groan and then the faint hum of the shower before I gather how to move again.

I am trying to figure out how to turn on the TV when Bastian reappears. The remote nearly slips out of my grasp when I take him in. My eyes do not know where to look and I freeze, but still take time to gape.

I notice his wet hair first, pushed off his face. My gaze then tracks a single drop of water gliding down his toned stomach. I barely have time to register his pierced nipples, and what looks like his only tattoo—some lettering across his chest that says *memento mori*—before my attention zeroes in on the dark trail of hair disappearing into the white towel tied around his narrow waist. Seeing him like this sends the same thrill I felt earlier zipping down my limbs. It makes me want to do something spontaneous, adventurous even, like walk up to him and trail my finger down the ridges and valleys of his naked torso.

When logic finally decides to catch up to my wandering thoughts, I suddenly realize I have been staring at Bastian for the past thirty seconds, but my eyes still linger. Finally, I peel my gaze away and snap back up to his face. My throat goes dry when I find heat in his dark assessing eyes.

"Your turn." His voice is low, but it is missing its usual chill.

"My turn?" I repeat without really registering what I am saying.

His head slowly tilts toward the bathroom and I land back on earth.

"Oh! Right." I smile, snapping out of my trance. "Shower. Good idea."

Releasing the death grip I have on the remote, I scamper past him without saying another word, avoiding his piercing look and locking the door behind me.

Under the hot jet, I try to wash away my wandering thoughts, my heart still beating wildly in my chest. But no amount of scalding water will wash away the image of Bastian from my mind. I let it take root, finding it a home, safe and far, far away from all the other memories that still continue to haunt me.

The vision of me discovering how Bastian's skin feels under my touch comes back in vivid colors. By the time I have dried myself off, I have decided that reality must feel even better than the imaginary.

11

BASTIAN

Seventeen years old

Reality still feels like a dream. The kind where the mind simply drifts, unencumbered and free. My eyelids are heavy, my blinks slow and unhurried. I perceive the haunting dance of the music still playing on my old stereo before I register where I am.

My bed.

My bedroom.

And my girlfriend Anna sleeping, her back turned, beside me.

I realize I'm still holding the needle in my hands, the shoe string loose, but still around my arm. Groggily, I take it off and rub the area distractedly. With strength I barely possess, I push myself up and sit against the headboard, patting for my pack of smokes beside me as I do so. My black-out curtains are drawn shut. It could be the middle of the afternoon—I wouldn't know. I snap my zippo shut after lighting a cigarette and take a long drag, pushing one of my palms into my eye socket. Reaching for Anna's shoulder, I give her a small shake.

"Wake up," I croak.

I'm not sure what I notice first.
Maybe it's all of it at once.
How her body feels under my touch. Her skin cold under the pads of my fingers. Or how her limbs feel rigid while I turn her towards me. Or maybe it's her pale blue lips when I finally see her face.
Whatever it is. It doesn't matter.
Anna's gone.
And I was the one with the needle full of death.

I HAVEN'T SHARED a bed with anyone since I was a street rat with a dead girlfriend.

All these years, I've successfully avoided it.

Until now.

Not to mention how fast I agreed to it.

I let what's left unsaid drift up along with the smoke from my cigarette while I look up at the night sky. The front door is ajar, I can hear Lucy coming out of the shower from outside. Continuing to smoke, I push away thought after wayward thought while I listen to her putter around the room until I finally hear a click of a lamp. Then silence.

I could just walk away. Leave and never return.

No one would care.

I sure wouldn't.

I push off the wall instead.

The room is dark when I walk back inside, save for a small lamp on the empty side of the bed. Lucy has her back to the front door.

"Move over," I order.

Lucy turns around to face me. "What? Why?"

"I sleep closest to the door. End of story," I mutter.

There's a pause, followed by a small huff, but eventually,

she does as I say, sliding to the other side of the bed. Her gaze is now fixed on me, although most of her face is hidden in darkness. The hazy glow of the light glints off her skin where it does reach.

I didn't bother with a shirt before heading outside. Her eyes linger like they did earlier and I don't stop her. I rake my hand through my hair and release a breath, licking my lips. My gaze slowly slides up to meet hers and I don't know what the fuck I'm doing. All I know is that I can't look away while my fingers find my belt, unbuckling it. Then the button of my jeans. The slow push down my legs, followed by the quiet rustles of fabric falling to the floor.

She hasn't stopped watching.

I don't think I want her to.

I lean over and push the duvet down. The movement makes the sheets fall off her shoulder, fluttering past her stomach. All she's wearing is an oversized t-shirt and black boyshorts. I swallow down the curse that nearly escapes my lips. She doesn't move, doesn't speak, her eyes never leaving mine. There's nothing left to do but slide beside her in bed and I do just that. I break eye contact while I slowly reach over her to turn off the light, the warmth of her body under me feels almost too good to ignore.

But I do.

I lay on my back, as far away as possible, one arm behind my head. The darkness only manages to heighten her presence beside me. Counting my breaths, I try to ignore every dirty little impulse seeking to manifest within me. I hear the glide of skin on cotton sheets before I feel her feathery touch on my chest. It's just one finger, but it could be her entire body on mine for the effect it has on me. By the way she was looking at me earlier, I'm not surprised she's daring to touch me. It rattles me just the same.

Her index finger traces my tattoo, letter by letter and I can barely breathe. My hand closes over hers and I hear her breath catch. I nearly succumb to one of my earlier impulses—to push her hand even further down. Instead, I gently place it between us on the bed. The silence pulses with tension, I can practically taste it on my lips. Suddenly, I crave another kind of taste entirely. Her skin on my tongue, soft sighs against my mouth.

Her quiet voice finds its way to my ear. Whispers in the dark. "Why?"

I close my eyes, trying to keep it together.

I let out a long sigh. "Why, what?"

But I know. I fucking know.

The silence that follows almost sounds like she's gathering the courage to say it. Then she finally does.

"Why can't I touch you?"

I swallow hard before answering.

"Don't make me answer that, Luce. I don't have a good enough reason."

Not when the very tone of my voice sounds like it's craving her touch.

For half an irrational second, I convince myself she won't listen and her hand will find its way back to my skin. But then I hear the mattress creak beside me and I don't need to look to know she's rolled over.

Listening to her even breaths, I stay stuck in the same position for most of the night. On my back and staring at the ceiling, unwilling to acknowledge why falling asleep feels so dangerous. Why, if I close my eyes, I'll wake up in the morning with another body to mourn.

71

12

"I t's time, Lucy," Imogene says with a too-soft voice that makes me want to curl up on myself. "I think you're ready."

I have been seeing her twice a week for six months now. I trust her. But what I do not trust are the memories desperate to be left alone. Because if left untouched and unspoken they cannot become this living, breathing thing. And maybe, hopefully one day I can just forget.

But if six months of therapy has taught me anything, it is this: Trauma never forgets. Trauma simply slumbers, burrowed deep inside its host, waiting to be heard. And it will be heard, whether it be now or decades later, it does not matter. Trauma has all the time in the world.

I simultaneously pick at the skin on my thumb and bite the inside of my lip, trying my hardest not to let the sinking feelings pull me even deeper still.

"When Lenix ran away, I was betrothed to Patrick in her stead," I mutter softly, looking out the window at the tree outside. I focus on how the rays of the sun peek through the leaves instead of the darkness hovering all around me. "I had just turned twelve."

I hear Imogene shift in her chair but I do not look away from the sun, the leaves, the tree.

"My brother Frederick, who was twenty-one at the time, became our shepherd when father died. And… well." I wring my hands, unsure how to continue. "He was now God's vessel and—and… it was his duty to take my maidenhead before I lay with my husband… my own brother…"

All these years and I am still desperate to normalize it, to convince my subconscious that what happened that day was holy. I never truly connected all the pieces until Lenix and I spoke about it, a few months ago. How our father had wanted to do the same to her before her wedding to Patrick, but instead she fought back and accidentally killed him. Somehow she understood what kind of battle was raging inside of me when I realized she defended herself and… and I did not. "You were much too young to understand, Lucy," she said into my hair, her voice cracking while she held me tightly in her arms. "You were much too young."

Slowly, I turn my gaze to Imogene, and we sit in silence for a few seconds before she finally speaks. "You were raped, Lucy." Again her voice is much too soft, too caring.

I did not even know that word existed before all this.

Before.

When I was sheltered and taught that Hell was Heaven on earth.

I close my eyes and let the tears fall. The sadness engulfs me and swallows me whole.

Instead of words, I simply nod and continue to mourn my innocence until I find my voice again. Opening my eyes, I take a deep breath and try to steady myself.

When I finally speak, my voice feels different, like a child's more than the twenty-five year old adult I am now. "I thought it was normal… I thought all of it was normal."

Imogene presses her lips into a waning smile and shakes her head. A simple gesture to convey so much. "It wasn't," she says softly. "None of it was."

THE NEXT MORNING, Bastian is already out of bed when I wake up. I blink blankly at the ceiling remembering what I dared to do last night. I try not to cringe, but I am somewhat unsuccessful. I do not quite understand what came over me to be so bold. The urge to touch him, to prove he was not just a figment of my imagination had been too potent to deny.

My body had heated beside him, my breath quickening. But these feelings... they felt so foreign. And still, now, I struggle to describe them. To put a name to my actions.

I am not a virgin. Still, in so many ways, I am inexperienced in my sexual history. And never did I ever feel like this with Patrick.

Never.

All I know is that I desperately needed to feel Bastian under my touch. To taste him. Or to simply press my palm against his chest and listen to his heart beat all night.

I should feel ashamed. But oddly, aside from the mild rejection, I feel—good? It is not as if we will need to have an awkward conversation about what transpired between us. At least there is one good side to Bastian never speaking.

Shaking away remnants of last night, I climb out of bed and freshen up. I find him outside, a book in one hand and a cigarette in the other.

"Have you even eaten yet?" I ask slightly disgusted, wrinkling my nose.

With his eyes still fixed on the pages of his book, he takes a long drag of his cigarette and shrugs. "Have you?" he drawls.

"I'm not the one smoking at eight in the morning," I state.

His gaze shifts, his head slowly tilting half an inch my way. His nose ring glints in the morning rays, and I can almost imagine the flicker of the metal as a wink—but not quite.

"Can't wait to discover one of your vices, Luce," he says while stubbing his cigarette in the ashtray on the small rusty table beside him.

My ability to process what he just said malfunctions for a few crucial seconds and I am left staring at him, mouth slightly agape. I might be inexperienced, but I can still pick up on tone. And that was… that is…

Is Bastian flirting with me?

He stands up, clearly unbothered by my surprise or lack of response, and stretches his arms above his head, squinting at the sun. My eyes dip to his hips, and the same sliver of skin I have witnessed before sends butterflies fluttering in my stomach.

"Car won't be ready for another day, but I got some of our bags," he says impassively.

That finally snaps me out of it. "Oh." I look at the ground, then back up at him, not quite knowing how to react to the news. Or the thought that we will be sharing a bed for another night. "What are we going to do until then?"

I END up convincing Bastian to come walk around town with me. Not that he has much of a choice, since he is basically stuck with me. The thought does not necessarily make me feel great. It leaves me mostly confused, never really knowing if the man—who acts more like my shadow—even likes my company.

The town center consists of one main road with one-story businesses and shops on either side, looking like any other small town we have encountered since this road trip began. It is surprisingly busy and filled with tourists aimlessly wandering the sidewalks. The clerk was not kidding about the circus being in town. I told Bastian we should get tickets, but the idea died a swift death as soon as I saw the daggers shot my way at the suggestion.

After lunch, I find a small boutique that sells cowboy paraphernalia and smile wide at Bastian while pushing the door open. The bell above signals our entry and the sales-person behind the counter greets us with enthusiasm. The smell of leather is heady, my eyes roving over all the merchandise, not knowing where to start. I leave Bastian to his quiet grumbling and peruse the aisles, my hand slowly trailing over the multitudes of cowboy boots I pass.

It reminds me of all the westerns I have watched with Lenix since I left the commune. She never really under-stood why I loved them so much, I do not either. I just know I like them and that is good enough for me.

My gaze falls on a cowboy hat on a top shelf. It is baby blue, and it is the most beautiful thing I have ever seen. I let my fingers trace the felt, my heart squeezing in delight. I look right, then left. When I am convinced no one is watching me, I pick up the hat and march my way to the mirror only a few steps away. I place it delicately atop my head, my one braid falling over my shoulder, and study my reflection.

I am suddenly overwhelmed with a bright, intoxicating feeling seeing myself like this. Just as quickly it is replaced by a small hiss in my head telling me this is too frivolous and completely unnecessary—the harsh tone of my brother's voice still telling me I should not desire such superficial things. My smile drops, and I hastily remove the hat. Feeling foolish, I look around, making sure no one spotted me, especially Bastian, and place the hat back on the shelf where it belongs.

I find him in the back of the store looking at the hunting knives. With one look and a small nod of the head, I tell him I am ready to go. He follows me out without a word. We spend the next hour shopping and wasting time, while my mind is still on the baby blue hat I did not allow myself to buy.

13

BASTIAN

The box I'm holding is burning my hands. I place it delicately on the ugly comforter before it scalds the skin of my palms clean off. My heart races as I move away from the bed, pacing in front of it, my fingers raking through my hair.

This is so fucking stupid.

I sit down in the old wingback chair in the corner and then immediately stand back up. I'm about to slip outside for a breather and a much-needed cigarette when I hear the bathroom door open behind me. My heart slams into my chest, then stops entirely before I slowly turn around to face Lucy. I'm convinced my face is unreadable but by the look of her questioning gaze, she might be picking up on cues I thought I was skillfully hiding.

Her light brown hair is still dripping from the shower, already curling at the ends, staining the cotton of her t-shirt over her shoulder. She's wearing my old band tee again. I swipe my hand over my face and clear my throat. I say nothing but point to the box instead.

"What is— I mean what's that?" she asks. The curiosity in her tone creates an odd feeling in my chest.

Shrugging off the discomfort, I look away and mutter, "Just open it."

She drops the white towel she was still holding on to the wooden dresser and steps closer to the edge of the bed. She shoots me a quick glance, eyebrows furrowed, and then looks back at the box again. She hovers over it, observing, and I grow impatient.

"It's not a bomb."

Her lips pull into a small grin, her eyes still fixed on the box until finally, her fingers curl over the lid, pulling it up and off. Her soft smile disappears as she grows unnervingly still.

I swallow hard.

This was a mistake.

I'm about to tell her that I'll return the damn thing, that it was a dumb idea in the first place when she finally turns to me, her eyes glimmering with unshed tears.

Her voice wavers when she says quietly, "You bought me the hat?"

I press my lips together but keep my gaze locked with hers.

I replay the scene in my head as we stand there, both not saying anything. The expression she had when she put it on and looked at herself in the mirror. The joy of a simple baby blue cowboy hat.

Not to mention the vague feeling of déjà vu it jostled free inside me. I knew if I went looking, I'd find the hat written somewhere in my notebook. First the map, now this. Another coincidence. Another memory I want to shove away and forget, but can't.

That aside, Lucy was breathtaking to watch.

Then her following reaction, so similar to heartache, scratched at my conscience, and it was too much for me to see.

I had to buy it.

I clear my throat and cross my arms. "It was made for you," I say with a shrug.

She stays silent for another beat, looking down at the box and the giggling squeal that follows takes me by surprise. She flies into my arms and a small *oomph* leaves my lips as she circles her arms around my waist and squeezes hard. The top of her head falls right under my nose and her still-damp curls tickle my face, while I try not to breathe her scent in through large lungfuls. My arms are stuck half-raised in the air, unsure if I should hug her back, so I stay unmoving instead until she pulls away and gives me a watery smile, mumbling a thank you.

She skips back to the bed and finally pulls the hat out of the box, putting it on with a flourish. Prancing into the bathroom, she disappears for a second and then walks back out, the baby blue hat still on her head and the widest smile on her face.

"Isn't it the prettiest thing you've ever seen?" she says, still beaming.

I lick my lips and give her half a grin. "It sure is, Luce."

Her smile falters as if suddenly nervous and blurts out, "Have a drink with me."

"You still have some vodka?" I say distractedly while I pick up my phone from the bedside table, quickly replying to a few of Connor's messages.

"No—uh, I mean, let's go out... to a bar... together."

I peek at her standing in the middle of the room. And suddenly the image of her still wearing that hat, her arms slightly swinging from side to side as she waits for an answer with a shy expression on her face, makes me want to agree to anything Lucy asks of me.

I nod, unable to look away as I pocket my phone. Her smile widens, sudden relief flashing across her gaze. "I saw a bar called The Arcade not far from here. Maybe we could go there?"

I give her another one of my nods while walking into the bathroom. "Let me just change first."

I REALIZE my mistake as soon as I open the door to The Arcade.

Lucy brought us to a fucking strip club.

I can't believe my oversight. How I didn't look this place up beforehand is beyond me. I bite back a groan and peer over to her walking in right behind me.

By the shock written on her face—she had no fucking clue either.

I consider shoving her out the door and finding another place to have a drink. A decent guy would find an excuse to get her out of here. That's before I watch Lucy try to steel her nerves, straightening her shoulders and sliding a determined look over her flustered nerves. I can't fight the amusement at the sight while I decide upon my next move.

Little Luce wants to pretend this doesn't bother her, does she?

Fine, I'll play.

"Problem?" I drawl, giving her a side glance.

Her laugh is forced. "No problem at all." She fidgets with her cowboy hat before blurting, "Table?"

"Lead the way," I say followed by a small hand flourish.

I place a palm on the small of her back and she jumps

ever so slightly but starts walking almost immediately. The place is busy, packed with inebriated and lewd hillbillies hollering at the dancers over loud dad-rock music. Weaving us around the main stage, she finds a darkened corner in the back for us to sit. I promptly settle in, purposely positioning myself so as to face the stage and the front door, patting the chair beside mine.

I shouldn't find such a sick thrill in Lucy's discomfort. Nonetheless, I can't help but fight back a grin while she slowly sits beside me, stiff as a board.

Thing is—I never claimed to be decent.

14

"How was your relationship with your husband?" Imogene asks in her soft voice, every syllable wrapped in silk. She typically uses that tone when the subject becomes too delicate.

Sometimes it feels like everything about me is too delicate... and it angers me.

I pick at a loose thread in the stitching of the chair cushion, facing my therapist, yet, avoiding her gaze as always, watching that same tree outside the office window.

I bite my lip, letting her question echo inside my head.

How was your relationship with your husband?

"Normal," I finally say.

I know my answer will lead to more questions but I do not know how else to describe the only reality I ever knew. How else can I describe the way of life I was subjugated to from birth?

What is normal anyway?

I can fight against my past and blame it on a lifetime of brain-washing. But both Imogene and I know that deep down I was vaguely conscious that normal was a synonym for abuse. And why I was so *willing to leave with Lenix when she escaped the second time with the help of Connor and the Sin Eaters.*

"Lucy… you were a child for half of your marriage with him. Nothing about that is normal."

"I am aware," I mutter, wringing my hands in my lap. "Most of us were children."

If I would look over to Imogene now, I know I would find her kind eyes looking tenderly my way. I would rather avoid that look as long as I can.

Her pity never tastes as sweet as my denial.

I AM IN A STRIP CLUB.

I am in a strip club with *Bastian*.

These two thoughts have been circulating in my head for the past fifteen minutes. I pretend to be riveted by what is happening on stage and ignore the heat rolling off of Bastian sitting so close to me.

I chew on the plastic straw that came with my vodka soda and finally sneak a glance over to the enigma sitting beside me. He looks displeased. But he looks displeased *anywhere*. Still, not an ounce of him looks uncomfortable or out of place here. If I look hard enough, it almost looks like the side of his lip is tugging upwards, a ghost of a grin wanting to shine through. I do not linger on the sight, quickly turning my gaze back to the crowd around us, the chewed straw still lodged between my teeth.

It is hard not to avert my eyes when I find a few of the dancers grinding on men's lap, it is an unconscious reflex as if trying to avoid anything that feels like it could further corrupt me.

To counteract that feeling I stare. Unabashedly so.

I manage to quiet my mind long enough to take in the woman on the main stage. The effortless sway of her hips and the twirl of her flexible body on the pole pinch at a confusing part of me. She looks so... free. And most importantly, sexually liberated.

The antithesis of the women back in Sacro Nuntio. We never spoke about sex, even amongst ourselves. I am sure it would not be called that even *if* we spoke about it freely— more like performing our matrimonial duty. Which is why it took me this long, after some private online investigation, to realize Patrick always took me from... *the back*. Why it always seemed to hurt no matter how *practiced* I was. And explained why, after even more research, the mystery of how I never bore children.

It might have not felt like it then, but never getting pregnant was a blessing in disguise.

After a few minutes of studying the dancer on stage, I finally recognize the nagging feeling for what it is —jealousy.

Or maybe it is closer to envy.

Both sinful emotions nonetheless.

Imogene's voice echoes in my head, reminding me that my feelings are perfectly valid. I take a deep breath and glance around the club trying to shake the thoughts away. The more I look, the more I feel inadequate. A reminder of my inexperience.

There is nothing inherently wrong with inexperience, I just—I just do not *want* it anymore. I am tired of feeling coddled by everyone around me.

Including Bastian... and maybe if I am being honest; especially Bastian. Ever since last night, I cannot seem to shake the low burning heat I feel when around him. It is not at all familiar but intoxicating nonetheless. And this environment is only heightening it.

How can I make him see me as desirable and not Lenix's little sister?

I shift in my seat, setting my drink on the table in front of us. Maybe it is time for me to act and not think. What is the worst that could happen? For once I do not dwell on the what-ifs and clear my throat, before licking my lips in anticipation, placing my hand on Bastian's thigh.

The rough texture of his jeans under my fingers sends a small thrill down my spine. His muscles flex under my touch and I freeze like prey trying to evade sudden death. My eyes are facing forward, still on the woman dancing on stage and I suddenly do not know what else to do.

Wonderful.

I can feel Bastian staring and my shaky resolve melts away as the seconds tick by. Finally, I turn my head to face him and give him a wobbly smile.

As usual, he does not speak. Instead, he stares me down and lifts a dark brow, his eyes falling on my hand still firmly planted on his thigh, then back up again. Suddenly, I am acting instead of thinking again and I dive toward him, aiming for his lips.

I am stopped by two strong hands around my arms before ever even coming close to my goal.

My eyes flutter open and my cheeks heat with the realization that Bastian has rejected me.

Again.

His dark brown eyes pin me in place, his eyebrows dipping low in scrutiny.

"What are you doing?" he says, his voice low but serious.

I fight the sudden feeling of embarrassment and shake

myself out of his grasp. He lets me go and I spring up from my seat. "It is nothing. Never mind," I stutter quickly trying to take a large step away from the table and far, far away from Bastian. But his long fingers circle my wrist and I am stopped in my tracks. I try to pull away but his hold only tightens, forcing me to look back and face his burning stare.

"Sit back down," he orders, with a small cant of his head. After a few seconds of weighing my limited options, I concede with a huff. I cross my arms over my chest and look anywhere but at him.

"Luce," he says, his tone steady and slightly scolding.

My cheeks continue to burn, and I push my hat further down to try to hide my face from Bastian's continued stare.

"I should not have done that. I am sorry, I will not do it again," I mutter, but in truth, I do not really mean it. I just do not know what else to say.

"Then why did you?" he says with a hint of curiosity.

I consider brushing him off with a non-answer, but mull over his question while anxiously biting at my lip. Wasn't this road trip part of me putting myself out there? To find the courage to just... live? So instead, I take a large centering breath and match his gaze, cocking my head.

"What is the point of this road trip if I don't live a little?" I answer with more confidence than expected.

I blink in surprise when Bastian smiles. It is gone as fast as it appeared like being visited by an elusive ethereal being in the dead of night.

"And you think this will add to your little adventure?" he says dryly.

His words are like ice pelting on my skin. His tone makes me feel childish. My heart slams into my chest in response. I try to stand up again.

This time Bastian's finger finds one of the loops on my jeans and tugs it forcefully.

"Sit." He takes a slow sip of his beer, his cold gaze on me. "I didn't mean for it to come off that way."

His finger lingers near my hip until finally he uncurls it and leans back away.

"So how *did* you mean it?" I manage to say, frustration dripping from every vowel.

His face is impassive but I can tell he is searching for his words, and my throat goes dry while I wait. "I'm not good for you, Luce."

I let out a small scoff, rolling my eyes. "I've had righteous before Bastian. It's all a lie."

"I didn't say *righteous*, I said *good*," he emphasizes both words as if it will further prove his point.

I study him for a beat, unsure how to proceed. I take a quick sip of my drink and then finally speak. "I do not—I don't want good, I just…" I swallow hard, my heartbeat rising with every word spoken. "I just *want*."

"*What* do you want?" he replies, a hint of taunt in his voice this time.

"You," I blurt out almost immediately.

I am suddenly so hot I wonder if I will turn to smoldering embers before Bastian decides to say anything else.

Letting the silence settle between us like an unwelcome visitor, he crosses one ankle over his thigh, settling back in his chair, his elbow resting on the table while his chin perches in his palm. "I don't think I'm actually what you want, Luce," he finally says.

My laugh is too nervous for how I am trying to act but I still answer him while I shake my head in disbelief. "Why do you think you know me more than I know myself?"

He gives me one of his blank stares, then eventually he

speaks. "I don't think you thought much about your answer, so I'll ask again—" he pauses, his body looking so relaxed while mine is far from it, before enunciating every single word, "*What. Do. You. Want?*"

His question feels innocent but the feelings clambering inside of me weigh much heavier. Suddenly my therapist's question from months ago floats back into frame.

How was your relationship with your husband?

Tears prick my eyes at the reminder of everything I am trying so hard to overcome. I blink them fast away before looking back brazenly at Bastian, shoulders squared and determination keeping my head held high.

"Pleasure," I say assuredly with a quick nod of my head. "I want to experience pleasure."

He blinks slowly, his reaction nearly impossible to decipher except for the slow swipe of his tongue over his lips, my eyes tracking the movement intently. He does not seem at all surprised. As if he knew my answer before I even voiced it out loud. He lets out a sound that could *almost* be described as a pleased hum, racking his fingers through his white-blond hair before taking another long sip of his beer.

"You want to use me. Is that it, Luce?"

"What?" I nearly yelp, my eyebrows jumping up. "No." My laugh is forced but I ignore the simmering discomfort for the more pressing matter in front of me. "That is not what I said."

He stays silent, taking another drink from his pint, his gaze still fixed on mine.

It is in that long stretch of silence that I am overcome with the need for Bastian not to have the upper hand in this conversation, suddenly tired of the pretenses and insecurities I seem to struggle with on a daily basis.

"You know what? Fine. Yes," I say with as much assurance as possible. "I want to use you. Happy?" I cross my legs and straighten my back. "Is that what you wanted to hear?"

Another pleased hum. Another drink of his beer.

"It did sound rather titillating coming from those lips of yours," he drawls.

My heart skips a beat, my cheeks suddenly heating for another reason entirely. And when he slowly leans over, his fingers curling around the seat of my chair, dragging me closer to him, it almost feels like the ground is crumbling underneath me the closer my body gets to his.

"Okay," he simply says.

I chastise my scrambled brain while I try to gather my thoughts. All I can manage is to parrot back his answer. "Okay?"

His eyes smoothly drag down my body and then up again, nodding.

"There needs to be ground rules," he says while standing up. I am left gawking at him, my head slowly lifting up with the action, unsure if I have imagined this entire interaction. He fishes his pack of cigarettes out of his pocket, propping one between his lips. "I need a smoke first," he mumbles, heading toward the exit without another word.

15

BASTIAN

The door swings closed behind me and the chill in the night air does nothing to cool my heated skin. The sparked flame I just lit smolders against the cigarette as soon as my foot hits the asphalt. I inhale deeply and then press my hand against my eye socket to try to even out my reaction to Lucy basically throwing herself at me... then me accepting.

It didn't take me long to analyze the innumerable outcomes of Lucy and I hooking up—all of them bad. Most of them involved Lenix slicing my balls off. Still, I accepted. I couldn't resist the idea of her using me for her pleasure.

What a fun way to die.

I hear footsteps behind me and I don't need to turn to know that Lucy has followed me out. I hear a small pebble being kicked across the dirt and take a long drag before turning around.

She couldn't be sweeter to look at. Her baby blue cowboy hat still firmly on her head, arms crossed as if to shield herself from whatever will eventually come out of my mouth and it inexplicably makes me soften toward her.

"Ground rules?" she says tentatively.

I flick my smoke further into the parking lot and turn to face her.

"Ground rules."

"Why?"

"Because this isn't a relationship. This isn't us dating. It's a…" I lazily wave my hand around looking for the right word. "An agreement."

Anger flashes across her face, her eyes narrowing. "So what? You think I'm so sheltered that I won't help but fall in love with the first person I… I—" she stutters, seemingly looking for the proper phrasing but her glare stays fixed on mine. "*Fool* around with. I managed to be married and share a bed with a man for over a decade without falling in love, I'm sure I can manage an *agreement*."

"I didn't assume any of what you just said," I say slowly, taking a step closer to her.

She takes a step back, her arms tightening across her chest.

"We just need boundaries for this to work, Luce. We can't just jump into the deep end without having even tested the waters first."

I don't mention that I'm incapable of love. And that it wasn't on the table in the first place.

"What's the deep end?" she asks curiously, and with all the innocence I know she wishes she could shed for good.

I bite back a smile. Even if love is impossible, it doesn't take away how alluring she is like this. Especially when she's looking at me with her furrowed brows and a perplexed expression.

I can't help myself and say something that will send her clear off the edge. "Full penetration."

She takes a step back as if physically pushed. And I am positively charmed. The front door of The Arcade opens and a crowd of five spills out, oblivious to us lingering to the side. We both follow them with our gaze until they're out of earshot, then Lucy's eyes snap back to mine. "You mean *sex?*" she whisper-yells.

I shrug and fight the urge to light another cigarette just to distract myself from the amusement it's giving me to watch Lucy like this.

"Sex can mean plenty of things. My cock in your pussy is just one of the possible variations," I say with light humor, expressly trying to taunt her.

Letting out a small gasp, she flashes me an angry pout, then stares at me for a few seconds before speaking. "I am —I'm not a virgin, Bastian."

I nod, having guessed as much. While on the subject I ask, "Contraceptive?"

She nods. "Lenix made me get an implant a few months ago."

Swiping my hand over my face, I take a long breath, snapping my gaze back up to hers. "We still need ground rules, Luce. Either agree or I'm out."

"Fine," she rolls her eyes, and I study her for a beat because I can't remember if I've seen her do that before.

We both stay silent until she gives me a look that seems to say *well?*

Finally caving into the urge, I slip another cigarette out of my crumpled pack and tuck it in between my lips, my lighter cracking with a flame not long after.

I drag my gaze back to temptation itself. "No kissing."

"No kissing?" she parrots almost immediately. "What else are we going to do?"

I fight the grin and mutter, "Oh Lucy."

She blinks owlishly looking like she's realizing she's shown her cards and steels her expression into something more assured. "No kissing then."

I nod and continue, "No physical contact outside of our little… *sessions*." I unfurl my fingers one by one as I'm enumerating the conditions. "No sleeping in the same bed," I pause, looking her up and down before she can interrupt me. "After tonight that is. And lastly…" I let the silence linger between us just to further rile her up before continuing, "I choose how, when, what, and where."

She reacts just like I thought she would, huffing and puffing loudly, lightly stomping her foot on the ground. "How is that fair? Why do you get all of the control?"

I smoke my cigarette coolly and lick my lips. "You get to use me, I get to choose how and when. Yes?"

Her breath hitches before answering, "Stop saying it that way."

"It's the truth, isn't it?" I reply flatly.

Her hands fall to her side while she looks into the blackened night, her fingers playing anxiously against the fabric of her blue-washed jeans before her eyes slip back to mine.

"Deal," she says.

"Deal?"

"I know you heard me the first time," she mumbles. Then, while staring at the ground she adds, "So when does it start?"

I take another drag of my smoke before dropping it and crushing it with the tip of my shoe. "Now." Reaching for the door, I step back into the strip club.

"Now?" I hear Lucy stutter out. This time, I do smile

knowing she's behind me and won't witness the thrill I'm getting from our little interaction. Still, I lead her back to our seats in the dark corner of the club. Sitting down, I order another round of drinks as if I didn't just agree to corrupt Lucy in ways she hasn't even dared to conjure up yet. The added delight of knowing I'm keeping her on edge and in the dark until I decide it's time for round one excites me more than most things in this shit life.

Maybe this road trip will be worth my time after all.

16

Bastian has not said a word since we started our way back to the motel. I do not bother coaxing him to speak even though the silence between us is… tantalizing.

Is he thinking about us?

About how he plans to show me all the things I cannot even begin to conceive from my limited experience. The thought of him teaching me what he likes, what makes him *feel* is more than enough for me to get tongue-tied while we slowly walk on the deserted street. The intermittent street lights expose his shuttered expression, his left eye still slightly bruised, looking like some wayward gladiator as we slowly pass them one by one.

In turn, I would learn what I like. What I desire— what… turns me on. Realizing how foreign that sensation feels drifting inside of me leaves a small ache in its wake. I was taught to please men, in servitude and in faith. We were mere tools for their own needs.

The thought of finally focusing on *my* needs thrills me. I bite back a small huff, exasperated with my inability to even think about those words without the heat of embarrassment prickling my cheeks.

How am I going to navigate this new territory if I cannot even manage to think salacious thoughts, albeit modestly, without wanting to cringe?

I have long ways to go, but I am determined. Even though Bastian is a block of ice and it feels like I will never have any legitimate tools to chip at his walls. Maybe deep down, that is what I prefer—it is safer if he stays behind his armor.

I much prefer indifference to what I experienced with my husband.

Experiences I now have words for. Sometimes I wish I did not.

They seem to always leave an invisible mark on my skin anytime I force myself to say them out loud.

Violence. Degradation. Humiliation. Subservience.

Imogene is always so proud when I do.

"You've come such a long way, Lucy," she told me the last time I saw her.

But how can I tell her it feels like taking a razor blade to my tongue?

The sound of a key sliding into a lock manages to snap me out of my drab thoughts.

How did I get here?

How did thinking about sex lead me to *him?* To my past. It is a rhetorical question, one I do not bother to answer. Everything always leads me back to my past. Never free, even thousands of miles away and a dead husband buried six feet deep.

"You should get some sleep," Bastian mutters while flicking the light switch on.

"But I'm not—"

"Get some rest, Luce. We're back on the road tomorrow."

He leaves me no chance to further interject, disappearing into the bathroom, the door firmly closing behind him.

Frustration curls around my lungs, *squeezing*. My jaw clenches followed by my fists, and I feel stuck, rooted to the carpeted floor, triggered by yet another man telling me what to do. I let out an irritated groan, taking off my hat and throwing it on the bed. I huff a curl out of my face, storming to the taunting closed door and bang on the wooden surface.

I am too emotionally heightened to take the time to realize how brazen my actions are, instead I just bang louder. The door swings open, Bastian appearing in a state of undress. I notice his bare chest first, the silver chain laying crookedly against his damp skin, the glint of his pierced nipples, my eyes then flicking down to his unbuttoned jeans. I jerk my gaze back up, refusing to get flustered. Not this time.

"You need to stop telling me what to do," I bite out in cold determination.

His face never falters, his eyes only growing darker as he lets the silence fall between us, like a loose thread waiting to be pulled and unraveled.

"Okay," he rasps, his mouth slowly wrapping around every letter as if finding it hard to even say one single word.

"Okay?" I cannot help but ask.

He nods, his tongue swiping over his bottom lip.

"Okay," I repeat, closing the door for him.

In the end, I still crawl into bed like he told me to, but what makes me doze off soon after is knowing that it was on my terms, and not anyone else's.

My eyelids flutter open before my mind questions why I was awoken. I keep perfectly still, the room cloaked in darkness as I lay on my right side facing outwards, my hand tucked under the colder side of the pillow. It takes me a moment to situate myself, my body still sleep-heavy and lethargic from whatever slumber I slipped into. Until I hear a slow deep breath in the room with me and remember I am not alone. Before I turn around, I can already feel the empty space next to me in bed. I must have fallen asleep before he ever even came out of the bathroom.

I slip the thin sheet down my torso and turn my body slowly around to face where I think the noise came from. I find Bastian tucked between the shadows, sitting on the only chair in the far corner of the motel room. I feel his dark brown eyes on me, although I can barely see the features drawn on his stoic face. He appears to be wearing the same thing as earlier, and still shirtless.

"What is wrong?" I find myself whispering, unsure if I even wanted to puncture the silence with something so plebeian as spoken words.

"Nothing's wrong," he whispers back.

My sight slowly pierces through the darkness, lost in the magnetic pull his presence has on me. I am not sure how long I stare at him, but my back grows straighter the moment I realize what *this* is—what is happening between us in the dead of night. I pull myself up, now on full alert. I watch as Bastian's lips curl into a smile, his nose ring catching the moonlight. It is so genuine—but beautifully lethal—that it even reaches his darkening eyes.

"Still don't want to be told what to do?" I swear his tone

is playful while he rests his chin between two fingers, his elbow casually leaning against the armrest.

I swallow hard, slowly shaking my head. More for myself, than for him.

"That is not what I meant, and you know it." My voice comes out hoarse and shaky, but in this moment, I do not care how I come off.

The only thing that matters now is what happens next.

He places both forearms on the armrests, widening his legs and leaning back into the chair. "Stand in front of me."

I sit still for another few long breaths before I act, flinging the sheet clean off me and climbing out of bed. I try to center myself, the motel carpet scratchy under the soles of my feet as I take one tentative step after the other, wearing only a thin white cotton top and sleep shorts.

Maybe I did imagine his playfulness because his face is as serious as ever. A marble statue chiseled into an intimidating human form. He leans toward me, his fingers creeping closer and closer to the bottom hem of my top but he stops before ever touching it.

"Take this off," he orders me all too casually.

"Take…" At first, I am startled by his demand, until I remember this was my idea to begin with. I steel my spine, refusing to feel ashamed by any of it.

The rustle of my shirt pairs with the staccato of my inhales, my nipples puckering as soon as the cool air hits my naked chest.

The same hand from before moves down my thigh, close but never touching, leaving my skin tense and yearning for his touch. "Take all of it off, Luce," he demands, his voice silky smooth.

The air is thick between us, charged with an indescribable buzz that leaves me lightheaded. It is addicting. It still does not prevent the trembling of my fingers when I slowly bring my hands to my waist and slip them under the elastic band. I gently push my shorts and panties down, letting them fall to the floor, while never breaking eye contact with Bastian, who is still firmly sitting before me. In this moment, it feels natural to share such intensity with the man sitting in front of me. As if we have done this countless times before. I take a deep breath in and step out of my clothes, my hands finding each other in front of my stomach, gripping them together to try to calm my nerves.

The darkness feels safe as I stand on the edge of another world entirely.

A world where I have the privilege to unabashedly watch Bastian like this.

I watch as his left hand finds the zipper of his jeans, his pants still unbuttoned, and pulls.

The sound tickles my senses in such a delectable way, I find myself taking a small step forward.

"Hands by your sides, let me see all of you," he says in a hushed voice.

I do as he says.

I drop my hands, palms splayed wide over each thigh as if trying to hold on to something. My eyes track his hips. They lift ever so slightly while he pushes his pants down far enough that I discover exactly where the trail of dark hair is leading to. And I need more.

Thankfully, my eyes have become accustomed to the near pitch-black room, gaining more and more of my sight back, eager—desperate to take in every inch of what Bastian is offering.

And finally, I see it.

Falling heavy onto his stomach, long fingers curling around it. He gives it a hard tug while resting his body into the armchair. His right arm finds the back of his head, leaning into the wall behind him, a few strands of blond hair falling over his forehead. I notice a glint of metal just above his shaft, but cannot make out what it is. His pose is so relaxed, I could barely tell he was touching himself if only looking at the top half of him.

Except for his dark brown eyes.

No, those are violent. But it is a different kind of violence. One I have never seen or experienced before. A kind that makes me want to fall to my knees and worship a different god entirely.

They are so penetrating I convince myself he is reading my every thought.

The silence curls around us. A writhing, breathing, living thing that slips through me and into the very center of my heart. It pounds and pounds as I watch with bated breath as he strokes himself long and hard. The sound of skin on skin is the only thing piercing the cloak of quietude encircling us.

I could live in this silence forever.

I squeeze my thighs together, my hands still firmly planted on either side while my core throbs in ways I do not think I knew was possible.

I have felt my body heat before, but not like this.

Not like when I have Bastian laid out before me.

His square chin slightly raised up toward me.

His eyes slowly raking up my legs.

They linger near my hips, slowly up my waist, then to my breasts, incinerating me when we finally lock eyes.

His breathing grows coarser, deeper as I notice his stomach tightening, his lips pressing together as he lightly bites down into his bottom lip.

The sound of his orgasm is sudden but quiet as he spills

on his hand and stomach, but it could have been a bomb, for the effect on me is the same. His eyes shutter, half-closed, mouth falling slightly open, while his head falls forward, the veins in his neck bulging with the exertion. When his dark eyes snap to mine, all I see is deep-seated *need*.

I let out a small whimper in response, my eyes locking on him while his movements slow to a halt, though his chest still heaves.

From what he just did.

What he just showed me.

I have never felt this alive.

This… free.

And I have done nothing but watch.

Suddenly, the possibilities are endless. And that in itself is intoxicating.

I watch as Bastian stands up, his right hand reaching over to my stomach, his fingers grazing the skin near my belly button as if he needed just a touch. Without saying another word he disappears into the bathroom and closes the door. Not long after, I hear the shower come on.

When I finally move, my heart is still beating wildly. With shaky limbs, I put my clothes back on and climb back into bed.

I pretend to be sleeping when Bastian eventually slips under the sheets beside me. But the adrenaline of what just transpired keeps me up for most of the night, while the widest grin I cannot seem to shake off adorns my face.

17

I am alone in bed when I wake up. I am neither surprised nor does it hurt my feelings. Bastian, in all his mystery, is rather predictable in his actions. Then I am reminded of what happened last night—my body heats up immediately like a warm wave, flowing smoothly through my limbs and veins. I hum in pleased delight while stretching, the same silly smile I have had since falling asleep still plastered on my face. I notice a lingering throb between my legs, like an ache but not painful, just… hard to ignore. I squeeze my thighs together, experimenting, and pleasure shoots up my spine. Swallowing hard, my hand travels down my stomach, eager to feel more of whatever Bastian kindled last night.

I hear the creak of the front door opening and I shoot out of bed like it caught fire. Bastian appears in the doorframe, stopping mid-step, hand still holding the doorknob while he takes in my appearance and the bed I just sprung out of. I let out a forced laugh, readjusting my tank top, finding it especially hard to keep eye contact this morning with the man with the thousand-mile stare.

"Car's ready," he says flatly, his face conveying nothing, immediately disappearing outside, leaving the door ajar—most likely for one of his morning cigarettes.

"I will be ready in a second," I respond loudly to the empty room, padding to the bathroom for a quick shower.

POPPING the baby blue cowboy hat on my head and sliding my heavy backpack on my shoulder, I head out finding Bastian reading outside. The morning sun alights on his dark furrowed brows as he sits on the ground, his back leaning against the brick wall right beside our motel room door. His beauty is at times shocking now that I let myself take it all in, like a modern rendering of a painted angel forced to experience the menial and mundane.

"Alright then," I say, making my way down the outside stairs. "Early worms get the bird."

I hear a quick low chuckle from behind but do not bother turning around, I am too distracted by all the signals my body is giving me to wonder what he finds so amusing. When we get to the car, I stand in front of the driver's side and spin around when I feel Bastian approaching.

"You can drive today," I say as I head for the passenger door.

"Why?"

"No reason." I try to keep my tone nonchalant, feeling anything but. I cannot tell him that the real reason I am opting out from driving is that I am not sure I could concentrate on the road ahead. Not when the close proximity to him is proving to be harder than expected.

When we have settled into our seats, Bastian hands me his phone, the screen opened to the maps app. Neither of us bother to say anything. I simply type in our next destination before handing it back to him.

"You brought us to a hole in the ground?"

I huff my frustration out loud. The *hole* Bastian is referring to is actually a natural freshwater pool in New Mexico, more than eighty feet deep and equally as wide. "You're boring, did you know that? Where's your sense of adventure?"

Leaning on the side of the car, hands in his jeans pockets, his eyes lazily travel to where I am standing, slowly sweeping up my body. "If an adventure is what you're looking for…" he drawls, pinning me with his dark stare.

It does not take an expert to understand his innuendo and like a match struck, my body flares in response. My first instinct is to want to touch him. To remember somehow through the language of both our skins meeting that I have not made this up, that last night was not just a dream that felt all too real. Then I remember Bastian's arbitrary rules.

I clear my throat and distractedly scuff my shoe in the dirt before changing the subject.

"Anyway, there are some public bathrooms over there," I say while pointing over my shoulder. "I'm going to change." Then eye him suspiciously.

"Did you even bother packing a swimsuit?" I ask with slight derision.

He stays silent for a beat, his eyes still steadily on me, then lets out a long sigh before nodding.

"Shocking," I say before turning my back to him. "I'll meet you at the entrance." I walk away, not bothering to wait for a response that will never come.

I find a stall to change. When my hand finds my black one-piece swimsuit tucked inside my bag, my nerves start to get the better of me as I fight a slight tremble. The thought of being around strangers, practically naked, has me questioning if this is even worth it.

It's your choice what you wear Lucy.

Lenix has incessantly reminded me since last year.

It's your body, no one else's. Keep it covered, or don't, as long as it's what you want, you understand me?

I understood.

And for a while, I did cover up when we'd visit the beach just us two. But I feel different now. How else can I know what feels right if I don't try it first?

So I take a deep breath and pull my swimsuit out of my bag with a hard nod of determination, trying to replace the nervous jitter that seems to follow me everywhere. I undress quickly and slip into the stretchy nylon, readying to face the world, or more accurately, Bastian, with his unrelenting stares and eyes as deep as the waters waiting for me outside.

FINDING BASTIAN NEAR THE ENTRANCE, in black mid-thigh swim trunks, I fight the urge to tell him that our swimsuits match, convincing myself it's childish and unimportant. Instead, I take the time to appreciate him like this. Tall, lean, stomach toned with muscles, his silver jewelry glinting, chest tattoo in prominent display in the New Mexico sun. As usual, he looks like he wants to be anywhere but here. But I don't let it hinder my excitement, instead, I smile wide as I approach him, my large striped towel tightly wrapped around my body.

"Can you swim?" Bastian says all too casually while we

start climbing down close to the edge, a few people already in the large pool of water, swimming and laughing.

"Yes I can swim," I say much too fast and with way too much ardor for someone who barely swam a day in her life. Frustration and a dash of shame flare inside my chest but I push it back down, refusing to have another thing to add to the list of *things Lucy cannot do*.

He shrugs and replies, "See you in there then," before diving in so gracefully that it barely creates any waves. I am left standing there, clinging to the rocks behind me, momentarily dumbstruck. He reappears a few seconds later. White blond hair falling into his eyes, water sluicing down his face as he whips his head to the side to get his hair off his forehead. Turning on his back, he faces me and arches an eyebrow.

Within that one small action, I understand everything he leaves unsaid, challenging me to admit that *all of it* is too scary, too much and that yet again, I am not enough. Unshed tears prick the back of my eyes as the harsh emotions wash over me and I look up at the blue sky, trying to hold down all of my emotions. Unable to spend another second watching him peel off all my layers until I am bleeding open.

"Luce." His voice floats up to me, and I spend a few more seconds watching the lone fluffy cloud drift by before looking back down. When I do, Bastian's expression has softened and that scares me more than anything else. We study each other for what feels like an entire lifetime but it must have been only a few seconds before he says, "Do you trust me?"

My fingers dig into the rocks even harder than before, my body still cocooned inside my towel. My throat tightens, those four words pressing into me like a clamp winding me tighter and tighter.

"Should I?" I ask softly, my voice trembling over the vowels.

He stays silent, his arms treading water to keep him afloat, his chin dipping just below the water as he nods.

Knowing I cannot stand here frozen all day, I close my eyes. While taking a large breath in, I drop the towel, and before I can think my way out of it, I jump feet first into the water. One second I am in the air and the next the water swallows me whole. Panic rises quickly like the tide, but I use it to propel myself upwards and when my head finally breaches the surface, I gulp in air, barely keeping afloat, trying to locate Bastian near me. I calm down when I finally see him only an arm's length away, I turn on my stomach and doggy paddle toward him. It doesn't take long for a strong arm to wrap around my waist, pulling me towards him. My reflex is to cling to him, the depth of the waters below twisting my stomach into knots.

"Wrap your legs around my waist," he says softly. I don't think twice and do as he says, as well as folding my arms around his neck for good measure. In a few quick kicks of his legs, he brings us closer to the edge and I begin to calm down, my rational mind settling back where it belongs. Which makes me realize how close our bodies are, wet skin sliding against wet skin, his face mere inches from mine. I can feel his breath on my neck and I can't help but wonder how the water would taste on his lips.

"I thought the rule was no touching," I say with a small smile, trying to cut some of the tension.

Instead, it only heightens it, his eyes boring into mine, arm still wound tight around my waist as the other hand finds the top of my thigh, his finger slightly dragging under the hem of my swimsuit near my hip.

"Exceptions can be made," he says gruffly, his chest rising along with his rapid breath.

Suddenly, the vision of him pleasuring himself floods my mind and I find myself pulled even closer to him, seeking friction against his hips. My breath hitches when I feel him hardening underneath me. I freeze, desperate to feel more of him, but not knowing what to do next or even how. I bite back a frustrated groan, annoyed with these chains that seem to hold me back with every step I take.

But all of it dissipates when I hear Bastian whisper in my ear, "How did last night make you feel, Luce?"

Part of me is astonished that he would bother to string enough words together to ask me that question, but when I feel his hips roll against mine I realize this is all part of this little game we are playing. And most likely why he's letting me touch him. And all I want now is to play even harder.

"Good," is all I manage to say.

"You're going to have to be more descriptive than that," he murmurs against my ear, the hand that was around my waist now traveling up my spine. "Were you turned on?" His heated whispers make me shiver uncontrollably, goose-bumps breaking out all over my body.

I nod, swallowing hard, my hips unconsciously seeking the hardness between his thighs, surprisingly unbothered by a few tourists swimming further out.

"Did it make you want to touch yourself?" he mutters darkly.

"Y–yes," I stutter out, suddenly shy but desperate to know where this will go.

"So why didn't you," he rasps, his fingers gently stroking my skin while he catches my earlobe between his teeth.

I jolt, a small gasp escaping me, hardly understanding how I could get such pleasure from his mouth on my ear.

"I am—I'm… not sure if I know how," I force myself to say, trying my hardest not to feel embarrassed but failing miserably.

Bastian stills beneath me, and for a moment I think I have ruined the moment. That he will pull away and finally tell me this was all one giant mistake. Instead, I feel him craning his neck as if scanning the area for something, then finally he pulls away and tells me to hold on to his shoulder while he swims towards an alcove receding into what looks like a small cave. Before I can ask him what he's doing, he turns me around and lifts me up onto the rocks slightly above him.

"What are we doing here?" I ask, my voice turning into an urgent whisper. From this vantage point, we are hidden but I can hear the voices of the other tourists bouncing off the cave walls.

"Teaching you how to come," he says, his tone hard and serious.

I freeze while my body responds to his words like butter melting on a hot stove.

"You cannot be serious," I sputter out with a half laugh, almost hoping he will start laughing too.

But this is Bastian, nothing he does is ever in jest.

"I cannot do that in public, with—with people around," I reply hastily.

"Yes, you can," he says as he nears the edge, his body still submerged. His hands find my ankles, and I barely contain the small jolt of surprise I cannot seem to suppress any time he touches me. They slowly slide up my legs, widening them as he makes his way further up. His eyes drop to the middle of my thighs. A small jerk of his chin and then, "Push it aside."

I do not need to ask what *it* is.

My body is trembling in anticipation, still my eyes dart to the side, worried we will get caught.

"It's just us, Luce," he says assuredly. "Trust me."

And for some inexplicable reason, I do trust him. Or maybe I am just looking for every possible reason to hit the wind with caution and just live a little.

My fingers travel down to between my thighs, pulling the thin fabric of my swimsuit aside, my heart beating so hard I am sure Bastian can hear it from where he is. His grip tightens around my legs but he doesn't move.

"Where do you want to touch yourself first?" he says much too calmly.

Instead of blurting out, *I do not know*, I take a deep breath and try to pay attention. After a loaded second, I drag my fingers down and show him where.

"Good," Bastian says, his voice seems to have deepened. "Now put some pressure on your clit and circle your fingers around it."

I hesitate, my hand trembling but still do as he says. My mouth falls open in response, shocked at how fast pleasure shoots up my spine, splintering my mind.

"That's it, just like that," he says while his hands push me even wider open. "Does that feel good?"

I nod eagerly, unable to form any rational thought as my fingers wind around my clit, chasing the pleasure building with every stroke.

"Now take your other hand and slide your middle finger into your pussy. I want you to fuck yourself with it." His dark eyes glinting with desire. "Can you do that for me, Luce?"

I eagerly do as he says, my finger gliding easily inside as my head falls back, biting my bottom lip while a small whimper flutters out of me.

"*Fuck*," Bastian groans, his fingers digging divots into my thighs. "You're so wet, I can see it from here."

Another small moan escapes me in response. My heels are pushed up close to my hips as my back rests on the large rocks behind me, propped up like a display, incomprehensibly thrilled by the idea that we could be caught at any time. It's my turn to pin him with my stare, needing to see him while my body coils tighter and tighter toward what I'm guessing will be my very first orgasm.

For a few loaded moments, we sit in near silence, the only sound being the water lapping against the rocks, and my own heated breaths. I am so caught up with how *amazing* it feels every time I slide my finger in and then out, while I continue to circle my clit that I do not understand the cues of what is building inside of me.

Then I feel it.

Sudden and indescribable euphoria.

I let out a shocked gasp, a long low moan following right behind as I suddenly grow very still, a wave of warmth crashing into me over and over again.

And I hope it never ends.

But all good things ultimately do.

While my grasp on reality solidifies, Bastian takes my hand, slowly sliding my finger out of me. When I feel his hot flat tongue lave up my finger, pleasure flares through me once more, my eyes slamming into his. He licks me clean, and then drops my hand, giving me a flash of a smile, gone in the span of a blink.

He holds out his own hand, and I take it, pulling me into the water once again.

"You did so good, Luce," he mutters into my hair before leading me back out into the sun.

The rays hit my skin as he swims us back to the stairs, while I idly wonder if I'll be the same, ever again.

18

BASTIAN

Staring at the popcorn ceiling of another middle-of-nowhere motel, the sheet pushed down to my waist in bed, I can tell sleep will once again be evasive, like a slippery eel disappearing under a rock. This time it's not my old haunts keeping me up. This time the ghost is real and is sleeping in the room adjacent to mine.

I could tell when we came back from the water hole that she wasn't all too pleased to revert back to our previous sleeping arrangements. But she didn't say a word, just gave me a soft smile when I pushed the keys into her palm and disappeared behind her respective door. I'm not sure I would've had the willpower to say no if she'd come crawling into bed with me— she didn't.

Lucy's no rule breaker. What did I expect?

I thought this was going to be easy. That I'd enjoy myself for a while, waste some time and tease Lucy for a bit, make her come once or twice and that would be the end of it. This already feels much more than just an illicit deal made between two practical strangers. It feels bigger somehow… like Lucy could never be *just* anything—like saying the sun is just a star.

Was last night, when I told her to undress and stand naked in front of me, really for her? No. That was all for me. I, on the other hand, was already bending and breaking the rules just to have more of her. *And fuck*, I can't remember the last time I came that hard. Just for a look.

She looked radiant cloaked in darkness, with small perfect tits, wide hips, curls falling over her shoulders, and a mouth that made me imagine all kinds of filth while I fucked my fist at the sight.

Then today happened.

I've never been into the teacher/student dynamic before… but I had never seen Lucy come after listening to my careful instructions either. And all the while, as I watched her splayed open before me, the echoes of having already seen her like this before pulsed all around me. It was powerful, yet incomprehensible. It's what made me reach out and bring her finger to my lips. She tasted like coming home. Like I had been away for far too long, hungering for something I thought forever lost.

I blink away the vivid memories, still staring at the off-white ceiling.

Absolute fucking nonsense.

Just my mind playing tricks on me. As if the part of my mind that will always crave an all-encompassing addiction had a taste of something new—a shiny new drug to get lost in. Something that could finally compare to the mind-altering opioids of my fucked up youth that left me sated and numb. Lucy leaves me anything but numb.

And that's more dangerous than anything else.

THE NEXT MORNING, I find Lucy waiting outside for me next to the car. Her now trusty baby blue cowboy hat snug on her head, and I struggle to ignore the small zing it creates deep in my chest. She raises her head ever so slightly to meet my gaze and her green eyes sparkle in the morning sun, specks of gold leafed inside her irises and I wonder if she's even real.

Maybe I'm imagining all of it. A drug-fueled doped-up dream and soon, I'll fall back to earth and be back there, eighteen with no life and no dreams. And most definitely no Lucy.

I push the absurd thought away and force myself not to graze my knuckle over Lucy's freckled cheek. Instead, I give the lip of her hat a small flick upwards. Her soft laugh wraps around my cold fucking heart and *squeezes*. I pay it no mind as I make my way to the passenger side, dropping my bag into the back before climbing in.

"Where to?" I mutter, pulling out my phone when she settles into the driver's seat.

"So, um…" she trails off, her fingers drumming on the steering wheel while giving me a look as if she's about to get in trouble. "I'm feeling a little tired of driving so much, and well, I was thinking maybe we could just stay in one place for a few days. I found this place with a pool and, so I thought maybe we could just… chill?"

I fight back a smile, watching her struggle through her faltering assertiveness.

"Chill?" I reply with a hint of amusement. "Did you read that on Urban Dictionary or something?"

"I don't know what that means," she deadpans. "Did I

say it wrong? I hear Lenix say it all the time." She gives me an innocent little shrug and I can't help but chuckle just a little.

"No, that was perfect, Luce."

Her smile widens, her eyes sparkling as if the small praise I just gave her made her entire day. Suddenly, all I want is to teach her something new, so I can praise her again and again.

I tuck the thought away for later. "This is your road trip, I'm just your plaything, remember?" She flusters exactly like I thought she would and my cock jerks at the sight. "We can do, or go wherever you want." I hand her my phone and she takes it tentatively, now avoiding my gaze. Challenging her limits is more entertaining than I previously thought it ever could be.

We arrive at our destination in the early afternoon, a motel on the far outskirts of Albuquerque. A little bigger than the ones we've been staying at and, as promised, a pool sits tucked into the courtyard of the property, the building squaring it on three sides. The pool walls are painted a faded pink and a quick look around the place tells me whoever owns this shithole loves that fucking color.

Lucy is acting as if she just arrived at a five-star chateau or some shit, my scowl not hindering her excitement one bit.

"How lovely!" she says genuinely, as if we didn't see roadkill on our way in, her wide open grin sharpening her cheekbones as she looks around.

We manage to snag two rooms facing the pool on the first floor. We're lucky, the receptionist tells us, as it's their last two adjoining rooms. A quick glance at Lucy and I can tell she'd much prefer if the winds of fortune would have blown in quite a different direction. Who am I kidding, a feral part of me was hoping the fucking same. At the very least, it would limit the excuses I'm starting to repeat to myself.

An hour later, I'm busy catching up on work that's been left on the wayside ever since this little road trip started almost two weeks ago. I'm on the phone with Byzantine when Lucy pops her head in the door, wearing nothing but her black one-piece bathing suit and shorts that match.

I hang up on Byzantine, not bothering to say goodbye.

She's holding tightly to her folded towel with both arms over her chest. I could tell yesterday that she was nervous about showing so much skin, and today is no different. Funny how she didn't act that way when she was standing naked in front of me. Quite the opposite actually. And that makes me want to take full advantage of that little piece of valuable information. Like telling her to strip for me everyday until this road trip's inevitable end.

"Are you busy?" she asks, a little shyly.

Yes. "No."

Her smile is immediate and infectious. "I was thinking we could sit by the pool while the sun is still out," she says, pointing her thumb over her shoulder.

"I'll meet you out there," I answer.

She nods eagerly, eyes twinkling like fucking galaxies. Turning on her heels, her braids swing over her shoulders, and I'm left staring at where she was just standing wondering how the hell I got here.

19

We have been at Casa Kismet for two days now. It feels nice to just do nothing for a little while. It's mid-morning, and I'm sitting on my now favorite plastic deck chair near the corner of the pool. The sun is already hot, sweat prickling on my forehead, so I reach over for my sunglasses and baseball cap on the table beside me.

That's when I spot her. Blonde hair loose down her back, the rays bouncing off the strands like wild bursts of light, a face and body full of freckles, and the bluest eyes I have ever seen. Today, she is wearing a white macrame top, frayed jean shorts that ride far up her hips, and bedazzled black wedge sandals. The way she walks around the property reminds me of Lenix; pure confidence and, according to what I have gathered from others, undeniable sex appeal.

Not that I would really know what that looks like… all I know is that it's instinctual and that I couldn't possibly have any. Not if I stay stuck in my suffocating shell of insecurity and inexperience, that's for sure.

For the past two days, I have locked myself in the bathroom at night pretending to shower but instead, I have been watching porno on my phone. I figured it would be a quick way to get familiar with all the things I know nothing about. Instead, I have more questions than when I started my covert investigation. Not to say that it didn't leave me heated and a little flustered. I tried masturbating like how Bastian showed me, but nothing compares to that time… to him watching… to him instructing me.

I lurch myself out of my wandering thoughts when I realize she is heading my way. I sit a little straighter chewing at the inside of my cheek while I watch her strut closer and closer, my notebook clutched tight on my lap.

"Hi, I'm Bridget!" she says, a bright white smile beaming like the sun itself while she stands in front of my chair, leaning closer to give me her hand to shake, bangles clinking together on her wrist with the movement.

I almost forget to speak, but then quickly clear my throat, reaching over to take her hand in mine. "Lucy," I say with, what I hope is, an equally bright white smile.

"Awesome, now we're friends," she says with a giggle as she plops herself in the chair beside me. "Where are you from Lucy?"

I slightly shift my body to face her, still clinging to my notebook for something to hold while I answer her. "California… You?"

She turns to me, sliding her large pink sunglasses down her nose. Her eyes have a mischievous glint to them, her fresh red-painted lips curling into a grin as she chews on gum.

"That's a secret," she answers with a wink. Leaning back into her chair, she stretches her arms over her head, crossing one freckled and tanned leg over the other. Her top rides up with the movement, revealing a pierced belly button. "I actually own this place." My eyebrows arch in surprise but I say nothing, letting her continue, "Well, my boyfriend Ritchie owns it, but I helped him decorate, it was my idea to paint the pool pink," she says with another effervescent giggle. I nod, not quite knowing what to say but not wanting the conversation to end. Luckily, she does not seem deterred and continues to speak. "So you're just passing through? I've seen you around with that silent blond guy, is he your boyfriend?"

This time I do answer. "Oh, uh, no," I say, laughing nervously. "He is just a, um… a friend I guess? We are on a cross-country road trip together."

"You guess?" she says with another giggle. "Oh, I just *know* there's a story behind that."

My stomach sinks thinking she is going to ask me more questions about Bastian, but instead, she moves right along and points to the notebook I am still holding.

"You write?"

I look down as a reflex and then back up at her. "No, it is more like a…" I trail off suddenly feeling embarrassed, but something about Bridget tells me she will not make me feel silly if I do tell her, even if I myself feel silly divulging it. "Bucket list," I reveal with a small sheepish smile. A term I learned while doing hours of research for exactly that—I just did not know that's what people called it.

"Oh my god, how fun!" she exclaims while twisting in her seat, placing her feet back on the ground, and facing me. "Can I see?"

I try to hide my mortification at the thought, my knuckles unconsciously whitening around the notebook, but Bridget immediately picks up on my reaction and laughs. "Oops," she says while bringing her hand over her mouth, eyes crinkling, freckled shoulders shaking. "That's invasive, sorry. You don't have to show me."

"No, um, it is—it's not that…" I answer, looking down at the notebook again as if studying it. How can I tell her that after my little porno investigation, this bucket list now includes a few *sexual* items too? "I can tell you a few?" I finally say, hoping it is a reasonable alternative than to hand it over.

"Sure," she says, flipping her long hair from one shoulder to the other, her facial expression open and inviting.

"Well, the road trip was one of them actually," I start tentatively, trying to shake off how childish I feel when Bridget is making me feel anything but. I exhale and then finally just start listing items off the top of my head. "Get a tattoo, skydive, fly in a plane—"

"Wait," Bridget interrupts and laughs. "Are you saying you've never stepped foot on a plane, but skydiving came first on your list?"

I shrug my shoulders.

"That's amazing, I'm obsessed with you now," she says in jest, flashing a smile while propping her chin in her hand, face tilting to the side, her elbow on her knee. "What else?"

"Um…" I mutter while I try to think quickly. "Singing at a karaoke."

"Oh my god," Bridget breathes out quickly, her hand flashing out to grab my forearm. "Honey, that one is doable." Her blue eyes widening in excitement.

"Doable?" I repeat, suddenly feeling nervous all over again.

"Yeah," she giggles. Letting me go, she leans backward, laying both palms flat behind her, holding up her weight.

"Don't you want to cross some of these off your list if the opportunity arises?"

My stomach drops picturing myself on stage singing in front of a crowd, but a tingle simultaneously zips through my veins at the thought of doing something so bold.

I nod. "I guess you're right." I give her a shaky smile, but it widens the more I let the idea blossom inside of me.

"Great!" she says while clapping her hands in conspiratorial excitement. "I happen to know just the place. We can go tonight, and we can bring our boys too."

"To—tonight?" I stutter as I watch her stand up.

She looks down at where I am still sitting and props her hands on her hips. "Yeah, carpe diem and all that right?"

I am not sure what any of that means, but I nod my head anyway, refusing to back down now. "You bet!" I say, trying to match her excitement.

She pauses and then giggles. "Perfect." She swings around and begins to walk away, yelling over her shoulder, "I'll come by your room later tonight!"

Watching her disappear into the building, I have not moved an inch for what feels like minutes, replaying the interaction I just had with Bridget. My smile drops when I realize I will have to tell Bastian what I agreed to do, especially because I managed to rope him into it.

My gaze swings to our rooms, and I find him sitting outside, staring directly at me. My first instinct is to wave but decide against it. Instead, I unclench my grip off of the notebook still in my hands and place it beside me. Bastian has not taken his eyes off me. I pretend I'm unbothered while I take my clothes off, revealing my black swimsuit underneath, and walk into the water via the built-in cement stairs of the pool.

I wish he would join me, but I know better. He's been

acting distant ever since we got here. More aloof than usual that is. I know it probably has something to do with whatever is happening between us.

Maybe it should bother me more than it does. But I find myself not really caring what he's thinking or feeling about all this. As long as our little deal is still on the table. Maybe it makes me selfish, but for once in my life, I want to be free to simply *take*, instead of always giving.

20

An hour later, I find Bastian sitting at the small desk in his room. It's where he has been spending most of his time since we have been staying at Casa Kismet. I do not bother asking what he's doing, he will only give me a vague response about algorithms that I will pretend to understand but ultimately will not. All I know is that what he does is illegal and most likely dangerous. My stomach turns, remembering how he told me he's been shot multiple times before. Suddenly, the urge to smooth my hand over his skin and find every single one of his scars throbs under my fingertips. I stay unmoving for a few too many seconds lost in the vision.

Hearing the chair creak in the otherwise silent room, I snap my eyes up to meet Bastian's gaze, his dark eyebrows slightly furrowed but otherwise intently fixed on me. The silence pulses between us as usual. This time, I welcome it. Like a language where the foreign dips and valleys of its vowels are now becoming familiar, or a soothing melody I find myself humming when I let my mind aimlessly drift.

"So I met someone," I say off-handedly.

I notice Bastian's shoulders straighten, his body infinitesimally growing rigid.

"Bridget," I quickly add as I walk further into his room, sitting on the edge of his bed. And then for more context, "The owner's girlfriend." His body does not relax, but his eyes soften, so I continue, trying to get to the point as quickly as possible, practically tripping over every word as they stumble out of my mouth. "So, uh, we were talking near the pool and I told her about this bucket list I have and that, well, that one of the items was singing at a karaoke, and then she told me she knew a place and that we should all go tonight."

This time, the silence that follows is not as comfortable as before, as I anxiously wait for Bastian to say something.

"A bucket list?" His voice, while carrying its usual flatness, finally pierces through the thick fog between us, his expression darkening which leaves me slightly perplexed.

Thinking he would have focused on the fact I made plans for us without telling him first, I am left surprised that he is focusing on my trivial list instead.

A small dry laugh escapes my lips before I answer him. "I know it is—it's silly, it's nothing really. Just... just something—"

"You've been keeping secrets from me, Luce?" Bastian says slowly while he stands up and comes to stand right in front of me, my eyes tracking his movements while my head tilts slowly upwards the closer he gets.

Not sure why he is acting so seriously about a bucket list, I try to cover up my nerves with false bravado. "You have plenty of secrets yourse—what are you doing?" I ask with slight panic when he drops to his knees in front of me, his strong hands traveling up my legs, long fingers digging into my thighs as he pulls me toward him.

"What about the one where you've been watching porn in the bathroom, thinking I wouldn't find out?" he rasps with a slight curl of his lips.

My eyes grow wide, heart slamming in my chest. "How did you know about..." The words die in my throat when Bastian pops open the button of my shorts, pulling down the zipper with a jerk. I swallow hard, licking my lips, my eyes glued to his hands. His gaze slides upwards to mine, his face smooth of any expression, nonetheless, my core throbs at the sight as if he has conditioned me to it. "Tell me about your bucket list, Luce," he says so quietly that I almost lean closer just so he can whisper it again into my ear.

"Tell you about..." Again, my voice trails off as his fingers curl around the waistband of my shorts and start tugging them down, pulling my underwear with it, my hips immediately lifting up to help him as if pulled by an invisible string. I fixedly watch as he discards my clothes somewhere behind him with a flick of the wrist, his hands finding my ankles. The metal of his thumb ring is cold against my skin as he slowly pushes them upwards. I follow his silent orders, lifting them up, my heels settling on the edge of the bed on opposite sides of my hips, my weight falling onto my palms placed behind me on the mattress.

My position is lewd, as if he is, once again, putting me on display, and I couldn't be more thrilled at the thought. I should feel vulnerable, but I don't.

All I feel is undeniable hunger.

His eyes flick up to meet mine, while he brings his thumb up to his mouth, dragging it down his tongue before finding where I am most sensitive, that same thumb now grazing up, parting me open, but never reaching my clit, his gaze still steadily on mine.

"Has anyone ever had a taste, Luce?" he asks just as hungrily.

My mouth opens but no sound comes out, the sensations of him there are already so acute I can hardly form a single rational thought.

I shake my head.

"Would you let me?" I only hesitate for a moment, but it is enough for Bastian to allow a trickle of desperation to be heard in his tone before saying, "*Please.*"

My mouth goes dry, nodding slowly, transfixed, and unconsciously widening my legs for him.

He smiles, and my heart explodes into a million pieces at the sight of the dimples appearing on his cheeks.

"What a good little student," he drawls as he puts pressure on my clit with his thumb. "Now tell me what made your list or I stop."

My tongue swipes my bottom lip in anticipation before I stutter, soft and breathless, "*Yes.*"

I scramble for the words—*anything*—eager to feel him on me. I start with the closest thing floating in my mind and tell him about me singing at an open mic. As soon as I start speaking, he dips down, his tongue replacing his thumb and I jolt, a small shocked noise escaping my lips.

Oh my...

The feeling of his tongue stroking, laving, exploring— the sensation is like nothing I could have ever imagined.

I stop talking, so distracted by the image of Bastian's head between my thighs, his fingers digging into my skin, that I suddenly wish I had a photographic memory so I could revisit this memory as many times as I pleased without any detail ever fading.

I watch with undivided attention as one of his hands crawls up my stomach, over my heaving chest, and catches the top of my neck, encircling the sides of my chin. My throat bobs into his warm palm as he lifts his gaze, his mouth still where I want him most. He stops, his one eyebrow arching questioningly. Then I suddenly remember that I should be enumerating items off my list.

"Sky-diving," I blurt out breathlessly, eager for him to continue whatever he is doing that feels this good.

Thankfully, his tongue returns, and he releases my chin from his grasp, the same hand disappearing in between my thighs.

My breath catches high up my throat, turning into a low moan when I feel one of his fingers enter me. This time, I listen faithfully to his command, too desperate to feel more of him, everywhere and all at once, to ever stop talking. Time slows down, or maybe that is just a greedy, hopeful prayer I make as I count my heated breaths, my core throbbing and clenching around Bastian's finger.

I must be saying nonsense, but at least he has not stopped and I tell him just that, my head falling backward, eyelids fluttering shut.

Don't stop, don't stop, don't stop.

Until I lose all sense of decorum, released from the voices still telling me how to behave, and reach for the back of Bastian's head, my hips arching forward, pushing his mouth, tongue, *everything* harder into me, until finally, something snaps and that same euphoric feeling washes over me.

Weightless. Free.

Lifting my head back up, my gaze slams into his and I experience another kind of freefall. I suddenly never want to reach the bottom if it means seeing Bastian like this. His lips glistening, cheeks flushed, hair disheveled. He wipes his face clean with one long drag of his palm, and then leans over, pressing his warm open lips against my right thigh. I cannot seem to keep the small shocked gasp from breaking the heavy silence.

"Can't wait to hear you sing," he says softly, before standing up, unabashedly palming his erection through his blue jeans, and disappearing into the bathroom.

21

B astian opens the door to the Dragon Star pub, waiting
for me to enter first. Taking in a large inhale, I square
my shoulders and walk in.

Bridget had been true to her word and came knocking a
couple of hours after Bastian's little lesson. She offered to
drive, but Bastian overheard the conversation and flat-out
refused, so I told her we would meet her there. She took his
scowls and lack of warmth in stride, giggling and smiling
wide. She gave us the name of the place and waved us
goodbye.

The pub is small, intimate even, a dozen tables scattered around near the small stage at the far back, someone
already on stage singing a song I don't recognize... Which
would be approximately ninety-nine percent of all songs
ever written. The bar faces the opposing wall, an eclectic
array of neon signs adorning the age-worn dark gray walls,
and the few windows in the place are so grimy that you can
barely see outside. Despite the less-than-desirable decor, the
place is packed and the atmosphere is warm and lively.

My nerves feel electric, like I'm holding on to a live wire and can't let go. I spot Bridget at the bar and she waves us over.

"Hi guys!" she says cheerily, pulling me into a hug and then quickly releasing me. She points to the man standing beside her. "This is Ritchie, my boyfriend," she says with a wide smile. "Ritchie, this is Lucy and her *friend* Bastian."

The way she emphasizes the word friend makes me want to die a little, but I swallow the embarrassment, waving hello to her boyfriend. Ritchie does not look like much, especially when I compare him to Bastian. His medium build, dull brown eyes, and shaved head make him easily forgettable. I'm not sure I would notice him in a crowd if we were never introduced. He barely gives me a glance, too busy staring at Bastian standing behind me to notice. Bastian does not help the situation much, giving a bored nod to both before turning to face the bar, trying to catch the bartender's attention.

Bridget looks my way and gives her head a little shake accompanied by an amused eye roll, not looking at all bothered by both men's lack of response. Her eyes shine with excitement when she starts talking again.

"I'm so excited for you," she gushes, her hand finding my arm and squeezing. "Are you nervous?" Not letting me answer, she adds, "I already spoke to the MC and he says that if you already have a song picked out he can cue it up for you and you can be on stage in the next twenty minutes."

The dread spilling into my stomach at an alarming rate must also be visible in my facial expression because Bridget's smile drops. She lowers her voice and leans in. "Do you know what song you want to sing already?"

"No—yes, I mean… I do have a song. I jus—I just do

not think I can do this," I say, my voice falling quieter with every word spoken.

She stays silent for a few seconds, studying me.

"Boys," she announces, threading her fingers through mine and pulling me away from the bar. "We'll be right back, we just need to powder our noses." She gives me a quick wink and tugs me forward. I am not sure what *powdering our noses* could possibly be, but I do not ask questions as we slip through the crowd toward the women's bathroom.

The music fades when the door closes behind us, and somehow it makes me breathe a little better. I watch Bridget strut up to one of the sinks, looking at herself in the mirror, adding volume to her hair with both hands.

"So," she says while looking down, rummaging inside her red tasseled suede purse. "What's your story, Lucy? Why was singing at a karaoke bar part of your bucket list?"

The real reason floats across my mind like a ghost seeking its grave.

I grew up in a cult where I was not allowed to sing outside of the church choir.

The truth is too bleak to share, so I decide on a safer answer. "I always loved to sing."

"What stopped you?" Bridget asks while reapplying her mascara.

I shrug a shoulder, looking down at the scuffed bathroom floor and then back up. "Everything?"

When she giggles in response, it does not feel pointed, instead, it feels friendly and welcoming. "I feel that," she says, dropping her mascara back inside her purse and fishing out her red lipstick.

I watch in silence as she applies a fresh coat, one lip,

and then the next. She finds my gaze through the mirror and smiles. "You'll do great, I just know it. Who cares about the crowd? What matters is that you're happy and having fun, right?"

Her words settle softly onto my heart, dissolving into small bursts of bravery, making me nod and smile back at her.

"That's the spirit," she says with a giggle, capping her lipstick. She walks up and hands it to me. "Here. For some luck." I blink up at her, a little surprised. "Take it," she says with a small flick of her wrist.

So I do.

"I'll give you a sec, okay?" her tone soothing while she squeezes my shoulder. "I'll be right outside." She opens the bathroom door, the music spilling back around me as she does. Then she pauses, looking back over to where I'm standing. "You'll knock em' dead, honey," she says with a wink.

Twenty minutes later, I listen to the MC call me on stage. With my heart slamming against my chest, I walk up on shaky legs and sit on the stool already set up in front of the mic for me. The lights are brighter than expected, but I still manage to find Bridget cheering me on, sitting close to the stage, both men sitting on opposite sides of her. My gaze locks with Bastian's and for a second I consider sprinting out of here and canceling the whole thing, road trip included.

Then I hear the melody start to play. Of a song I have listened to on repeat, for months now. One of Lenix's favorite—and now mine. I know every single verse by heart. I could even sing it without the tempo guiding me through the notes. I keep Bastian's gaze until the very last moment, his little nod of encouragement making my heart squeeze in my chest.

Finally, I close my eyes and begin to sing.

22

BASTIAN

L istening to Lucy sing on stage, eyes closed, a soft soulful smile etched on her red-painted lips, feels like finally receiving the answer to a prayer I never even made. Goosebumps break out all over my arms and up my nape as her voice—quiet but clear and so eerily beautiful— surrounds me, like smoke carrying the scent of the divine.

Shifting in my seat, I give a quick glance beside me, wondering if I'm the only one being affected by Lucy's voice this way. The twinkle in Bridget's eyes confirms my suspicions, and I can't control the pang of jealousy making my jaw clench at the thought of anyone experiencing Lucy like this, other than me. The thought startles me more than the feelings accompanying it.

Feeling a little out of it, my eyes sweep back to her on stage. I jolt slightly in my seat when I find her staring back. I match her golden green gaze, my mind turning hazy the more I study her like this. Like witnessing a transformation in real time. Like a pearl recovered from the bottom of the sea.

I don't realize time has even passed until Lucy sings her last note, the music fading along with it. When the room explodes into applause, she finally breaks eye contact with me. I realize then that what she was seeking within my own gaze was support, and maybe even strength. I simultaneously feel honored and unworthy of such a connection. Her eyes sweep around the bar, her smile growing even wider as she giggles into the microphone.

I've never heard something so fucking perfect.

"Thank you," she says softly, jumping off the stool and bouncing off the stage.

I'm out of my seat in an instant, and I catch her mid-air as she jumps into my arms, her legs wrapping around my waist.

Fuck the rules, and fuck everything I've ever fucking said, if it means having Lucy's giggles tickle my ear while her hand trails up my neck into my hair.

I've never seen her eyes shine so brightly.

"That was amazing," she says breathlessly.

You were amazing.

I have so much I want to tell her, but the words catch in my throat when I realize how fragile this moment is. How quickly feelings like the ones she's experiencing can be ruined.

She takes my silence as discomfort.

Suddenly serious, she says, "Right." And pulls away. My arms slacken around the small of her back and I let her plant her feet back on the ground. "I forgot. Rules," she adds with a sheepish smile, as if she forgot who she was for a second. And I was the piece of shit to shove her off the cloud she was on. I clench my fists, but say nothing, forcing myself to smile. At least just a little.

A squeal coming from my right bursts through my

eardrum as Bridget nearly slams into Lucy, wrapping her arms around her and jumping up and down. Lucy laughs, and I'm left wondering if maybe I'm just a black hole selfishly swallowing up her light whenever she comes too close.

The urge to turn on my heels, walk out and disappear is so acute that I can feel my muscles protest when I don't. I sit back down at our table, ignoring whatever the fuck Ritchie is trying to tell me over the music, and down the rest of my beer in one gulp. It doesn't help much. Only dulls the edge some. With all the emotions clambering up my throat, I can't help but wish I could feel even less... Nothing will ever compare to the dull edges of my youth.

Nothing compares to the feeling of *nothing*.

A FEW HOURS LATER, I'm still stuck at this fucking table. Bridget carries most of the conversation, Lucy chiming in when she can get a word in. I'm not shocked to discover Ritchie is a fucking dud, and if it wasn't for Lucy looking like she's having the time of her life, I would have dragged us back to the motel a long time ago.

"I'm not lying!" Bridget says followed by one of her constant and unnecessary giggles. Most likely finishing up another one of her pointless stories that I haven't paid much attention to. "I'm telling you, God's honest truth," she tells Lucy, still laughing while raising her hand up and placing the other over her heart.

"You done?" Ritchie barks from across the table.

"What?" Bridget says, her laugh a little dryer than before.

"You 'bout giving me a headache with all that fucking talking of yours. Go get me a drink would you?"

I sit up a little straighter, my chin between my index and thumb while I study Bridget's shift in demeanor from bubbly to insecure, her eyes jumping from him, to me, then to Lucy. It's quick, and only lasts a few seconds, before she smiles back at him. "Of course." Her usual laugh pouring out from her lips. "I'll get us a fresh round—Lucy want to come?"

Lucy appears a little nervous but smiles back and nods, glancing at me quickly before standing up and walking away. The table falls silent, Ritchie and I both face the bar as we watch the girls find a spot to wait for their drink order.

Finally, the asshole speaks.

"Thought she'd never shut the fuck up," he chuckles while he fishes something out of his pocket. "This usually helps." He snickers, holding up a vial for me to see between his finger and thumb. I watch him dump the clear liquid into Bridget's drink. "Makes her much more pliant for later, you know what I mean?" he says with a wink, his conspiratorial tone so effortless that the edge of my vision reddens at the thought of how practiced this all looks.

I don't move until he's settled back into his chair. There are too many witnesses to do anything worth my fucking time, so I settle on making him believe I will. Making sure the girls are still waiting at the bar, I slowly slide my chair closer to his and lean in, catching his collar in my fist. I jerk him toward me, his neck snapping backward with the force, a small yelp spilling out of him as it does. "Hey man, let me go!"

I don't.

My voice is cold when I spit the words into his squirely fucking face. "You know," I say, as his hands find my wrist, trying to pull himself out of my grip. I just yank him even closer, twisting my fist even deeper into his shirt. "I once buried someone alive for far less. You'd be surprised how easy it is to make someone disappear," I growl into his ear while he continues to squirm. "What makes you think I won't do the same to you?"

"I was just joking, man," he says in alarm, still trying to tug his shirt out of my hand. "I swear the bitch is in on it, she *likes* it."

I don't believe a fucking word out of this piece of shit's mouth. The tether I have on my control snaps and I wrap my hand around his throat, pulling him out of his seat by the neck. I grab the laced drink with my other hand before slamming his back onto the table. The sound of glass breaking around us doesn't deter me, it only spurs me on as I pin him down, my hand moving up his throat and over his chin. I squeeze his reddened cheeks, forcing his mouth to open, and pour the alcohol—as well as what I'm guessing is GHB—down his throat.

"Drink every last drop or you'll disappear just like the rest of them," I order.

He sputters and chokes on the liquid but ultimately heeds my threat and swallows everything down, eyes round with terror.

I feel a pair of hands shake my shoulder.

"Bastian, stop! What are you doing?" Lucy says in alarm.

Keeping my arm straight, hand still gripping Ritchie's face, I slowly turn my head to find Lucy standing close by, her face painted in shock. My eyes snap to Bridget behind her, looking a lot less upset.

I lean over the table, hovering close to Ritchie's ear. "Do something like that again? I *will* find out. Understand?"

He nods profusely and I finally release him.

Not bothering to placate the crowd forming around us, I grab Lucy by the arm. She doesn't protest when I drag her out of the bar and into the car. I can tell she's rattled but doesn't utter a word the whole ride back to the motel, and I don't bother breaking the silence—or try to comfort her and whatever feelings she might be having.

I unlock the door to my room and walk in, Lucy following close behind. Adrenaline is still pulsing through my veins, my skin feeling tight. I reach over and grab the back of my shirt, tugging it over my head, and then off me. Rolling it into a ball, I discard it somewhere near the bathroom and turn around. I'm slightly startled to see Lucy still standing in the middle of the room, having assumed she'd disappear into her own room.

Maybe I should apologize.

"The guy deserved it," I say flatly.

Not an apology.

"I didn't mean to scare you," I mutter a little gentler, my eyes fixed on hers.

"I'm not scared," Lucy says softly, tucking a loose curl behind her ear. "Actually, I'm uh…" She lets out a quiet nervous laugh as she looks down at the floor and then back up. "I'm actually a little…"

My brow arches, curious, as her throat bobs on a hard swallow. But then watch in utter fucking rapture as she sinks to her knees, her eyes never leaving mine.

"What are you doing?" I manage to croak out, my mind already flooded with images of *what* I could make her do while down there. My cock swells and presses against my jeans, but I pretend to be unbothered while I'm *still* high off the taste I had of her this afternoon, and the adrenaline still pumping in my veins from what happened at the bar.

"You know…" she says, elongating the words, her voice trailing off as she sits back on her heels.

I can't help myself, magnetized by her eyes fixated on me, I step a little closer.

"Use your words, Luce," I say slowly, tauntingly.

Her eyes grow wide, and I almost laugh at the sheer terror in her gaze.

She presses her lips together, the red lipstick freshly reapplied.

"I want to suck…" She closes her eyes, eyebrows cinching together as if I'm torturing a forbidden secret out of her. Finally, she takes a deep breath and blurts it out. "I want to suck your cock." I watch as her gaze turns defiant, but smooths quickly into something much closer to innocence. "Please?"

Fuck.

I've never been this hard in my fucking life.

Slowly, I step closer to her. Then even closer. Until she's straining her neck to look up at me. I let the silence sink its claws into us while I reach down, cradling her cheek into my palm. Her gaze burns into mine, her mouth falling slightly open as I drag my thumb across her bottom lip, smearing her lipstick onto the side of her freckled cheek.

"Such a teacher's pet, aren't you?" I rasp.

She gives me a slow, lingering nod, and I grin. The sight of her beaming up at me, lipstick smeared and on her knees nearly does me in.

Instead, I drop my smile. "No."

I let her go and take a step back.

"What? Why?" she whines, her arms flying up in irritation.

I attempt to concentrate, my face expressionless, while I

try not to get distracted by the thought of her lips around my cock.

"That wasn't the deal. It's not about me, remember?"

"What makes you think this is about you?" she says with the same defiance I glimpsed earlier. "I want… I want you to teach me. I want you to show me what it's like to be used… and like it."

I groan, my head falling toward the ceiling. My balls tighten almost painfully, my pulse thumping with the cadence of her words. "Don't say shit like that. You don't even know what you're implying."

"So teach me," she whispers.

I stay unmoving for a few seconds, and then—

Fuck it.

I stalk back towards her and she perks up, still on her knees, looking almost giddy as she licks her lips in anticipation.

"You want me to take advantage of you. Is that it?" I say darkly as I finally, fucking *finally*, unzip my jeans, and pull my cock out. "Sweet little Luce wants to be ruined?"

She stares at my dick for a beat, until her gaze slowly lifts up to find mine. I've never seen it this steady—no question, no hesitation—as she opens her mouth wide, flattening her tongue. I bite back a groan and just fucking give in.

"Put your hands behind your back and keep them there." My order almost violent.

I idly stroke my cock as she does what I say, my stomach muscles contracting with anticipation. Then, as I wind my hand around her long hair, I slide my cock inside her hot, wet mouth. "Relax your jaw. Let me in," I groan.

I feel it when she does and I slide even deeper inside. She gags around my dick, and it only makes me want to push deeper down into her throat. "That's it," I mutter, slightly breathless. "That's so fucking good."

She moans around me, sounding so pleased that it sends shockwaves up my spine. Tightening my grip on her hair, I watch her lips stretch around my shaft.

My restraint finally snaps.

I grab her head with my other hand and start dragging my cock in and out of her mouth, my hips pitching back and forth with the movement. I hear her small little choked gags while she tries to swallow around me and my mind is *burning*.

"Does that turn you on, Luce? Does me fucking your tight little throat turn you on?"

She tries to nod, humming in response.

"Show me. Unbutton your shorts and *show me*," I growl, my eyes falling closed for half-second as I get lost in the sensation of Lucy sucking me off. At first, I think she might not know what I mean. But after a few seconds, she raises her hand up, her fingers glistening with proof.

Fuck.

"Such a good little student," I groan.

Leaning over, I take her fingers into my mouth. Her taste bursts on my tongue, successfully rewiring my starving brain to crave that, and *only* that. Straightening back up, I thread my fingers in her curls and her eyes flit up to meet mine between her eyelashes, one lone tear trailing down her cheek.

"Now, swallow," I command.

I hold her with both hands as I bottom out, unloading down her throat in hot, mind-numbing spurts.

I'm trying to catch my breath when I finally come down. Suddenly, I'm worried I've gone too far. Worried, I showed her too much, too fast.

But then she slides me out of her mouth, and she's fuck-ing... beaming—eyes glazed and pupils blown wide. If I didn't know any better, I would say she looked high. Still smiling, she lets out a satisfied sigh and stands up.

I stand frozen to the spot as she gives me a quick kiss on the cheek and whispers, "Thank you." Then she turns her back to me and vanishes into her room.

23

I wake up late. There is a soreness in my jaw that makes my stomach flutter. It's hard to explain the feeling without wading through the muck of my past. I'd rather not kill my good mood. It has been raining all morning, the wind fresh and less dusty than usual. I decide to open the door to the room while I lay in bed to read. The earthy smell wafts from outside comforting me as I am equally lulled by the sound of raindrops falling and falling.

It's quiet on the other side of our adjoining rooms, all I hear is the distinct click of a keyboard while Bastian is busy working. I see him pass by the open door connecting our rooms once in a while, wearing nothing but jeans, his gaze at times lingering on me and the bed I am laying in. I wonder if he's replaying what happened last night. I know I am.

It has been five days since this deal between us started and my nerves seem to have settled along with it. It's hard to explain with words how I feel when everything I experience is somehow life-changing—as if I've been finding a piece of me in the palm of my hand every time I surmount something new.

Even this distance between Bastian and I is somehow comforting, like the rain falling outside my room. It might have made me feel wary at the beginning but now I expect it. Embrace it even. It is not the typical silence I've had to endure my whole life. A kind of silence that would carry an unknown threat. It would keep me on edge until the threat materialized… usually as my husband.

No, this silence feels like breathing.

Lungfuls of oxygen, when I've been suffocating my whole life.

I hear my cell phone ringing from somewhere at the bottom of my bag and I scramble to find it before the call ends. I know it's Lenix.

"Hi, sister of mine," she sing-songs when I pick up. "How's your second week of being on the road?" Without letting me answer, she adds, "I hope Bastian isn't giving you much of a hard time. He can be such a prude sometimes I swear to God."

All of the things we have done in the past week flash in quick succession in my mind and I breathe out a choked laugh, trying to disguise it into a few forced coughs.

"You okay?" she asks.

"Yes." Laughing more effortlessly now. "Yes, I'm fine. Everything is great actually. We've been staying at this one motel for the past few days just to relax."

"Oh?" The pause that follows feels pregnant with questions, but eventually, she only asks me one. "So, like, what have you been doing if not traveling?"

"You're doing it again," I tell her, my tone amused but with a slight bite.

"Doing what?" she says, but then laughs. "Okay fine,

sorry, I can't help but worry. I just want you safe—are you safe?"

"More than safe," I say with a smile.

I stay on the phone with Lenix for another twenty minutes, catching up on what is happening back in Noxport. As always Connor is getting on her nerves but she loves him to death. Sunny, her best friend, bought a boat for her seaside cottage in Midnight Cove, and how her boyfriend Byzantine wants to christen it Windflower. In turn, I tell her all about how I sang at an open mic last night. As expected, she chokes up and then gushes about how proud she is of me. She then reminds me of how much she loves me and I do the same.

After I end the call, I let my head fall back onto the pillow, staring at the ceiling while my thoughts ebb and flow like a soft breeze in my mind's eye. It's not long until I land back on Bridget and what transpired last night. I still don't know all the details since Bastian didn't offer much information on the ride home or after we… did what we did.

It is now early afternoon and I decide it's a better time than any to go check up on her. I do not bother telling Bastian where I'm going, it's only a few doors down. Finding my flip-flops near the door, I slip out. I rap on Bridget's door, hoping Ritchie is miraculously somewhere else, so I can speak with her without him overhearing. The metal awning protects me from the rain, the water rattling against it while I wait.

I'm about to turn back to my room when the door opens and Bridget appears, wearing large dark sunglasses. They feel out of place. Especially with the overcast weather outside. My stomach drops. Something is wrong.

"Lucy!" she tries to say cheerily, but her voice sounds hoarse and slightly forced. She peers over my shoulder as if looking for someone and then back at me. "Look, uh, I'm kind of busy right now. I don't really have time for a visit."

Her tongue darts out of her mouth, it's subtle as if unconscious. My gaze narrows on her upper lip, realizing it is split under her red lipstick.

"Bridget…" I whisper in shock. "What did he do?"

My heart starts to beat wildly in my chest at the thought of Ritchie putting his hands on her. I try to push the door open, but Bridget resists.

"I'm fine, Lucy," she says hurriedly, looking over my shoulder again. "It's fine. You don't have to worry about me. Now is just not a good time, okay?"

My throat tightens, not knowing what else to do but let her feed me her lies.

"I'll talk to you later, okay?" she says reassuringly, but I do not believe her.

She doesn't let me answer, quickly closing the door, effectively shutting me out.

I stare at the door, my mind racing, unable to move for what feels like an eternity, this helplessness growing larger and larger inside of me.

Images of my mother pretending the same. My older sister Claire. They would disappear until the bruises faded, split lip mended. Everything was always fine.

Everything *needed* to be fine.

Just fine. Fine. Fine. Fine. Fine. Fine. Fine.

The paralyzing hopelessness suddenly takes a new form, my breathing accelerating, fists clenching. I am feeling untethered. Snapped. And I no longer care.

I storm back into my room slamming the door on my way in, I do not stop until I'm standing in front of Bastian. I must look like an angry bull, nostrils flaring, arms locked to my sides, fists still clenched, nails digging into my palm.

"Why?" I say, my voice cracking as if I am about to cry, and that only makes the anger burn brighter behind my heaving chest.

Bastian at least has the decency to stop what he is doing and swings around to face me. He doesn't answer, simply cocking his eyebrow in question.

"Why?" I repeat with more heat this time. "Why do they keep doing this?"

His face stays passive, and I let out a groan of frustration knowing that I am not making any sense. I pace across the room and then back feeling caged within all these repressed emotions trying to claw their way up. Caged, like I have felt for so long, not knowing when it would end.

"I hate them," I say through clenched teeth. "They deserved to die. Every single one of them." I don't feel like explaining myself, my thoughts burning, melting into one.

Muddled, jagged, and sharp.

This is beyond words. And if I do not let it out, it will swallow me whole, once and for all.

Needing to just *do* something, I turn to the bed and start ripping the sheets off the mattress in small bursts of anger, throwing them on the ground and then stomping on them. I have just enough self-awareness to realize how I must look, and stop, my legs tangled in white sheets at my feet.

"Sorry," I breathe out.

The look I find on Bastian's face is not one I have seen before, and I am too upset to truly take it in. It is different from the other times I have found him studying me. It is intense. Like he has gone beyond curiosity this time and into another realm entirely. His eyes snap to mine, and I am left breathless when he smiles.

"You can do better than that," he drawls, now standing,

leaning back onto the small desk, his arms folding over his bare chest.

I blink back at him a few times, unsure what he means, until he pushes the chair toward me as if that gesture will coax me into understanding. But when my eyes lift back up to his, the words I was missing are written clearly across his irises.

Wreak havoc.

It is not permission. But an invitation.

My breathing quickens as my gaze falls back to the chair. I untangle myself from the mess at my feet and step forward, the silence now promising something greater than just a simple outburst. I curl my fingers around the chair, and when the wood meets the wall with a loud crack—my anger turns to rage.

My vision narrows and I lose all sense of thought. All that matters is my hand finding the next thing to break, to destroy, to shatter, smash, or splinter.

I hear myself scream, it is primal and guttural but I barely register it. For the first time in my life, I do not care. I allow myself to become consumed. The memories, the pain, the feelings attached to such decaying thoughts. All of it.

And in turn, I destroy everything around me and it feels *good*.

More than good.

Like the cage door finally swinging open.

It feels like freedom.

24

BASTIAN

I thought seeing her sing was mesmerizing.
But this?

This is a masterpiece.

A rebirth through destruction, and I have the privilege
to witness all of it.

All of her.

I stay leaning on the desk and give her all the time she
needs. And she takes it, willingly and unabashedly. The television is the last thing to crash to the floor before she seems
to settle back into her body, like a kite wound back to
earth.

She's out of breath, her t-shirt askew when she finally
looks up at me, a few strands of hair falling over golden
green eyes. My body hums in need, desperate to feel her
under my touch. To feel that level of destruction still strum-
ming underneath her veins while biting into her skin. I
white-knuckle the desk behind me, as I try to stay perfectly
still, trying not to take advantage of the moment. Wanting

for her to take it all in after being cracked open without me muddling it.

But then she smiles, and I stop breathing, like being struck with blinding white light.

Her smile drops, her expression turning into something much more carnal when she sees me move. Two long strides and we slam into each other, my hand reaching up to her nape and tugging hard so her head lifts up to mine. A soft, shocked moan slips out of her as I catch her bottom lip between my teeth. I run my tongue along it, but then I remember myself and release her lip, dragging my nose near her ear, taking in her sweet scent.

"How did that feel, Luce?" I rasp and I feel her shiver under my touch.

"Good," she says a little mindlessly while I push us toward the wall behind her.

"That's it?" I say almost playfully.

I expect her to respond but then I feel her fingers fumble with the clasp of my jeans, and I suddenly don't really give a shit about her answer.

"Just shut up and fuck me," she says so breathlessly I would have missed it if the words weren't like heroin shooting straight into my veins.

The silence yawns around us as we both grow unnaturally still, I lift up my head to find her staring at me, her eyes wide in surprise.

I don't let her internalize what she just said, instead, I tug her shorts down with a jerk, and she kicks them off as soon as they're down her legs.

"Sweet little Luce wants to get ruined," I say tauntingly.

Her mouth falls open, but no sound comes out as she hurriedly fumbles with my jeans, my hips pitching forward as she does. But she's not fast enough. I push her hands away, ignoring her protest as I jerk my jeans down my thighs, not bothering to even take them off all the way.

I grab Lucy by the upper thighs and push her upwards, her back sliding against the wall as she instinctively wraps herself around my waist. As soon as she's steadied, I position myself against her entrance, the thick head of my cock finding her wet and dripping, while I slowly push her open. I rip my gaze away from the prettiest cunt I've ever fucking seen, up to her even prettier face, my hand smoothing her hair away from her cheek. I'm suddenly desperate to kiss her.

But I don't.

Instead, I cup her chin with my palm, pushing her head against the wall.

"I won't be gentle," I growl.

I'm not sure who I'm telling this warning to. Her or me.

"I'm not fragile," she answers immediately, pushing her weight down, my cock sliding deeper inside of her as she does. My mind blanks when she clenches around me. I let my restraints snap, slamming my hips into hers, her body jerking upward again and again as I pump in and out. I can tell that the piercing just above the top of my shaft drags against her clit with every thrust, her soft mewls punctured by breathless yesses. My fingers dig into her thighs, half aware that I'm most likely leaving marks and I'm getting even harder at the thought.

"You feel…" she says in a low moan. "You feel… *amazing.*" It almost sounds like disbelief, a sated smile appearing on her lips as if she never knew it could feel this good. Her eyes fall shut, her head falling against the wall behind her, while I mercilessly pound into her as she grinds on me just as hard.

I let the silence fall between us, the sounds of our erratic breathing and skin on skin enough to fill my head with all the things I want to do to her, as her whimpers drift like a prayer around us.

"Look at you, Luce," I say hoarsely, not able to drag my eyes away from her, and why would I? "Such a sweet little student fucking herself on my cock."

She hums in response, spurring me on, and then finally her mouth falls open. "I'm going to…" she starts to say with a small furrow of her brow as if she's concentrating, her teeth biting her bottom lip. "I think I am…"

She falls silent, eyes pinned to mine. Her hand finds her clit between us, stroking herself while I continue to slam into her, my balls starting to tighten.

I can feel her orgasm before I even hear the moans escape in sharp bursts from her lips, and barely resist the urge to tell her all the lewd thoughts currently lighting my mind on fire.

Mine to own.

Mine to corrupt.

Mine to breed.

"*Bastian,*" she says in whispered awe as she comes. I pin her to the wall, grinding even harder into her while her pussy tightens over and over around my cock and I can't hold it any longer.

I let her feet drop to the floor. But before I can even find the words, she falls to her knees in front of me, expression eager, eyes dazed, mouth open, and tongue wide and flat.

What's the point of having words like *breathtaking* when it doesn't even come close to describing the sight of her like this?

She's so fucking perfect, it hurts.

I smile, my thumb dragging across her cheek as I do so.

I lift her chin even higher, her darkened gaze throwing me into the deep end.

"What a sweet little slut you're becoming," I whisper.

Her eyes flare with heat and my mind splinters.

Then, finally, I let go.

I lean one of my forearms on the wall above us, my other hand jerking myself off as hot white ropes paint her pretty face, her eyelids fluttering closed.

When it's finally over, I try to catch my breath, my chest heaving up and down. Lucy is still peering up at me, a small grin on her lovely lips. I give her a half smile in return. Smearing my fingers in my cum, I rub it into her skin. Slowly, I drag those same fingers into her mouth, her lips closing around them as soon as she tastes me on her tongue. Her quiet little mewl is suddenly fucking with my head and I take a step back, as she releases me with a long drag of her tongue.

I take her hand and pull her up, resisting the impulse to circle my arm around her waist and press her warm body against mine.

"You should shower," I tell her while pulling up my jeans. Then look around the wrecked room. "I think it's time to leave."

She nods, still standing half-naked in front of me like it's the most natural thing in the world, but then her smile drops, looking worried.

"I just want to know that Bridget will be okay before we go," she says softly while making her way to her own bathroom.

"Why?" I ask, but, *shit*, I already fucking know what she's about to say.

"Ritchie hurt her. He *hurts* her."

"How do you know?" I press her.

"I saw the bruises," she says dejectedly.

My mind is already ten steps ahead, Ritchie dead and rotting somewhere dark, but I keep my face blank, and nod. "We'll see what we can do for her, okay? But we can't stay here. We need to go."

She studies me for a few seconds and then lets out a long exhale. "Okay," she says, a little defeated.

I'm out of the motel room as soon as Lucy closes the bathroom door.

25

BASTIAN

A few hours later, and a short hiatus from the room on my part, we're back on the road.

"Is that your bucket list?" I glance toward the passenger side as Lucy slams her notebook shut. She asked me to drive today and I happily obliged, needing some distractions from everything that transpired in the past twenty-four hours. We've been on the road for over an hour, and she's been silent for most of it.

My gaze falls on her closed notebook, a pink flamingo illustrated on the cover. I bring my attention back to the road, but that same prickling feeling at my nape sends shivers down my spine. It's that same—and now ever-present—feeling of having already seen such a random and innocuous thing, like this fucking flamingo notebook, before. I just know I'd find it somewhere scrawled inside my notebook back home.

"Uh, yes…" Lucy replies as if harboring a shameful secret.

"What are you hiding in there, Luce?" I say playfully—only half-jokingly.

The hit of jealousy straight to the gut I felt when I learned that she had told Bridget about her list before telling me was... shocking, to say the least. It's ridiculous that I'd feel anything other than apathy. Instead of letting that feeling linger any longer, I did the first thing to come to mind—just so happens that thing was to make Lucy come on my tongue.

"Nothing." Her tone is higher than usual while she shoves the notebook into her backpack at her feet. "It's silly really," she adds with a quick sigh.

Nothing about you is silly, Luce.

It's at the tip of my tongue, I can taste every single ridge of every word. Still, I keep my mouth shut, staring at the road ahead, hating myself.

Thankfully, my phone rings, relieved that I don't have to stew in whatever was happening just now.

I snatch it from the drink holder, seeing it's Kenzie calling before pressing it to my ear.

"Yeah?" I say.

"Been a while, pal," he drawls in his Scottish accent. "How's life?"

My nostrils flare, gripping the steering wheel a little tighter, knowing this isn't just a social call.

"Life is life. What do you want?"

His chuckle travels through the receiver. "Still a sorry cunt I see," he says, then pauses before continuing, "Remember that favor?"

As if I'd forget what he did for me.

"I remember," I mutter.

"Good, 'cause I need your special skills set in Colorado Springs."

"I'm busy."

He laughs. "Tough."

I stay silent, my eyes traveling over to Lucy who's looking out the passenger window, most likely pretending not to listen. Dread circles around my throat like a snake at the thought of bringing her with me—to one of Black Plague's chapters no less. The image of Lucy in a room full of bikers is enough to give me fucking hives.

But then…

I'm not fragile.

Her heated words float back to me, the clear determination in her tone before I fucked her against the wall. *And fuck.* How good she felt when I finally did.

I clear my throat, my attention landing back on the road ahead, trying not to derail figuratively and literally.

"How did you know I was close by?" I finally say.

Another laugh. "I didn't. Just a happy little coincidence, isn't it?"

I grunt in reply.

"When can you get here?" he asks.

I check the time on the dash. "Late tonight."

"Sounds good, see you then."

I hang up and throw my phone back in the middle console.

I let the silence fall inside the car. Half lost in thought, the other annoyed that I'm about to disappoint Lucy.

She's the first one to speak.

"What's going on?" Her tone is light and airy.

I chew on my words but then finally say, "There's a job up in Colorado Springs." I drum my fingers on the wheel, looking at her. The disappointment I was worried I'd find is missing, instead, her expression is curious and open. "I have no choice, Luce. Only for a couple of days, I promise," I say, trying to sound apologetic.

She studies me for a few seconds. "You're taking me with you?"

"Of course," I answer immediately.

Staying silent for a few beats, her eyes brighten. "Okay," she says with a wide smile.

"Okay?" I repeat while looking back at the road. "You're not disappointed?"

She settles back into her seat with a pleased sigh that shoots straight to my balls.

"Part of the adventure, Maxwell," she says breezily, wiggling her eyebrows.

This time, I can't help but smile along with her.

THE SUN IS HALFWAY down the sky and we're still hours away from our destination when Lucy holds up a joint in her hand.

"Look what Bridget gave me last night," she says, her tone hushed and conspiratorial as if her joint is some kind of government secret. But the pleased look written on her face tells me she's more excited than nervous.

I hum in response, holding in a laugh. "You ever smoked weed?"

"Once with Lenix—surprised?" she says a little defiantly.

"You surprise me every day, Luce. It's my favorite thing about you," I say a bit too seriously.

The words hang heavy between us, as we both fall silent.

Fuck. I shouldn't have said that.

I keep my eyes glued to the road, not knowing what else to say, while hers are burning the side of my face.

"So?" she says, and at first I think she's trivializing what I just said, but realize from the corner of my eye that she's still holding up the joint between us.

"You want to smoke it now?" I say, a little surprised.

"Why not," she says with a shrug. "We can take a quick break... watch the sunset." And then, as if catching herself. "Or sorry—do you *do* drugs?"

Her lingering innocence is at times so refreshing that I can't help but grin a little.

"Just not hard drugs," I answer frankly.

"I'm not sure what that means," she answers.

I breathe out a small chuckle. "Yes, Luce. I smoke weed."

"Oh my goodness look, that's your name!" Lucy shouts out of nowhere, pointing to the interstate sign that says Maxwell, amongst other things. "How perfect," she says, beaming back at me.

"How is that perfect?" I say, my tone coated in amusement, still planning on taking that exit anyway so we can stop on a side road somewhere.

"I don't know," she says with a small shrug. "Fun coincidence, don't you think?"

That word again.

I chew on my lip before answering. "If you say so," I mutter, now slightly distracted.

After a few turns, I park on the side of the road, the car facing the setting sun.

"Come on," I tell Lucy, opening the door. "We can sit on the hood."

Her face lights up as if I told her something much cooler than I just did. Putting on her cowboy hat, she scrambles out of her seat and out of the car. Then stalls in front of the hood seeming a little lost.

Her laugh is a little nervous when she turns her head to look up at me. "What's the easiest way to get up there?"

"Turn around and face me." My voice having dropped an octave.

Her face falls serious. The scuff of her soles against the pebbles underneath is the only sound lingering in the sudden silence, as she slowly faces me, her back to the car. When my hands find her waist, it's purely instinctual, then I remember, according to those stupid fucking self-appointed rules, I shouldn't be touching her. I don't know if it's her following my lead or she forgot just as easily, but her hands fall delicately on both my shoulders before I lift her up and place her down on the hood.

Her legs fall open and again, I'm lured into the space between them, my palms resting on either side. The scent of warm florals and mandarin lingers between us. I fight the urge to bury my nose in her neck and lick her warm skin just to remind me that she's real. If I didn't know any better I would swear I felt electricity pulsing between us, bouncing off one another eager to merge into one. My eyes flit up to hers as I try to ignore how easy it would be to have another quick taste while she's up there.

"How are you feeling? After..." I suddenly feel stupid even asking.

Lucy blinks as if lulled out of a spell. Picking up on what I'm trying to ask, she smiles, her gaze finding the sun. Her expression is pensive as if lost in thought, or the past— who knows.

"This is not a relationship, remember?" she says softly. "You don't have to ask me how I'm feeling." Her attention is now back on me, and I wish it wasn't, because somehow those words sting and I step back in response.

She studies me for a beat, and I hope my face is as closed off as I think it is, then pats the hood beside her. I swipe my hand over my face, concealing a sigh, and jump up, joining her on top of the car.

I take the joint from between her fingers, bringing the flame from my lighter to the rolled tip, lighting up a cigarette at the same time. Taking a deep inhale of weed first, I pass it to Lucy but keep it between my fingers so she needs to lean forward. Her eyes are fixed on me when she does, her lips slightly parted while her mouth closes on the filter of the joint, inches away from my heated skin.

"Small drag," I mutter.

The stern look she sends my way promptly reminds me that she hates being told what to do. It would even be comical if I wasn't currently suffocating in emotions, craving my usual detachment. Eventually, she takes it from me, and I watch her as she takes a few more puffs, coughing in between all of them, but still holds her own as the setting sun dances across her golden green eyes.

Her giggle breaks the silence we've settled comfortably into. I reach over, my fingers grazing her own, and I linger, lost but not really wanting to find my way. Her eyes flit to mine and I snap out of it, taking the joint out of her grasp.

"That's enough, Luce," I say a little sternly, but with a small dash of amusement.

She giggles again. "Okay," she says with a long satisfied sigh. "This feels nice."

"The weed?" I ask.

She presses her palms to the hood on either side of her thighs, leaning her weight into them as if trying to get closer to the sunset. Her skin glows with the dying rays and I'm left breathless.

"All of it," she states. The few tokes she's taken have clearly loosened her tongue because then she adds, "How much do you know about what happened to me?"

I fall silent not knowing how to answer.

"Some," I finally say. "Not the details."

"Would you like to?" she says tentatively.

I study her for a bit. I nod.

She takes a large breath in, her face chasing the last rays of sunlight. Then she begins to speak. And a shameful part of me wishes she didn't. Because I'm left powerless, listening to a past I can't change. Of men who are already dead when all I want is to kill and maim—in her name. She tells me about her brother first. How he raped her before her forced wedding with Patrick. How her husband Patrick treated her... and abused her. And how her life was not her own. She was simply what Sacro Nuntio told her to be. And for most of her life, she believed exactly that.

I don't feel worthy of her confession. But still I ache to hear all of her, of what made her who she is now and keep all those jagged edges of herself locked safe inside of me.

Eventually, we fall into silence. I'm lacking the words to comfort her and I hate myself for it.

"Did you always want to be part of the Sin Eaters?" Lucy says after a while.

"I never had much of a choice."

Never thought much ahead either.

"How so?"

"Family business," I answer with a shrug. The conversation is as close to mentioning or even thinking about my father as I can stomach so I try to quickly change the subject, and somehow land on the reason why I'm on this road trip in the first place.

"Connor paid me to chaperone you, you know?" I don't mean for it to come out so harsh, but it still feels like it does.

But Lucy doesn't sound affected by it, simply answering, "Yes." She falls silent and then, "How much?"

I flick my cigarette into the road before answering. "Half a million." Her eyes widen, her head turning to face me but before she can express her shock, I say, "Have it. I don't want it."

She giggles, and I'm reminded that the weed is probably hitting her a lot harder than me. "What do you mean?" she says with another laugh. "I must admit I don't think I can even comprehend how much money that is."

I don't know how else to tell her how uncomfortable this money now makes me feel. As if she's nothing but a paycheck. When in reality she's... well—

I jump off the hood and reach for my phone inside the car. It takes me less than five minutes to find Lucy's bank information and transfer the money over. "Well, I guess you'll have to figure it out, because it's yours now," I declare with a shrug, pocketing my phone.

Lucy laughs, studying me with quiet amusement.

"I'm not joking, Luce."

Her smile falls. "What? You can't be serious..."

I don't feel like placating her, the words sticking to my tongue even if I wanted to.

Finally, after a long breath, she murmurs, "I don't know what to say."

I shrug my shoulders. "So don't."

Her gaze turns soft, almost shy, her eyes bouncing back and forth.

Then suddenly, her face lights up as if she just had the greatest idea.

"Let's eat, I'm starving," she says with zeal, followed by a giggle.

I grin, letting out a small laugh too.

I hold my hand up toward her. "Sounds like a plan."

The rules can go fuck themselves.

Her palm finds mine, her fingers curling into my grasp. We stay like this for a few seconds too long, her gaze fixed on mine. Then she smiles, and my heart is suddenly beating a lot faster than before. With my help, she pushes herself off and jumps down. As soon as her feet touch the ground, her hand leaves mine. The emptiness that follows feels all too familiar.

And for the first time, I wish it didn't.

26

I t's the middle of the night when we finally arrive at the private compound.

Bastian wakes me up with a small shake of the shoulder and I jerk awake, looking around trying to situate myself, groggy and disoriented.

"We're here," he whispers, quietly opening the car door, and climbing out. "Grab what you need for tonight."

I stifle a yawn, still half asleep, but grab my bag and a change of clothes, popping my cowboy hat on my sleep-flattened hair. The smell of pine is heavy in the air as soon as I'm out of the car. The property seems to be surrounded by forest, cloaked in darkness, but I can see light further ahead, through the trees, distant music and laughter accompanying it.

On our way here, Bastian enlightened me on what to expect around one-percenters like the Black Plague MC. What I got from it was that these motorcycle clubs were very similar to the Sin Eaters, but lived by a strict code that involved bikes and a whole lot of illegal activities.

I find Bastian near the trunk, speaking to a man with an accent I've never heard before. Curiosity gets the best of me, making me walk up without my usual nerves just to hear him speak.

Stopping mid-sentence, the man turns to me, his face mostly hidden by the surrounding night. "And who's this bonnie lass?" he says with a smile.

All I hear are words, half of them carrying no meaning. I fight back the embarrassment of somehow always being slightly confused about everything at all times and turn to Bastian for clarification.

"Lucy. Lenix's sister from Sacro Nuntio," he responds coldly.

Hearing myself being described as such by Bastian stings a little, but ultimately those descriptors are not wrong, so I say nothing, simply nodding with a smile.

The man makes a sound of recognition, which leaves me a little weary, wondering what he's heard about my family and the commune we grew up in.

He holds out his hand. "Name's Kenzie. Pleasure to meet you, Lucy." We shake hands as I mumble the same.

When Kenzie drops my grasp, his eyes lift to Bastian. "Two rooms?" he asks.

I answer yes at the same time as he answers, "One."

Kenzie's brown eyes catch the moonlight, twinkling in mirth as he looks from Bastian to me and then back to Bastian.

"New rules," he says curtly, staring me down as if challenging me to protest in front of his colleague. I'm peeved but say nothing, giving him the smallest of nods to show that I understood.

"You can stay in Doc's old room," Kenzie offers.

He leads us up the road, a large rectangular building

appearing like a mirage in the middle of the forest. The closer we get, the louder the voices and music become. My throat tightens, not particularly ready to meet a mass of strangers who, by the sound of it, are quite rowdy. Luckily, Kenzie walks us around the left side of the building and away from the noise. Opening a side door, we follow him down a darkened hallway, eventually unlocking a door near the end.

"Not much, but it'll do," Kenzie says, pointing to the room with a flash of a smile, then handing the key to Bastian.

He grunts a "Thanks," herding me inside, and then closes the door on Kenzie without even a goodbye.

"See you in the morning, ya cunt!" I hear through the door, and then footsteps fading away.

"You don't have to be so rude all the time," I say, while I drop my bags on the floor, taking in the small room and decor.

Kenzie was right, there is not much to look at. A dilapidated white dresser to my right, a yellowing calendar with a naked woman on the cover hanging askew atop it, a nightstand with a light, and a bed to my left that barely seems big enough to fit two people. The door in the back is ajar, and through it I see the bathroom.

"He's used to it," he says with a bored shrug, dropping down onto the mattress.

"And what was *that* all about?" I say crossing my arms, still standing in the middle of the room.

Bastian's face is serious when his dark eyes begin to slowly slide up my body, his gaze lingering on my hat for a few seconds and then back down to lock eyes with mine. "What?"

"New rules," I say with a petulant lilt to my voice, repeating what he told me earlier.

Bastian's slow curl of his lip is anything but amusing. "You don't understand this place, Luce. I can't protect you if they think you're fair game."

It takes a few seconds for me to connect the dots, but when I do, anger blasts through me leaving me breathing that much heavier.

I narrow my eyes. "This sounds a lot like you're trying to protect my virtue," I scoff, stepping forward, my arms still crossed tightly over my chest. "Or staking your claim, when I never asked you to."

Bastian lets out a dry laugh, his head falling down and to the side for a few seconds before he's up on his feet, stalking toward me. Startled, I step backwards until my back hits the dresser, his arms trapping me.

"You have no idea what the fuck you're saying, Lucy," he says darkly.

I match his burning gaze, trying to stand my ground. "Stop saying that," I say a little too quietly.

He stays silent, his glare only intensifying. "You think if I truly staked my claim there'd be any doubt in your mind?"

One of his hands flicks my hat off my head, his fingers finding my nape, fisting my hair. I swallow the shocked gasp traveling up my throat, my heart beating wildly against my ribs. His other hand then travels down to my shorts, his fingers unfastening the button with a hard tug, and before I can even catch my breath, he thrusts his hand down my panties. His fingers find my clit, stroking me with slow deliberate care, while his eyes are still stripping me bare.

My mouth falls open on a silent whimper but I say nothing, transfixed by Bastian's ability to control my every thought with his body, his hips pushing me into the dresser. "Sweet little Luce wants to be fair game. Is that it?" he says tauntingly.

"That is not… that's not what…" But I forget what I'm even saying when Bastian travels down my slit, slowly but forcefully pushing two of his fingers inside of me, and then circling them around while deep inside. This time, my moan is nowhere near quiet, his hips continuously grinding against me, the hard curve of his cock pressing into my hip. His face falls closer to mine, his lips barely grazing the column of my neck. "Make that sound again, and I'll put a baby in you. Really stake my claim," he groans next to my ear.

I would not expect his words to have such an effect on me but my inner walls squeeze around Bastian's fingers, my palms clambering against the dresser behind me for some-thing to hold. His chuckle is lewd, and all I want is to hear it again and again.

In the span of a blink, he's off me, taking a few steps back, his typical apathetic glare slipped back into place. "I'm going out for a smoke, lock the door after I leave," he mutters.

He stalks out of the room, the door closing behind him.

After a few seconds, I force my body to relax and peel myself off the dresser. My mind clambers to make sense of what just happened. Slowly, I strip down to my underwear and bra, the drag of my clothes on my heightened sensitive skin sending shivers down my arms and legs. I ache for release but do nothing about it, too rattled by our latest interaction. I try to stay awake, but exhaustion overtakes me, falling asleep before I hear Bastian come back into the room.

27

BASTIAN

I kick the exit door closed with my foot, my nostrils flaring, huffing out frustrated breaths as I fish out my pack of cigarettes. Palming my still, *raging*, erection through my jeans, I groan out loud, wishing I could just go back inside and fuck Lucy against that dresser. But I know I won't. Especially after what she said. No matter if she meant it seriously or not.

The strike of the lighter, followed by the spark of the flame coming to life has almost the same effect as the nicotine waiting for me on the other side of that first drag. My hand shakes, trying to light my smoke as fast as possible. I close my eyes, inhaling deeply, my head falling back between my shoulders. I can still smell her on my fingers while I smoke my cigarette, and it only exacerbates the barrage of thoughts in my head.

Opening my eyes, I stare at the night sky, the stars looking like loose glitter, breathing life into the vast expanse of darkness. When in reality, they're all dead. Extinguished.

Gone. Their shining light, the only thing left of them, traveling across the universe to reach us. I focus on the irony of it all for a little while, trying to calm down and finish my smoke.

I wasn't lying when I told Lucy that the one room was for her own good. It's just a matter of time before these MC fucks start sniffing around her like she's fresh meat. A new little challenge and the winner gets their dick sucked. My vision starts to blur at the thought of any of these losers treating her like she's just another chick passing through the clubhouse. At the very least, if we're sharing a room, the smarter ones will stay away. And for the idiots? Well, we'll just have to see about them.

My head snaps toward the approaching footsteps, tension releasing when I realize it's Kenzie.

"Didn't think I'd find you out here. You seemed quite pressed to be alone with the missus," he drawls, taking a swig of the bottled beer he's loosely holding.

"She's not mine," I mumble, the words tasting like rot as they leave my mouth.

"Could have fooled me, pal," he answers with a chuckle.

I ignore him. Although, a swift punch to the Adam's apple might do him one better.

"So, are you going to tell me what was important enough that you had to call in your favor?" I ask with as much disinterest as I can muster.

He takes another swig of his beer, looking up at the sky before answering.

"Gravediggers are out for blood. This time, they're trying to hit us where it counts. We keep getting activity on our server that looks like someone's trying to hack in. We have some… sensitive files that need some heavy-duty encryption. We have a guy," he says, then looks at me with a crooked grin. "But he's not you. We need that shit done fast and as usual, it needs to not just be hard to crack—but impossible. If they ever get their hands on that info—" he pauses, taking a sip of beer. "It could mean war."

I'm familiar with the Gravediggers. They've been the Sin Eaters' rivals for as long as the Black Plague have been allies. I don't bother asking what they're trying to keep hidden. It's not my job to care. I'll find out eventually anyway.

"Give me full access to your system, and I can start now," I tell him as I light another cigarette, still feeling on edge.

"Now?" he says with a laugh. "Shouldn't you get some sleep first?"

"Do you want this shit done or not?" I say with a blank face but a bite of annoyance leaks into my voice, taking a drag.

"You haven't changed," he replies with a shake of his head. "Come on, I'll show you where everything is."

I flick my half-smoked cigarette to the ground, stepping on it with my heel before following him back into the club-house, the party somewhere near the front of the building not seeming to have let up even if it's close to dawn. We're both silent as I follow him through a series of hallways and locked doors.

"Lucy's off limits." The words fly out of my mouth like I'm fucking possessed and I try not to externally cringe while Kenzie looks back over to me with one of his casual smiles.

"I thought she wasn't your bird," he says with mirth.

"She's not—but I want her treated like she is."

"If you say so," he replies, unlocking a fortified door and leading us into a room filled with monitors, keeping the lights dimmed. Their set up looks a lot more state of the art than I expected.

"Here's everything you'll need. And this," he says pointing to a series of camera feeds, "is for your peace of mind."

I sweep my gaze over all the different camera angles until I finally find the hallway right outside our bedroom door. I suddenly feel a little less on edge.

"Thanks," I mutter, heading for the computer. "I need coffee," I say as an afterthought, settling into one of the chairs.

Kenzie laughs as he heads for the door. "I'll get a prospect. They'll bring you whatever you want." Closing the door behind him, the room falls silent. I let out a long sigh, already twenty steps ahead, thinking of what needs to be done. My gaze lands back on the video of the hallway, wondering why the fuck I'm here when I could be in bed with Lucy. Like a self-inflicted punishment for something I didn't even fucking do.

I stare at it for a little while longer, wondering if she's sleeping, imagining her under the sheets, her sleep-warm skin just waiting to be stroked and caressed. Her mouth asking to be kissed... to be licked, and sucked. As some kind of self-soothing reflex, I check her phone for any activity. I wonder if she's watched any porn since last time, but she hasn't browsed her phone since we were in the car together. The thought of Lucy watching porn makes my brain over-heat, the image of her masturbating in secret making me groan out loud. I clear my throat, shaking my head, and stretch, facing back toward the screen in front of me. Eventually, I fall into a cadence, the clack of the keyboard almost meditative, while my mind stays distracted. Still, my eyes periodically fall on that one camera feed of the hallway, like a lured fish just waiting to be hooked...

Maybe, I already am.

28

I wake up alone. For a groggy second, I think Bastian came back and then left again, all before I woke up. But it doesn't take me long to gather that he never came back to the room. I have woken up in enough empty beds to know the difference.

What a walking oxymoron. What was the purpose of his hard rule yesterday when he didn't even spend the night here? My heart pinches, but I pretend it does not. Refusing to let my mind drift to the what-ifs, I stay on my back for a few wandering minutes, staring at the ceiling, wondering what my day will look like today.

I could call him. He must be somewhere on this property. At least, the music and ruckus seem to have died down.

There is a knock at the door that makes me spring up in bed, the sheet fluttering down to my thighs. For a second I think it's Bastian, but then remember he has the key. I stay paralyzed, staring at the closed door for far too long until a second knock makes me clamber out of bed. I smooth down my frizzy curls, not knowing what else to do but open the door. I creak it open, and poke my head through, unsure who I'll find on the other side.

"Hi!" the young woman says with a bright smile. Her head slants to the side, her short bob, swishing with the movements as if trying to take a better look at me. My eyes fix on the color of her hair, a rainbow of bright vivid shades. I have never seen anything like it. "Lucy, right? I'm London. Kenzie sent me, he wants me to show you around while your man is busy working."

"He is not—" I stop myself. Not important. I change course and smile, opening the door fully, hoping it's a genuine expression she finds on my face. "Nice to meet you, London. Let me, uh, refresh myself and I—and I will be right out," I stutter, internally hating how easily flustered I still get.

A few minutes later, I am out the door wearing jeans shorts and Bastian's band t-shirt. Might have been a calculated move to wear it today, but after his stunt last night who is he to care?

"Nice hat," London says with an open smile, eyes twinkling, realizing then that they're different colors—one green, the other crystal blue.

"Thank you," I reply shyly, touching it instinctively while I answer. The baby blue cowboy hat is now becoming a thing of comfort rather than just a silly accessory.

"You hungry?" she says from over her shoulder, leading us closer to the front of the building. "I can fix you something."

I nod and smile. "That would be very nice of you," I answer, trying not to sound as meek as I feel but failing miserably.

"Great, the kitchen is just through here," she says,

walking through two swinging doors. As soon as I step foot into the large space, which looks like the common area, I freeze.

At least a few dozen people are strewn around, men and women in various states of undress, slumped on couches sleeping, or face first on tables seeming to be doing the same. There are empty bottles of beer and alcohol everywhere and the place reeks of stale cigarettes. I sweep my gaze around the room, suddenly hoping I won't see a certain someone amongst the pile of slumbering bodies.

The giggle beside me snaps me out of wherever I was just now. I must be making a face similar to shock because London laughs again and says, "Wait, is this your first time at a clubhouse?" Her words do not carry any ill intent but I feel embarrassed nonetheless.

I nod, my smile sheepish.

"Oops," she says with a chuckle, her fingers brushing against her lips. "Should have warned you. Don't worry most of them are harmless," she says, waving me off with her hand. She puts a hand on her waist, popping her hip, her eyes looking upwards as if thinking. "Well... except Alley Cat... and maybe Napalm." Her gaze snaps back to mine and she smiles. "Anyway, come on, the kitchen is this way."

We weave through knocked-down chairs and bodies, my stomach sinking when I notice more than one discarded gun laying around. Bastian had warned me, but *seeing* it is different than the mental expectation. I have been around guns before, especially having Connor as my brother-in-law, but it's the carelessness of it all that surprises me most.

When we finally exit the room, I exhale, my shoulders relaxing. The kitchen is big and bright with exposed brick and large wooden beams close to the ceiling—pots, and pans hanging off them. I offer to help but London shoos me off, telling me to sit. She hands me coffee and I happily take it, the cup hot under the pads of my fingers. I watch her in silence as she starts breaking some eggs, a pan already heating with oil on the stove.

"So, um," I say, taking a sip of coffee before speaking again. "What's your role here?"

I'm unsure if the question is impolite, but the way Bastian explained it to me, it sounded like everyone had their specific function within the club. I could not help but notice how similar it was to the commune I grew up in.

"I'm club property," London says breezily, her back to me.

My heart drops, along with my voice. "You are here against your will?" My mind instinctively tries to find ways to get her out.

Her laugh leaves me confused. "It's not what you think," she says with a giggle. And I relax just a little. "It means I work for the club, keep this place clean—among other things." She turns and winks at me, and I'm surprised at how fast I pick up on her innuendo, feeling a bit proud of myself. "In turn, I get room and board plus protection. Sweet deal really," she adds.

I nod while listening, my eyebrows slightly furrowed. My mind is having a hard time grasping the difference between this and Sacro Nuntio.

"And you're happy here?" The question holds more weight than she knows, but the answer feels too important not to ask.

"More than I ever could be out there," she says, placing a plate of toast in front of me while she finishes cooking the eggs. I thank her and we fall silent.

"Are *you* happy, Lucy?" she asks after a while, and when

I look up her expression surprises me, as if she genuinely wants to know and isn't asking just for pleasantries. So I decide to answer truthfully, taking a bite of toast while I think. My mind drifts to Bastian and how he's made me feel in the past few weeks. And how the road trip has brought a much-needed sense of peace I have been seeking for a long, long time. Although, I fear all of it is temporary... ephemeral.

"Maybe someday soon," I respond finally with a smile.

I END up spending the day with London. She shows me around the property, patiently answering all of my questions about club life, and who is who within the hierarchy of the Black Plague MC. Eventually, we end up back in the common area, the place looking better than when I first saw it earlier this morning. And a lot less crowded too.

"Hi, boys," London says to two heavily tattooed men dressed in black jeans, boots, and leather vests, hanging by the pool table. I learned earlier that the vests are called cuts, their road name—a nickname given to them when they join the club—stitched in large letters to the back. "Have you met Lucy?" she adds while strutting up to them. "She's here with Kenzie's friend."

Both of them smile and nod. The way they look at each other seems to say that they know who Kenzie's friend is, and why he's here.

"So you're Bastian's girl?" the one with dirty blond shoulder-length hair says with a flash of a bright white smile.

"He's just a friend," I say a little too quickly.

Although, I barely believe the words coming out of my mouth.

"Gotcha," he answers with a wink, leaning in to give me his hand. "Well, nice to meet you, Lucy. I'm Barker."

We exchange a handshake, his clear blue eyes sweeping over my body from head to toe, then back up again. I am surprised by the small flutter in my stomach in response.

"We were about to play a game of pool, you want in, ladies?"

"Oh, uh, I don't know how to play," I answer softly, shaking my head.

"That's okay. I'll show you, I'm a great teacher," Barker responds and then looks over to London. "Isn't that right, honey?" he adds with a playful smile and a wag of his eyebrows.

She giggles, popping a hip and then tucking her hair behind her ear. "I'd say so."

I am self-aware enough to pick up on the flirtatious tone, but can't seem to pinpoint who it's directed at, so I decide to simply ignore it.

I nod, and give him a smile. "Okay."

"Great, Catfish, you be with London, and I'll make sure Lucy beats both of your asses," Barker says.

The group laughs, and I laugh along with them. My shyness is not doing me any good in this situation, but I try to power through it nonetheless.

We spend the next hour playing pool, Barker teaching me how to properly hold the cue, and tips and tricks on how to sink the balls into the holes. Eventually, I warm up to him, his charisma infectious, and I let myself relax and have a little fun.

But all the while we play, Bastian lingers at the back of

my mind, wondering what he is doing and why I haven't seen him all day.

Eventually, I excuse myself, feigning a headache, and head back to the room by early evening. Hours pass slowly by and still, I haven't seen or heard from Bastian since last night. I don't bother texting or calling. I am less than thrilled, but I will live. Ultimately, he doesn't owe me anything, and he's here for a job, I just happen to have tagged along.

His behavior makes me wonder if he's suddenly mistaking my inexperience for dependency. As if now that we've had sex, I suddenly need him. That I am craving something deeper than what he's offering. I was in a forced marriage for more than half my life—he should know that the last thing I want is a relationship.

I decide to go to bed, my musings all speculation anyway. No point in spending any more time on them. I must have been dozing, unsure how much time has passed, when my eyes snap open in full alert due to a rustling in the room, followed by a long sigh. Somehow, I recognize Bastian's breathing and relax, my back to him, facing the wall. I stay still, pretending to sleep as I listen to every little sound he makes around the room.

The rush of the water in the sink while he brushes his teeth. A lighter placed on the dresser. The swish of a shirt pulled over his head. The clink of a belt. The sound of jeans falling to the ground. Bare feet on hardwood floors. The push of the sheets, and finally the creak of the mattress.

The weight of his body on the bed makes my body fall toward him, but I try my hardest to stay huddled next to the wall. The heat of him so close makes me break out in goosebumps, and I shut my eyes trying to pretend I can fall asleep now that he is here beside me. It takes him a few minutes to move again, but when he does, his hand finds the curve of my waist, traveling down and over my stomach, reaching over to the other side and pulling me into him.

I forget to breathe. Or maybe I refuse to, intent on hearing every little sound he makes as his body slowly curves into mine. His lips press a soft kiss between my shoulder blades as his hips press into the back of me and I suddenly realize all of this is happening because he thinks I'm sleeping. He lets out another small sigh, settling even closer, the room now completely silent. Trying to relax into him, I absentmindedly count Bastian's breaths with every rise of his chest. I eventually manage to fall back asleep, his arm a warm weight around my waist throughout the night.

29

BASTIAN

I'm out of bed before the sun has time to rise over the Black Plague compound. I pad through the room in the dark still feeling the imprint of Lucy's body on my skin. A moment of weakness maybe—to have pulled her into my chest while she slept soundly next to me.

I'm stepping into my jeans, distracted by all the shit that needs to be done when I hear a rustle coming from the bed. My gaze snaps to hers as I straighten to my full height, buttoning my jeans in another one of our loaded silences.

I can just make out the soft lines of Lucy's face, her wide eyes the only thing penetrating the shadows.

"Are you doing this on purpose?" she whispers.

She tucks the sheets under her chin as if trying to shield herself from me—or maybe even my answer.

"Doing what?" I reply. My voice gravelly like I haven't used it in a while. I'm not sure why I ask, because I already know. Better to play dumb than be truthful.

Her own voice is still low and full of sleep when she answers. "Avoiding me."

My heart squeezes knowing I'm the reason for the insecurity in her tone, letting the silence fight my own battles while I think of how to answer. In the end, I go with a lie. "I'm not."

She sits up in bed, eyebrows furrowed in anger, the sheets falling down to her hips. I track the movement, my gaze lingering near her thighs.

"Look at me," she says sternly, my eyes snapping back up immediately. "You haven't talked to me since we got here," she says defensively.

"We're talking right now," I answer without thinking, which only makes the tension between us simmer.

"Don't be obtuse, Bastian. It does not suit you." Her words are cold when they reach my ears, her arms folded over her loose shirt in protest.

"I'm sorry," I say much too quickly. I mean it, but it doesn't sound genuine while I turn around to reach for a clean shirt in my duffle bag. "I'm just really busy," I add, throwing the shirt over my head. "This job is going to take longer than expected. I have to undo all their work. I can't believe these idiots had any security at all with the jacked-up code they had written, and—" I stop myself mid-sentence, realizing my words must be bouncing off Lucy's skin without making much sense to her.

I step closer to the bed, pushing my hair off my face as I do so. With the same hand—and without much thought—I reach over, my fingers hovering inches from her cheek.

I never get to feel her warmth under my touch before dropping my hand to my side. Her gaze slowly lifts up to mine and I let out a long sigh, dragging my palm over my mouth, before speaking. "I'll come find you sometime today, okay? In the meantime, stick with London, yeah? I don't want—"

I don't finish my sentence, chewing on my words, deciding not to mention how I watched her through the cameras, playing pool with Barker yesterday. It shouldn't have bothered me. But it did.

I should be the one teaching her how to play, not that dumb club fuck.

"You don't want what?" Lucy repeats, defiance in the gleam of her eye. And fuck, am I enjoying watching her starting to push back. The fire she's been forced to smother all of her life is now burning brighter and brighter every day.

I'm addicted to the sight.

"You're beautiful to watch, you know that?" I say, too caught up in the sight of her to make sense of what she's asking and answer her question.

Her eyebrows rise, mouth falling slightly agape, chin still raised up so she can keep my penetrating gaze. I wish I could just fall to my knees and cradle her face in my palms while I spend the morning counting the freckles across her nose and cheeks.

Instead, I force myself to leave.

"I'll see you later, okay?" I say, my voice so tender that I can barely recognize it.

Lucy seems to have lost her voice, simply nodding, her stare still steadfast.

I suddenly feel pulled apart. Naked and vulnerable. So I give Lucy a half-hearted smile and turn on my heels, dashing out of the room like a bat out of hell.

I'VE BEEN STARING at the screen for so long that my vision starts to blur. It must have been hours by the kink in my neck. I lean back into the chair, rolling my shoulders, then stretching my arms above my head. My eyes fall to the cameras—where else would my attention be if not working?

My entire body jerks forward when I realize Lucy is leaning over top the pool table, cueing up a ball while Barker is standing right behind her.

The blinding and sudden rage that roars through me is undefinable, like trying to describe the different hues and colors of a dying star. I've never been out of a room so fast. It might be the first time in my miserable fucking life that I don't overthink what I'm doing. My mind takes the backseat as I let my instincts take over. Stalking through a few half-lit hallways, I light a cigarette, leaving it propped between my lips while I slam the doors of the common area open, heading straight for the pool table.

Lucy notices me first, her eyes growing wide before I rip the cue out of her hands and turn to face Barker. He doesn't even have time to protest before I take a swing, the wooden rod whistling through the air before hitting him square in the jaw. The brunt force makes him stagger back and before he can even think of shielding himself, the cue connects again with his forehead. This time he goes down.

"Bastian! What are you doing?" Lucy yelps in alarm.

I ignore her, swinging around as I take a long drag of the cigarette before flicking it on the ground. My gaze sweeps around the room. A few fuckers are staring, looking like they're not sure if they should intervene. I find Kenzie standing near the bar with the president of the Colorado chapter, and he must see what I can't articulate myself because they give each other a look before the prez speaks.

"Everybody out. This isn't club business." His voice is strong and clear, and the effect is immediate, bodies filling out of the room within seconds. Kenzie sends me a look of warning before disappearing into the hallway.

"Bastian?" Lucy says hesitantly. My gaze snaps back to hers. "He was just teaching me how to play pool."

Even her just saying those words makes me want to hurl a chair through a window just so I can hear something shatter. I march over to Barker who's still groaning on the floor near the wall. I grab him by his leather cut and pull him up as he tries to scramble to his feet.

He looks dazed, barely putting up a fight while I drag him to the couch closest to the pool table.

"Eyes on me," I growl, while he falls into the cushion. "Got it?"

I don't wait for the nod. I know he'll listen.

Instead, I turn back to Lucy, consumed by thoughts of what I'm about to do next.

30

I watch Bastian take one quick step after another, every stride bringing him closer to me—I should fear him. I should see his face smooth like marble, like a war mask slipped onto his features, and want to shrink, to hide, to run. But his eyes tell a different story—I have never seen him look so *alive*.

And whatever he has planned for me now, I'm ready. I can already taste it on my tongue, and it tastes like sweet victorious debauchery. I crave it. No. I *need* it.

His fingers are busy unbuckling his belt when he finally addresses me. "Bad, *bad* little student," he drawls, pulling his belt out in one seamless motion, the leather slapping against every single loop on its way out. The sound makes me flinch, but the anticipation brewing like a storm inside of me keeps my gaze steady as he finally comes up toe to toe with me. I lean my weight into the pool table behind me, waiting for Bastian to speak again. Needing his voice to stoke the lustful urge I can feel between my thighs.

"Turn around and face him," he orders. His voice sends

shockwaves through my veins. I suddenly wonder if I have ever felt this alive. It takes a few seconds for my body to catch up, but I eventually turn, my hips now digging into the edge of the table. My eyes catch on Barker's, sitting on the couch facing us. He still looks dazed, his body slumped back, knees wide, arms loose and resting on his thighs, his head lulling slightly backward, his split lip noticeable even from this distance. His eyes are the only thing steady about him, fixed, and trained on Bastian behind me.

Instead of feeling dread at the thought of someone witnessing us like this, it's a thrill, so acute, that it sparks like an electrical charge through my limbs. My arms are then tugged forcefully behind my back, making my chest stick out. The feel of leather against my wrists sends my heart slamming in my chest.

"If you want to know something, you come to me," he growls behind me, looping the belt around my wrists once, then twice. "If you want to learn something, I'm the one who teaches you," he continues, his voice deadly yet intoxicating while he loops the belt one last time around my wrists before tightening it. He gives it a hard tug as if testing it, and then before I even have time to gasp out my shock, he pulls me up by the taut belt, plastering me against his heaving chest. "Do you understand?" he presses against my ear, a shiver slithering down my neck and arms at the sound.

I don't question what comes flying out of my mouth, only that it feels natural. "Yes, sir," I answer breathlessly. "I will not do it again. I promise."

The guttural groan I hear tells me I said exactly what he wanted to hear and I can't help but smile in delight.

"I think sweet little Luce needs to be taught a lesson, wouldn't you agree?" he asks while bending me over the pool table, his wide palm keeping my head down, the green felt rough on my cheek. "Now, you be quiet and take it, while *Barker* over there obediently sits and watches like a good dog." He pauses while the hand that was holding my head down now drifts down my spine. "Yes?"

From my bent position, I can still lift up my eyes to see Barker. I find him nodding at the same time as me, his eyes now hooded, still fixed on Bastian, and I can feel myself growing more aroused.

"Good," he says, almost as an afterthought, while my hips jerk backward with the hard tug of my shorts being pulled down my thighs. Bastian knocks my feet apart and I widen my legs as much as the shorts will allow me. The shock of the air on me heightens the already heady sensations. I mewl into the table when his fingers swipe along my slit. It almost feels clinical, as if needing to find proof of his suspicion.

He hums, circling my clit with the help of my arousal, then drags his fingers back up to my entrance. "Someone can't wait to be punished," he says with a taunt and a hard tug of the belt around my wrists.

"*Please*," I beg, my legs starting to shake. From what? I can no longer tell. "Please," I repeat, hearing my own desperation in my voice, somehow only heightening my need for him.

My cheeks flush when I hear the tell-tale sounds of his jeans being pulled down, his strong thighs pushing in between mine. I whimper when he slowly drags the head of his cock down and then up my core. My mouth opens on a soft gasp when I feel him push into me, his hand trailing up my spine and wrapping around the back of my nape.

"You beg so sweetly," he rasps before slamming his hips forward, his cock impaling me to the hilt. I let out a long drawn-out moan, and I can hear Bastian do the same, his grasp tightening around my neck.

My eyes snap to the couch, finding Barker still and transfixed. My arousal skyrockets, my inner walls clenching around Bastian as he thrusts in and out, pounding harder and harder into me while using the belt as leverage to sink even deeper inside. "I can't tell what's making you so wet," he goads, while he slowly drags his hard, throbbing shaft out, then slams back in. "Is it me tying you up and fucking you over this pool table? Or is it the fact that sweet, sheltered Luce likes being watched?"

I moan out a *yes, yes, yes*, as my eyes practically roll back into my head, not even sure what I'm agreeing to, the sensations dizzying my thoughts, unable to formulate a coherent sentence. Suddenly I'm lifted up, my back against Bastian once again, his hand collaring my throat. His cock is practically pulsing inside of me while his hand travels down my stomach, his fingers finding my swollen, sensitive clit.

I'm so close to the edge of oblivion. So close to what I already know will be the strongest orgasm I have ever felt. "Look at him when you come all over my cock," Bastian groans into my ear. He circles my clit even harder, his fingers sloppy with my arousal as he continues to piston into me.

My hazy gaze finds Barker once more, his hand palming the crotch of his jeans and it doesn't take me long to splinter. My vocal cords freeze, not one sound coming out as I am thrown into the blazing sun, bliss flaring through my veins, and then turning my bones to ash.

I don't even have time to blink back into existence or catch my breath before Bastian addresses Barker. "Come here," he says, snarling the words.

He immediately stands up from the couch, quick steps rounding the pool table, while Bastian swiftly unties the belt from my wrists, pulling my shorts up and spinning me around. My limbs feel like jelly as he lifts me up and sits me on the pool table. His eyes burn with white-hot need, his pupils blown before he presses a quick kiss onto the curve of my neck.

Bastian then turns to him and begins to stroke himself, his cock still hard and glistening from my own desire. "Take it out," he orders, and Barker is quick to unzip his jeans, his erection already pushing to get out.

It only takes a few frantic tugs for Bastian to spill all over Barker's erect dick and jeans, while Barker strokes himself, rubbing Bastian's release onto his own shaft. The sight sends me spinning into an even more heightened state of arousal, my mouth agape, my eyes locked on the scene happening in front of me.

The silence that follows is so full of unspoken desires, I can barely take in a full breath. Barker's eyes tentatively slide to meet mine, and I see the same want written clearly across his face.

"Let's go," Bastian says coldly, while he mechanically zips himself up, and then helps me down the table. Without another glance, we leave Barker behind, exiting in silence, my mind still reeling, busy replaying every minute detail of what just transpired.

BASTIAN MAKES me sit beside him for the rest of the afternoon while he works on whatever he is here to do. His hand intermittently finds my wrist, his thumb smoothing over where he tied me with his belt. My heart feels like bursting every time it does, but I say nothing.

Eventually, he gives me a book to read, but I am too distracted to do anything but stare at the pages. As usual, he pretends like nothing of importance has happened while I find myself staring at the wall most of the time. I am not sure how to even describe the rift in the fabric of my reality. How my life has been flipped upside down, and all I can think about is *more*.

It must be late evening when we finally get back to the room. Words are still limited on both sides, but it's not as tense as before. As if we have both figured out a way to walk across the tightrope that exists between us without the fear of making the other person fall.

I can already hear people partying in the common area, the loud thudding music dulling the sharp yells and cheers.

"Drink?" I find myself asking Bastian, feeling restless and full of jittering energy.

He licks his lips and gives me a quick grin. "Sure, Luce."

My stomach flutters, but I say nothing, simply smiling back.

After showers and a quick change of clothes, we head over. My anxiety spikes when we push through the doors, heads snapping to look at us and I suddenly wonder if everyone knows what happened after Bastian hit Barker with a pool cue.

"Maybe this was a bad idea," I say quickly, my nervous gaze finding Bastian's steady one.

"Nonsense," he assures, placing a hand on the small of my back, ushering me in.

Luckily, the attention does not stay on us long, the

dispersed crowd eventually going back to their conversations. While Bastian leads us to a few chairs near the bar, I spot London sitting on Alley Cat's lap, but I do not bother waving, her lips glued to his. While we wait for drinks, my gaze is continuously lured toward the pool table on the opposite side of the room. Every time I realize what I am doing I startle, quickly looking away as if people would surmise what happened earlier just by me looking at the scene of the crime.

"Here," Bastian says, handing me a vodka soda.

"Thank you," I mutter, happy to have something to hold.

His eyes sweep over my face, studying me. "You okay?" he says, but he doesn't sound worried. No, instead he sounds amused. "Remembering anything of importance?" he adds, and the small grin he lets slip should infuriate me, instead it just makes my cheeks heat.

I try my best to look unbothered, innocent even, while I answer him, happy to play along. "No, nothing of importance."

He keeps his darkening gaze on me while he hums, taking a sip of his beer, and then slowly sets it down. When he breaks eye contact with me, it's only for a split second, but I suddenly feel the space between us become so charged, I know exactly who he just spotted before I turn around and look.

As soon as I swivel my head, my eyes land on Barker standing near the corner with some other men from the club. I don't bother being subtle, his interested gaze already on us. The right side of his face is bruised, his shoulder-length hair covering some but not all of it, his split lip a little swollen but his blue eyes still hold the same need as before. Lust coils low in my stomach at the sight.

I turn back to Bastian, matching his questioning gaze.

We do not exchange a single word. I simply nod before taking a slow sip of my drink.

Bastian stands up and then leans down close to my ear. "What Lucy wants, Lucy gets," he rasps, and I am left breathless, squeezing my thighs together as I watch him walk away.

I turn in my seat, mesmerized as he approaches Barker in slow, assured steps. Leaning close to his ear, Bastian whispers something to him and then points his chin toward me. Two sets of piercing eyes slide to mine. My heart skips a beat as I clutch my vodka soda with both hands. Barker nods, telling something to Bastian I am too far away to make out, and then turns around without a second glance, disappearing behind the double doors.

Bastian gives me a jerk of his head toward the exit, and I'm up on my feet before I can convince myself otherwise. I discard my drink on the bar and take quick strides reaching him in record time.

I follow him out, through the now familiar hallways, all the way to our room. The silence is thick, tasting like honey on my tongue. When we finally turn the corner, I spot Barker waiting outside our bedroom door. With the limited experience I have of him, I have never seen him so serious. His casual smile has disappeared, replaced with serious intent while he tracks our movements. The words are left unspoken while Bastian unlocks the door, letting me walk in first, Barker second.

I step into the room, and face the bed, slightly dazed. When I hear the lock latch, the sound snaps me back to attention. I turn on my heels to find both men watching me. I expect nerves, apprehension even, instead, all I feel is elation, mixed with needy anticipation.

"Take off your clothes, lay on the bed, and keep your

legs spread wide," Bastian says, cutting through the silence. He takes a step closer, and then another. "Don't move until I say so."

A small gasp escapes my lips at his demand.

I stay frozen for only half a second before I pull my t-shirt over my head, my curls tumbling over my shoulders when I let it drop to the floor. The bra follows quickly after. I hear a throat clearing close to the door but I don't look as I diligently continue to take my clothes off, pushing my shorts and panties down my legs, and slowly stepping out of them.

Again, I wait for the usual feeling of shyness, of needing to hide my body from prying eyes but it never comes. I sit on the bed, the mattress creaking under me and then slide myself closer to the pillows. I first glance at Barker, his body tight, eyes hooded. Then, I look over to Bastian, similar heat emanating from his expression, and let my legs fall wide.

Both men move forward, like an instinctual half-step, lured by the sight of me displayed like this and I can't help but feel powerful for that small fleeting moment.

Bastian's voice slices the air, low but steady. "Barker, make my girl feel good, won't you?"

For a small, quiet moment, I am not quite sure what he means, but one look at Barker's sudden debauched grin answers my question. I feel my chest and cheeks flush, my legs falling even wider open at the sight of him prowling up the bed on his hand and knees. My eyes snap to Bastian as if unconsciously looking for permission, but then Barker's hot tongue finds my clit and I let out a small whiny moan, my head falling back onto the pillow.

"No need to be gentle, she won't break," Bastian growls, a lewd grin dimpling his cheek. "Isn't that right, Luce?"

All I can manage is an enthusiastic nod while his voice lifts above us like a depraved sermon, instructing Barker step by step. Licking, sucking, thrusting. Two of his fingers slide inside of me, and I tumble into a state of lustful stupor, my hands fisting the sheet, my mouth open on a continuous mewl. I don't even realize I've closed my eyes, victim to my senses until I hear Bastian's voice.

"Open your eyes." And I do so immediately, finding him sitting in a chair next to the bed. "Look at me when I allow Barker to make you come." Leaning on his knees, his dark gaze slides to Barker. "That's a good boy, don't stop. I can tell she's close," he says in a low, heated voice as he pushes Barker's face into me.

Barker's vocal reaction to Bastian's words is the same as mine—mindless and needy.

Even with all these lustful sensations overtaking me, I can't help but wonder how Bastian always seems to know when I'm close to an orgasm—as if he already knows the secret language of my body.

Barker's tongue is laving me at just the right spot, my core clenching around his fingers. That, alongside Bastian's burning gaze, fractures me. My hand snaps to grip Bastian's wrist as I come on a long moan, shamelessly grinding myself on Barker's face.

I'm breathless, chest heaving widely, small curls sticking to my heated cheek, while I pull myself up to sit against the wall, my eyes still fixed on Bastian.

"Woah…" Is the only thing I find to say, the side of his mouth lifting ever so slightly.

I hear Barker sit up further down the bed, and when I feel the mattress dip close to my hip, I turn my head over to him. His devilish grin is back, pupils wide and glazed over. I realize then, maybe a little too slowly, that he intends to kiss me.

But the kiss never comes.

Instead, Bastian grabs him by his cut and lifts him off the bed. He scrambles to his feet, their faces mere inches apart. "Who gave you the right, pup?" Bastian growls, releasing him with a shove. With a bored flick of his wrist and an index finger pointing down, he says, "Kneel."

I watch in absolute fascination as Barker doesn't balk, sinking to his knees at Bastian's command, while reaching for his belt. To my surprise, Bastian lets him, crossing his arms over his chest as if all of this is a mere inconvenience. Until his dark eyes slide to meet mine, and I see for myself how affected he really is. I can tell the very second Barker takes him into his mouth, because his eyes flutter shut for a quick loaded moment, his head falling slightly back, before he snaps them back open.

I've never seen someone so magnificently stoic, so cold in his beauty.

My gaze falls to Barker, his pink lips wrapped around Bastian's thick cock, his cheeks hollowing out as he takes him even deeper. The sounds he's making are choked and guttural.

Even though I just had an orgasm, my sudden arousal engulfs me, legs falling open once again as I cannot help but find my already swollen clit with two of my fingers.

Bastian watches me casually as if I am doing something as mundane as folding laundry. His eyes then move up, languidly traveling up my stomach, pausing on my breasts, up my neck, my open mouth, and then finally latching onto my own frenzied gaze.

"Do you need me to fuck you, Luce?" The dichotomy

of what Barker is doing to him and his relaxed tone makes my head spin, but I eagerly nod anyway.

"Please," I say softly.

His face hardens when he looks down at the man at his feet. "That's enough," he says while pushing him off. Barker's already split lip seems to have reopened, blood dripping down his chin while he looks up at Bastian. "Up."

Hurriedly, Barker gets up to his feet, both men of similar heights and now face to face. Bastian grabs Barker's jaw in his strong grasp and pulls him toward him, licking the blood off his chin in one long depraved lick. My eyes widen, and then widen even more when Bastian spits his blood back onto his face.

For a loaded moment, I think Barker has been pushed beyond his limits, that he will snap and attack. But then he smiles as if taunting Bastian right back, his tongue swiping over his split lip before he wipes his face with his palm and says, "Woof."

Bastian's smile is devious in response. I don't bother to attempt to understand why I find all of it so unbelievably attractive, both men kindling something inside of me that I am not sure I even knew existed.

A soft whimper slips from my lips and both men's heads turn, their eyes as dark as the chasm I'm desperate to fall into. Bastian moves first, stepping closer to the bed, pulling me by the ankles, and dragging me closer to the edge. I let out a surprised shriek, Bastian chuckling darkly, his tongue swiping over his bottom lip as he pushes my thighs wide.

From over his shoulder, he tells Barker to kneel back down and wait for instructions and I continue to be astonished by his complete willingness to follow Bastian's order. Even though I know firsthand how irresistible it feels to follow Bastian's commands.

"Good dog," he drawls, as he pulls his t-shirt over his head.

Bastian turns his full attention back on me while pushing his jeans further down his thighs but never taking them off. He sits on the edge of the bed, and I scurry close to him, eager to touch him whenever I am given the chance.

"Stand up, and face him." His tone so much gentler now that he is speaking to me. I do as he says, his hands finding my thighs and caressing up to my hips. He guides me backward, making me sit on top of him, legs on either side of his. "Show him how wet and eager you are for my cock, Luce," he says by my ear, a shiver traveling down my spine. I let my back fall into his chest, as his hands find my sex and spread me open. "Such a desperate little thing, needing to be stretched full." His palms slowly smooth up my chest, kneading my breasts while he rolls my hard nipples between his finger and thumb. I bite down on a whimper trying to be quiet. "Now Lucy," he says, finding my hips again. "Raise yourself up, and then sink your perfect little cunt on my cock, will you?"

This time, I don't bother to hide my whimper as I do exactly as he says, feeling myself stretch around him the more I sink down. I start rolling my hips experimentally, and the sharp curse behind me and the hard grip on my hips tells me I am doing something right. I start getting into a rhythm, my sharp breaths in time with Bastian thrusting into me from underneath. My eyes are barely focused, Barker still kneeling in front of us, his gaze never wavering.

Bastian's hand slithers up, his bracelet dragging over my chest as he does so. Collaring my throat, his hips move faster and faster as my own movements start to grow more feverish. "I should chain you up," he growls in my ear.

"Keep you all to myself and pump you so full of my cum, you'll have no choice but to have my babies."

My body flares like a star being born, his words the tipping point to my own sanity.

"Please, please, please," I beg him breathlessly. He can do whatever he wants as long as he keeps making me feel like this. I stroke my clit mindlessly, barely hearing myself breathe out Bastian's name over and over while I grind myself harder and harder on his throbbing cock.

I don't even feel the orgasm coming, it surges like a deadly tide, like the air has been sucked out of the room one minute and then launched into space the next. I stop moving entirely, sinking as deep as I can onto Bastian, my nails digging into the skin of his thighs.

He groans behind me, his forehead falling between my shoulder blades, *"Fuck,* you're going to make me come, you're squeezing me so fucking tight." Before I even know what's happening, he pulls me off of him and spins me around, my back bouncing on the mattress, as he lets me fall onto the bed. He kicks off his jeans, now fully naked, and brackets my body with his, his cock thrusting back where it belongs in a matter of seconds. His hips slam into mine, I can't comprehend how my body already wants *more, more, more.* My nails create divots into his back, as I breathe out *harder, harder,* and he complies, his balls slapping against heightened sensitive skin, his piercing rubbing against my clit, leaving me craving everything he can possibly give me.

The groan Bastian makes when he comes inside of me is nearly angelic. It suddenly makes me wish I could sink to my knees every morning and worship, just so I can hear it again and again. His head falls into the crook of my shoulder, his breath choppy and erratic. We lay still for a beat, as he catches his breath, and I, in turn, try to catch every detail of this moment so I can imprint it in my mind forever.

Finally, Bastian pushes himself off the bed, his hand stroking my warm cheek as he stands up, and then snaps his fingers. "Clean her up, and make her come one last time before you leave," he says so offhandedly that at first, I don't even know who he is talking to until I remember poor Barker still kneeling on the ground.

He stands up, a grin forming over his bruised face. "My pleasure."

"Wait—I... I don't think I can come again, I'm too sensitive," I answer truthfully, and maybe a little sheepishly.

Bastian softens when he looks down, but his voice is still smoldering when he rasps, "You can, and you will. Let's give our boy his treat, yeah?"

I can feel my nipples tighten at the thought, Bastian somehow tapping into an insatiable part of my psyche. *Our boy.*

I fall even deeper into the chasm of my desires and lean back into the pillows, opening my legs for Barker. He's eager as ever, but this time one thing is different. I can feel Bastian's release dripping out of me, and it only seems to spur him on even more, dragging two fingers in it, smearing it all over my clit, and then slowly pushing them inside of me.

Barker's chuckle is wicked when he hears the moan his actions create. Bending down, he circles my clit with his tongue. My first instinct is to close my eyes, but instead, I find Bastian's gaze, sitting in the chair, dragged back into the corner of the room. His jeans are back on but unbuttoned, watching me steadily as Barker goes down on me. I am so sensitive that it doesn't take long for me to come, this time it arrives hard and disappears fast, my eyes never leaving Bastian's proud gaze.

It only takes me a few seconds to crash, my eyes suddenly hard to keep open, as I hear Barker stand up from the bed. Bastian stands up and meets Barker halfway. They talk in low hushed voices, Bastian sliding his hand over Barker's shoulder, then down to his arm, giving it a soft squeeze, and a slow grin. When I hear the door open and close, my mind starts to drift, and by the time Bastian finds me in bed, I'm falling asleep. Still, I'm conscious enough to feel the warm towel against my thighs as Bastian cleans me up. The last thing I remember is his arms around my waist pulling me into him.

31

BASTIAN

Pushing off the desk, the computer chair rolls under me, and I let out a long exhale. Rubbing my eyes, I stretch my neck from right to left, stand up, and grab my phone, shooting Kenzie a quick text. I leave the surveillance room, my mind calm after hours of coding but the rest of me is still wired from last night.

Lucy was still sleeping when I left the room this morning. I kept her close and in my arms all night, the rules I first made up on a fucking whim in a strip club parking lot not feeling all that vital anymore. We're beyond them, washed up ashore somewhere in the middle of a whole new fucking reality.

I don't know what any of it means. I just know that when this road trip ends, we both won't be the same people who met outside of her building on a sunny Noxport morning.

But this isn't love. Because love hurts, and well—this is the opposite of that.

I'm restless to get back to her, to look into her eyes and

see what new part of her blossomed last night, like the rarest flower discovered on a snowy hilltop.

Pushing the exit door, I walk out, fishing out my pack of cigarettes from my pocket, the sun making me squint. Taking a long drag, I press a palm against one eye as I head toward the garage knowing I'll find Kenzie working on his bike. When I get there, he's outside sitting on a dilapidated couch near the huge open garage doors, the trill of machinery emanating from inside.

I sit on the couch with him, neither of us saying a word while we each finish our smokes.

"I'm done. Everything is recoded," I finally say as I peer at him from the corner of my eye. "It'll be nearly impossible to hack into and take someone way smarter than me to decrypt. You know how hard those are to come by," I add while flicking my cigarette further out into the yard.

Kenzie chuckles beside me, most likely about my last comment, but he knows I'm right so he doesn't bother contradicting me. Instead, he changes the subject completely.

"Are you going to tell me the truth about the bird?" he says with a smirk.

"What's to tell?" I answer out of defensive reflex.

"You're off your head if you think I'll believe that lie, pal," he says in jest, but I still pick up on the hard edge of his words and know he won't put up with my shit for much longer if I keep this up. I smooth a hand over my mouth while I think, not sure how to even approach the subject.

My feelings for Lucy are like a tangled web, and for an unexplainable reason, they're starting to feel like they stretch much further out than the three weeks we've been together on this road trip. Maybe because it's Kenzie, one of the only people in my life who I know listens when I speak that I decide to lead with the unexplainable first.

"Sometimes, when I'm with her, I feel like I've done all this before," I mutter.

Kenzie leans his forearms on his thighs, turning his head to look at me directly. "What have you done before?" he questions seriously.

I bite the inside of my cheek, thinking about how to answer before speaking again. "You remember when I got clean?"

His laugh is dry. "How can I forget?"

My throat grows tight, and I tensely pull out another cigarette, offering one to Kenzie but he waves me off. I focus on the flick of the lighter, the blaze of the flame, followed by the crackle of the burning cigarette before I figure out how to continue. "I have this notebook. Used to write in it a lot after my last overdose. Most of the pages are just filled with random objects. Never thought much of it. Never made any sense. The shit I wrote was so random that I've managed to convince myself that it was just remnants of my doped-up brain," I pause, knowing I must be rambling, while I take a slow drag, rubbing my forehead with the back of my thumb, suddenly incapable of looking Kenzie in the eye, before saying, "Until this road trip with Lucy started... then, well some of the shit on that list started showing up in real life. All of it feels vaguely familiar and I'm probably just crazy." I let out a small dry laugh. "But I can't seem to shake the feeling."

Kenzie is silent beside me, and I let loose a long exhale before finally meeting his gaze. I expected, at the very least, an incredulous expression on his face, but what I find is *recognition* which leaves me confused.

"Do you not remember what you told me those first few

days at the ranch?" he says slowly as if weighing every word coming out of his mouth.

I scoff in disbelief. "You left me alone those first few days, remember?"

"No, I didn't… who do you think brought you your meals?"

Disbelief forms a crease between my eyebrows as I study Kenzie for a beat.

"What are you trying to tell me, Kenz?" I say, trying to ignore my heart beating inexplicably faster.

His smile is mischievous as if he's getting a kick out of this, and I fight the urge to just stand up and leave.

"You told me you saw your future. Said you were older, had a lass too—built her a house near the water."

"You're full of shit. I don't remember any of that," I say dryly.

"Maybe I am," he says, standing up and giving me a knowing wink. "Or maybe life is much more complex than even that big fucking brain of yours," he says, tapping my forehead with his index finger, and I'm too stunned to wave him off. "Anyway, I gotta get back to it. Find me before you leave, will you?"

I nod, the words lost somewhere in my chest, and watch him walk back into the garage as I'm left sitting on the shoddy couch, wondering if I even understood what he was alluding to.

Or am I just that desperate for a genuine connection?

32

I had been surprised to find a vegetable garden on my first day on the compound, tucked in a small patch of greenery before the thick wilderness of the forest began. It looked alive and healthy and I wondered who was taking such good care of it. It reminded me of the gardens back ho–in Sacro Nuntio. But somehow this garden did not carry the usual ache of my past, it simply reminded me of community. Something I, at times, vaguely missed when feeling lonely in the big city of Noxport.

When I woke up this morning, my body sore but my mind feeling so alive, I decided to take a walk to the garden. I've been here most of the afternoon, laying on a blanket I brought from the room, my cowboy hat covering my face from the sun.

I feel a little nudge on the sole of my foot before hearing Bastian's playful voice above me.

"What are you doing over here, Baby Blue?"

The new nickname hangs in the air between us as I

slowly pull my hat off my face, my heart beating that much faster as my stomach does a little somersault in response. Then I see him... and tumble into a state of breathless awe at the sight.

I have never seen him smile so freely, reaching all the way up to his eyes, crinkling the thin skin on either side of them. Backlit by the sun, the rays bouncing off his head, his hair a white gold halo as he continues to look at me with such openness I feel like I might cry.

I am not really sure why.

I clear my throat trying to shake off all these sudden surging emotions, and push myself up into a sitting position. "Just enjoying the fresh air," I say, forcing a casual tone into my voice. Shielding my face from the sun with my hand, I meet his gaze.

Bastian's expression turns into one of curiosity when he bends over next to me, and I realize too late that I've left my notebook open beside me.

"Don't!" I yelp much too loudly, as my hand snatches at the air, my notebook already in Bastian's hand above me.

"What are you hiding in here, Luce?" he says with an amused chuckle.

I am up on my feet in one swift movement scrambling for the notebook, but Bastian has it raised up above his head, his other hand palming me in the forehead and with the few inches he has on me, I cannot reach far enough to snatch it away.

"It is nothing I swear." My voice coming out high and shrill, still fighting against his grasp.

"Sure it is," Bastian says with a taunt and a smile, squinting at what I have crossed off my list. "Does that say..." he pauses, squinting even harder. "Threesome?"

"Give it back!" I say in horror. Next thing I know I'm climbing up on him, ready to do anything for him not to read anything else out loud.

"Sweet little Luce has a dirty bucket list," Bastian says with a shocked laugh, wrapping his free arm around my waist while my legs circle his hips trying to gain some height.

"You were not supposed to see that," I retort, suddenly laughing with him, my hand finally on the notebook. He lets it go, and I hold it against my chest like a guarded treasure. My laughter transforms into a giggle. Bastian is still smiling so widely I think my heart will burst if I keep staring at it head-on.

We fall silent, both breathless, chests heaving, our smiles fading into something a lot more serious. Bastian's hands lock together, grabbing me from underneath and pushing me higher up his hips. I let my notebook fall to the ground, hearing the muted *thud* of it landing on the grass at his feet. Circling one of my arms around his neck, I thread my fingers into his hair before interlocking my hands behind his head.

Bastian's eyes dance all around my face, studying me with growing intensity, and for a small hopeful moment, I think he's about to kiss me.

"It's time to go," he says softly, gently placing me back onto the soft grass.

Disappointment swoops low in my stomach, but I ignore it.

What an outlandish thought to begin with.

"Go where?" I ask, bending down to retrieve my notebook, and maybe to also avoid his gaze, while I snap myself out of the daydream I fell into.

"Wherever you choose, Luce. I finished what I came here to do." His quiet smile is almost nervous when I look back at him. "So where to next?"

Straightening back up, I answer with a wide smile, "Texas."

>

WE'VE BEEN on the road for a few hours now. I've let Bastian drive again, something about it feels almost soothing—like I can relax and daydream, still knowing that I'm safe with him at the wheel. A quiet peace that I didn't have the privilege to experience around a man before.

Back in Sacro Nuntio, everything I did was monitored but we didn't call it that. We called it being under God's watchful eye. Even in my home life with Patrick, I was a role. Nothing else. I needed to adhere to severe expectations or I would be punished. The violence was sometimes physical, but it was the psychological kind the men there preferred, including my husband. For a very long time, especially when I was still a child—although I wasn't considered as such—I would pray to be good.

But I never *felt* good.

My entire life felt suffocatingly structured, and when I saw Lenix for the first time after thirteen years of separation, a part of me I didn't know could exist *sang*. I knew without a single shadow of a doubt that my prayers had been answered.

Now looking back, I can't tell if I was just naive to think God had always been on my side. Not when it was the same God who let my brother rape me under his watchful eye.

I am close to dozing off when a phone call startles me

out of my daydream. It's coming from the bottom of my backpack and I scramble to find it. Expecting to see Lenix's name flash on the screen, I am surprised to find Bridget's. I have not talked to her since we left the motel days ago.

Answering with an upbeat tone, my smile drops when I hear sniffles through the receiver.

"Bridget, what is wrong?" I say urgently.

"I can't find Ritchie," she says meekly. "I didn't know who to call. I just—I just don't know what to do."

"What do you mean you can't find Ritchie?" I repeat back, my eyes slowly sliding to Bastian's and discovering that he's already watching me intently. His gaze falls back to the road, seemingly unbothered. But I am beginning to see his mask, and the pang in my stomach tells me Bastian already knew about this.

"I *mean*, that he's gone," she says through small sobs. "He hasn't been back to our room since the afternoon you two left."

It could sound like an accusation, but her tone tells me she is just blindly recounting back facts without really piecing anything together.

"I'm sorry," I tell her genuinely, while Bastian turns into a middle-of-nowhere gas station. "Is there anything I can do? Bastian is really good at finding people…" My voice trails off when I see the glare Bastian shoots back at me, and I just shrug my shoulder in response.

"No…" she says followed by another few sniffles. "I mean—it's not like he hasn't disappeared like this before. I just—I just thought maybe you would have seen him or something before you left," she pauses, then sighs. "He's not… he's not a bad guy you know? He just—he doesn't know how to manage his anger sometimes."

My tongue is on fire, needing to tell her how *wrong* her statement is, but I swallow everything back down, having an inkling that this is not the right moment to tell her that. Instead, I find a few soothing choice words, hanging up shortly after.

The news of Ritchie's disappearance hangs between us when I finally look over at Bastian.

"You knew," I say after a stretch of silence. I could have said *you did it*, but something keeps me from wanting to know the entire truth. Exhausted by my own secrets already so heavy on my shoulders. And there's also the simple fact that I am unable to find any sympathy for a man who could do such a thing to the woman he claims to love.

He keeps my gaze for a beat, then breaks the spell, opening the car door. "I told you I'd take care of it, Luce," he mutters before stepping out and closing the door behind him.

Well, then.

I guess the conversation is over.

Feeling a little dazed, I stare out the front window taking in the scenery.

Deserted roads, pine trees, and wildflowers. Not much to look at anyway, until my eyes catch on the steeple of what looks like a church behind the gas station. I don't know if it's because it looks so out of place or if I just feel inexplicably pulled to it, but something makes me reach for the car handle and open the door.

I round the building, the sun low and bright orange in the sky, when finally the whole facade of the church comes into view. It's then I realize that it's boarded up. My steps stutter to a stop, the dry-packed dirt leaving dust on my shoes. I look behind me to see if I am alone. I should just turn around. But I don't. I continue the twenty-odd steps, approaching the small wooden church like it could physically harm me if I startled it out of its slumber. The two small steps creak in warning as I walk up onto the landing, the windows nailed shut with some aging plywood.

It might be luck, or maybe I am being led here by the same God I have so recently questioned, but the front door is ajar, crooked, and slightly off its hinges. I slide my body into the building, expecting disarray, but instead, it looks somewhat well-preserved, the pews all lined up neatly as if still waiting for the next sermon to begin. I avoid the rotting planks of wood as I step into the main aisle leading up to the altar, a huge cross still fixed on the wall above.

The silence is so dense it's almost deafening. Finally reaching the front, I sit at the front pew staring up at the cross. Shivers wreak havoc down my spine, and I am left questioning if my body's reaction is good or bad. Tears prick behind my eyes, my nose tingling as if I'm holding in a sob. I'm left confused as to what emotions are trying to speak to me—what feelings or memories are trying to be heard.

I hear the floorboards groan behind me, and I know I will find Bastian stepping into the aisle if I turn my head. It's almost painfully predictable to find me here. I keep my eyes fixed on the cross while Bastian sits beside me, his movements careful as if trying to make as little noise as possible.

My brother used to preach that you could find God in silence, if only you would sit long enough, or pray hard enough, you could find answers in silence.

The silence now is different. It does not seem to want to reach into my soul and teach me how to be good. This silence is just silence—reflected back at me. I find it much more comforting than the one I used to endure.

There are no expectations here, with Bastian witnessing it alongside me.

"It's funny…" I say fissuring the silence with my voice. "It seems like the more I experience life, the more the question becomes murkier."

"What question?" Bastian asks, still looking straight ahead.

"Of what I believe in," I say gingerly. "What happens if I never find the answer?"

He doesn't speak for a small stretch of time, his eyes roving around but his body unmoving, seemingly thinking. Then finally he says, "It'd be boring to know all the answers, wouldn't it?"

I breathe out a little laugh. "Of course, you'd say that." He looks at me from the corner of his eye, a small dimple appearing on his cheek. "Doesn't the unknown scare you?" I add seriously.

He falls silent again, eventually turning his piercing gaze directly on me and there's emotion written so close to the surface I can almost see it. But then it's gone. "There's a lot that scares me. The unknown isn't one of them, Luce."

I suddenly want to dig that much deeper, to crack his chest open and find out what he's hiding underneath. But I don't. I never do. I look away, swallowing hard, my gaze back on the cross, allowing the silence to slither back around us for a while.

"Sometimes I miss the act of prayer though," I say feeling like I plucked a thought out of thousands clambering in my head to speak out loud.

Bastian looks genuinely confused when he glances at me before asking, "Why did you stop?"

The chuckle that falls out of my mouth is dry. "Isn't it obvious?"

"Prayer isn't inherently religious, Luce. Everybody does it one way or another. Wiccans call it making a spell, New Age folks call it manifesting. Prayer is just prayer. *You* decide what it means."

I look at him then, surprised by his answer, but also a little thrilled by it. No one had ever described it like that to me before. And a little seed of hope burrows itself in my mind at the concept. "So, I—" I lick my lips, looking up trying to find the words. "So I... I can just—do whatever I want?"

Bastian's smile is mischievous, his arms stretching out behind him on the pew.

"Of course, you can, Luce."

Again, his beauty strikes me like a bolt of lightning straight from the heavens. His hard facade sharpens the edges of a face that could almost look innocent if he wasn't so stern.

When I stand and kneel in front of him, it feels more like being compelled by a greater force than a rational choice I am making.

Bastian doesn't react until my hands are on his belt. "What are you doing?" he rasps.

I'm reaching into his unzipped jeans, his cock hardening under my touch when I look up and match his hooded gaze.

"Worshiping."

Bastian chokes on a groan, but doesn't say a word, licking his lips instead, dark eyes intensifying with every slow breath he takes. Helping me push his jeans down his thighs, I slide myself even closer to him, remembering how good he felt on my tongue the last time I had him in my mouth. I keep my movements slow and deliberate, like a ritualistic act, imbued with respect. My hands slide up his thighs in wandering adoration, trailing my fingers over his piercing just above his hard shaft and Bastian flinches as if already too sensitive.

I smile, peering up at him, pleased to know the effect I have on him. He doesn't smile back, but his expression is soft as I watch his chest heave up and down.

"How does it feel to be worshiping a sinner, Luce?" he says quietly.

There's an edge to his voice as if he's trying to find my limit. As if somehow looking for the suffocating and dutiful innocence I carried for so long like a protective cloak.

But all I crave now is to lay naked at his feet.

"Liberating," I profess before wrapping my lips around his cock.

A LITTLE OVER six hours later, we arrive at a motel twenty minutes away from Adrian, Texas. The small town is known for being the midpoint between Los Angeles and Chicago, the café with the same namesake the only real attraction the town has to offer, and I am beyond excited to visit.

Bastian shot me one of his classic unimpressed looks when I told him the destination. My heart squeezed at the sight having somehow missed his grumpy attitude toward practically everything about this road trip.

When we check in, I don't bother asking for two separate beds, suddenly very uninterested in that deal. Bastian doesn't mention it either while grabbing the keys for the one-bed motel room. Nothing feels awkward about us anymore, as if sharing a bed is now natural and expected.

Maybe I shouldn't be getting used to any of this.

Maybe the last thing I should do is to allow my mind to sketch a blurry future with Bastian at my side. But for now, I settle into the quietude and ease between us, hoping to stay in this moment just a little while longer.

Bastian is reading beside me in bed, when I suddenly sit up, phone in hand.

"Oh my goodness!" I nearly shout, still staring at the screen.

"What's wrong?" he asks, his tone laced with worry. His eyebrows soften when I turn to face him and he sees the excited look I'm sporting.

I lower my voice, and mouth the words slowly as if I'm telling him the most sensational news ever. "There's a tri-state fair and rodeo fifty minutes from here."

Bastian gives me a blank and unblinking stare, clearly not matching my excitement. Unfazed, I readjust myself under the covers to face him directly.

"We have to go," I press, feeling giddy like a child, my fingers finding his arm, the skin warm under my touch. "Imagine if there's a Ferris wheel? I've always wanted to go on one of those," I say a little breathlessly.

He quirks a smile, his haughty mask cracking. "Always?"

"Well, maybe not always, but ever since I watched a movie with one in it last year with Lenix," I say with a laugh, looking up to the ceiling and then back down at him. "Imagine the view," I add willfully.

He studies me for a beat, a faraway look in his eyes.

"Fine," he says flatly, but I still spot the gleam in his gaze.

Shaking my arms in front of me, hands in fists, I make a small squeak of celebration and fight back the instinct to kiss him on the cheek as a thank you. I fall back into the pillows instead with a happy sigh, suddenly excited for the future—even if it's only one day ahead.

33

BASTIAN

Lucy has barely finished parking the car before she scampers out, her energy humming with excitement. It's nighttime, and the multicolored lights emanating from the fair replace the glimmer of the stars as they dance atop her irises like iridescent fire, while her cowboy hat sits snugly on her head.

She fits right in.

"Look at this place," she utters, her mouth opened in awe, head swiveling this way and that, trying to take everything in. Her enthusiasm is so pure, I can't help but take in our surroundings from her perspective. The rows and rows of booths filled with games or sugary foods, and all sizes of stuffed animals promised as prizes for the crowd's hearty efforts. Live country music fills the air, the stage on the far left. I hear Lucy gasp and I know she's just spotted the Ferris wheel towering like heaven's gate over the carnival.

I give her a furtive glance, her face still so gleeful, and a feeling akin to happiness blooms in my chest. Her gaze slides to mine and for a split second I find myself wanting to pretend her energy isn't contagious. Instead, I indulge and smile. Lucy's eyes widen, her fingers finding my hand, interlacing them together. My eyes fall to our joined hands. And the same throb of *knowing*, the one telling me that I've somehow experienced this with her before, makes me squeeze her hand a little harder, her face smoothing into something a little bit more serious when I look back up.

"Show me where we start, Baby Blue," I say with a smirk.

And her golden green eyes light up with the same thrill as before.

"I don't even know," she says with a giggle, tugging on my arm to follow her inside the fair.

"Thought you would have said the Ferris wheel," I respond in jest.

"I want to save that for last," she says a little breathlessly as if stuck in a dream. She lets go of my hold as I pull out my wallet to pay for two entrance tickets, and as soon as we've paid I find her hand again, her warm palm pressed against mine starting to feel like the highlight of my fucking life.

"Why keep it for last?" I ask.

She shrugs her shoulders and flashes another one of her beautiful smiles, her eyes focused on all the possibilities before her. "I think I've always enjoyed delayed gratification."

I can tell she hasn't realized she's given me a lot more than just an answer to the current question. Tucking that information away for later, I'm now suddenly aching to explore that side of her further.

For the next hour, I watch her flutter from booth to booth like a butterfly exploring a field of flowers. I buy her cotton candy, her eyes growing wide with wonder when the spun sugar dissolves on her tongue and this selfish, addicting need to witness everything else she possibly has to discover in this lifetime barrels right through me.

"Oh my goodness, look!" she says while walking to a booth that looks to be some kind of duck shooting game. She's pointing to a large flamingo hanging from the ceiling. "Just like my notebook," she adds, her gaze finding mine. "Can you get it for me?"

I stare at her for a second. "You want me to play a carnival game?" I deadpan.

"Yes," she answers flatly, a defiant look now curling her lips. "Why? Do you think you will lose?"

Intellectually, I know what she's doing but my pride doesn't seem to care. Next thing I know, I'm throwing cash to the attendant, snatching a gun from the counter, half listening to the instructions while I get into position. I shoot, missing the first floating duck. Lucy giggles beside me and my irritation at this stupid game spikes, but I keep my face stoic, taking a large breath in. I don't miss another duck after the first, my attention far too laser-focused for just a game, the sharp ping of the cork bullet hitting its target one by one.

Lucy yelps and claps with glee, pointing to the flamingo as her prize. The carny hands it over, and she takes it, thanking him profusely. Her gaze flits to mine, and I smirk, dropping the gun back down on the counter. She holds the stuffed animal under one arm, the little bird legs dangling in the air while her hand finds mine again.

I'm getting used to this, I realize. To Lucy. To *us*.

My logical side knows I should nip this in the bud. Prevent future disappointment on both sides. But then Lucy looks at me, still charmed by a state fair in the middle of nowhere, and I wouldn't want to be anywhere but here.

My hand never leaves hers.

Eventually, we find the line for the Ferris wheel, and Lucy pulls me into it. She falls silent, her head tilted upwards watching the ride slowly spin.

"I am a little nervous," she says with a quiet but slightly tense laugh, her gaze still skywards.

"You've never been that high up?" She shakes her head. "And you want to go skydiving without ever knowing if you're scared of heights?" I ask with a small chuckle.

Her eyes find mine, and she gives me a mischievous smile. "I guess I'm about to find out."

After a few minutes of waiting, it's our turn to embark. The passenger gondola slightly sways as we settle into our seats, Lucy's grip whitening around the metal bar placed just above our thighs. As the ride starts to move again, and we are lifted from the ground, I watch her throat bob on a hard swallow, her gaze avoiding mine.

I lean close to her ear and whisper, "You're safe. I'm here."

I settle back into the seat, Lucy matching my gaze with a look so profound I'm not sure I can or *want* to venture into the meaning of it. I notice her hand move, hesitating for a moment as if releasing her grip could potentially have her falling out of this thing, but eventually, it finds my own on my lap and I cover it with the other.

The higher we move up, the less noticeable her nerves become, replaced by wonderment at the view unfolding in front of us. We're nearing the top and she still hasn't said a word since we climbed in.

I can't help but break the silence, eager to know what she's feeling. Needing to be involved in whatever moment she's currently experiencing.

"So?" It's not much, but enough to have her gaze flick to mine.

She licks her lips and smiles. "Remember the wishing well?"

"The one back in Arizona?"

She nods, her eyes shining. "This is it."

I blink, letting her words bounce around in my mind until they suddenly make sense. "Riding a Ferris wheel was your wish?"

She suddenly looks shy, closer to the person I first met a year ago. "I needed a wish I had the power to make come true," she says softly.

My heart cracks and suddenly nothing on this forsaken earth can hold me back from what comes next. I slip her cowboy hat off her head, placing it gently on her lap, brushing her hair behind her ear.

"What are you doing..." Her gaze is wide and searching. My eyes dips to her mouth and she lets out a small gasp when I cradle her face with both hands and pull her lips to mine.

She freezes for half a second, then melts into me, her free hand finding my neck, her nails raking my nape as her lips part, deepening the kiss. I swipe my tongue over her bottom lip, teasing, and then find her tongue waiting for me, hot, needy, and demanding.

I groan into her mouth, my fingers lacing through her curls, my hips wanting to press into hers but realizing there's nowhere to move, stuck on this fucking Ferris wheel.

We're making out like two teenagers on a first date and still, if I had to choose one of my favorite moments with Lucy, this one would be at the top of my list. And I can't believe I've denied myself the pleasure of the taste of her lips for this long.

A fucking fool.

Half-aware that we're nearing the end of the ride, I break away. It might be the hardest thing I've ever had to do, especially when I see Lucy's dazed *fuck me* look in her eyes and I know I'll have to conceal a raging hard-on when I climb out of these seats. Her pleased hum that follows our heated silence shoots straight to my balls.

When the seat finally arrives back at the bottom, I press another quick kiss on Lucy's soft lips before popping her hat back on her head, my thumb smoothing over her chin before standing up. I hold my hand out for her to take, and I pull her up as she beams up at me. She falls into my side as we walk away from the ride, giddy and effervescent.

We're making our way toward the exit when Lucy points to the bathrooms. I decide to go as well, and pull her in for one more kiss, insatiable now that I've had a taste. I watch her walk away, her flamingo still tucked under her arm, and only make a move when she turns the corner and disappears from sight.

I'm distracted, punch-drunk, and dazed when I turn the corner of an empty booth looking for the men's bathrooms. Next thing I know I take a blow to the back of the head, my knees hitting the packed dirt hard. I don't have time to react when the second blow lands even harder than the first. My eyes roll backward, and I lose consciousness.

I should have known that nothing good lasts forever.

34

There's a lightness to my step when I walk back to where I left Bastian, a permanent smile on my lips, the same lips still tingling from the kiss. The moment we shared atop the Ferris wheel can't be described as anything other than magical. It's hard to believe I'm the same person who dropped the coin down the well three weeks ago, when this version of me—the one who was kissed amongst the stars—feels so different.

How can three weeks change a person at such a molecular level?

Maybe there lies the mistake. I was always this person. Bastian just somehow intuitively knows what layers to peel off. A lifetime of brainwashing, and trauma, suppressing who I am, and still, I can feel myself blooming when I'm around him.

Then it hits me.

Maybe I am falling for him…

Maybe the one thing I told him I was not going to do *is* happening.

But unexpectedly, the thought does not accompany the anticipated dread.

Instead, it brings me joy—a fragile feeling, but one I will never take for granted.

Snapping out of my wandering thoughts, I realize I've been standing here, waiting for Bastian, for an unusually long time.

My smile fades but doesn't disappear entirely, the corners of my mouth still holding on to the feelings I was just daydreaming about. My eyebrows dip, tucking the flamingo Bastian won for me tighter under my arm as I look around. Instinctually trying to rationalize his where-abouts, I try to ignore my rising heart rate. But after another ten minutes, my smile has disappeared. Still unwilling to entertain my fears out loud, I convince myself that he must have told me he'd be waiting for me by the car, and head for the parking lot.

When I get there, my throat grows tight, hand shaking when I unlock the door and grab my phone from the glove compartment. Although I am well aware that Bastian knew I left my phone in the car, I foolishly hope to see a missed call from him. My heart drops when the only notification I find is from Lenix.

Where would he have gone?

He wouldn't leave like this… would he?

I scurry into the driver's seat and lock the doors, now paranoid that someone might be watching me. My sweaty palms wring the steering wheel, my eyes locked on the carnival exit, hoping to see Bastian appear.

He never does.

I sit, rigid in my seat, for an hour, the muted sounds of the fair accompanying my ragged breath as I watch the minutes tick by. Finally, I snap. I rip my hat off my head and throw it onto the passenger seat just to have something to do with my hands. My face falls into my hands and I let out a long groan, fear melting into the sound I am letting out while hot tears fall into the cracks of my fingers. Everything in my being is screaming at me that something is wrong, that something bad has happened to Bastian.

He would never leave like this. Not after... *everything.*

I do not know what to do. I know crying is not the answer. The tears fall nonetheless as I tumble into a well of frightening possibilities, the feeling of loneliness so acute I think it may suffocate me. After a few minutes of drowning in the terrifying possibility that Bastian might have been kidnapped, I take a few long breaths—in from the nose, out from the mouth—trying to figure out what to do next. I slam the wheel with my palm, anger piling on top of the fear. Sniffling back the tears, I shake my head as if trying to clear my thoughts—enough to drive at least. I start the car, furtively looking all around for any suspicious figures, but find nothing but a sea of cars.

The fifty minutes back to the motel by myself is pure torture. I do not bother turning on the music, the silence acting as a fellow passenger as I continuously check the mirrors hoping not to see a car following me. As far as I can tell, there is not.

I scurry across the motel parking lot, a dim street light in the far corner, the only glow piercing the dark of the night. Shivers rake down my arms and legs. By the time I turn the doorknob to our room, the back of my neck tingles, and fear stabs through my heart while the door creaks on its hinges, terrified of what I will find on the other side.

35

BASTIAN

I return to consciousness by coughing up the frigid water that was just thrown in my face. My senses are suddenly so heightened that my mind has trouble catching up to my surroundings. *Feeling* everything, but having trouble turning any of it into coherent thoughts. I'm in a dark, barren room. It's cold in here. Cement walls and floor, the strong scent of moisture clinging to the air. This must be a basement of some sort.

I hack up more water, tasting blood in my mouth, not quite sure where it's coming from, only that I'm spitting it onto the ground next to me. It takes me far too long to realize I'm chained to the wall by the neck, my arms and legs shackled in front of me. I'm still disoriented, my head throbbing from the multiple hits I took before blacking out, chains rattling alongside my protest when my glare flicks up to find the asshole who's still holding an empty bucket.

I don't recognize him.

Then my mind latches on to the one thing I should have thought of as soon as the water hit my face. The guilt is already hot and consuming when I pull on the chains with all my strength growling out her name. *"Lucy."*

I immediately regret speaking her name inside these suffocating walls, realizing I just unwittingly showed how important she is to me.

I feel myself grow feral at the thought of her chained up somewhere without me. *Or worse.*

And like a conjured-up nightmare, a deep voice from the shadows confirms that hell really does exist.

"Lucy? Mmm, you mean that pretty little thing that was with you?" The voice drawls. I still can't see who it is —only that it's a man's timbre. He hums like he's reminiscing on something delicious, smacking his lips. "Screamed real pretty. Pussy as tight as a virgin—cried like one too."

No, no, no, no, no, no, no.

I fight against the harrowing reality that he just painted. Unwilling to let his words sink in.

Because if they're true, it's all my fault.

The agony is unbearable. The shackles dig into my skin as I fight against the restraints. It compounds with the overpowering shame and guilt that I've failed Lucy. Told her she was safe with me and got her—got her *raped.*

My eyes latch onto the flame of a lighter struck, the man's face illuminated while he lights his cigarette. I suddenly realize who's addressing me. Lee Beauman, the notorious leader of the Gravediggers, and one of the most despicable people I've ever had the displeasure of keeping tabs on for the Sin Eaters—like knowing he's involved in human trafficking.

He takes a long drag, then steps into the glow of the single lightbulb above his head. I would recognize this lunatic anywhere. Shaved head, diamond studs, script tattoos above both eyebrows, and a scythe and noose where his sideburns should be.

"You know," he muses, tapping his finger on his chin, "she was calling out your name the whole time. Real heartbreaking shit." He laughs and shoots me a pleased look.

"You fucking piece of shit, I'm going to fucking kill you!" I shout so loud, my neck strains.

He lets out another dry chuckle and I've never felt so powerless.

"Come to think of it," he says, snapping his fingers. "Should have recorded it—have you listen to the noises she made when I was balls deep inside of her. I just *know* you would have loved the sound of her voice. Makes my dick hard just thinking about it."

His words are the cruelest of tortures, and I can't listen to him any longer without going deaf from agony.

"*Where is she?*" I hiss through clenched teeth, continuously pushing and pulling against my restraints. I'll take any physical pain over *this*.

"She's dead," Lee states.

I never knew pain could be this lethal.

I refuse to believe him.

"You're lying," I growl loudly. My voice is raspy and hoarse, similar to the sound of the chains digging into my skin as I fight against them. Murderous and full of so much hate, I wish I could just rip his head clean off his neck and pulverize it against the wall over and over again.

"What's the point of keeping her alive when I've already had my fun?" he says with a laugh, approaching me. "Besides, all I needed was you."

All the while I'm sinking.

She can't be dead.

Can't be dead.

Can't be…

He points the two fingers holding the cigarette my way. "You're the only one to blame, Lover Boy," he pauses, his eyes narrowing. "Was it worth it?"

Doesn't take a genius to understand why I'm here. Whatever I encrypted for the Black Plague was a lot more valuable to the Gravediggers than I previously believed.

I don't think I can despise myself more than I do now.

The more I allow the reality that Lucy has been killed to take hold, the more I feel the life force slowly seep out of my body.

Lucy's dead.

Dead, dead, dead.

And Lee is right. I only have myself to blame.

When I don't answer, he adds, "Didn't your daddy teach you not to stick your nose in other people's business?"

I spit another mouthful of blood, now realizing it's coming from a split lip, and keep my face blank, feeling empty. Nothing really fucking matters anymore. "Didn't think to ask him for any last words of advice while strangling him in his sleep."

Lee chuckles. "Funny." His grin is malicious while he takes another drag, his thumb rubbing his chin as if thinking. Then he strikes. It's so fast that I barely anticipate the blow. The heel of his boot connects with my jaw, my head snapping to the side, molars slicing open my inner cheek with the force, the taste of blood intensifying in my mouth.

Lee orders his lackey still loitering behind him to leave. He's out of the room seconds later.

I tongue the gash while I wait for him to speak, the whole right side of my face now throbbing with every heartbeat.

"Did you think I wasn't going to find out you were

helping those club fucks up in Colorado?" he spits, his voice now low and cold.

I feel vacant. Automated. "I don't spend much time thinking about you, Lee," I answer flatly. I know my taunt will most likely warrant another blow, but suddenly don't care if I live or die. What I don't expect is him crouching in front of me, squeezing my face into his grip, and extinguishing his cigarette on the thin skin below my left eye.

My first extinct is to scream out in pain, but if suffering through a childhood full of daily beatings has taught me one fucking thing it's this: Don't give them the satisfaction. I shut it out as fast and effortlessly as I used to, like a light switch I simply have to flick off inside my mind's eye. Doesn't prevent me from smelling the putrid burning skin, or the pain radiating all the way down to my teeth. The same ones I'm clenching now while Lee stands back observing his handiwork.

We remain silent. His is calculated. Mine usually is too, but this time it's to prevent the agony from slipping from my lips.

Finally, he says, "Are you going to give me the encryption key?"

I spit up a bit more blood but don't answer him. Even that small movement makes my face sear in pain, and I try to hold in the wince. What does it even matter if I give Lee what he wants now?

Lucy is gone, and I'll be buried next to her no matter if I survive this or not.

Lee lets out another dry chuckle, turning to the door. "You'll crack," he says while turning off the light. I listen to the steel door lock, then footsteps disappearing into the hallway.

Although I'm surrounded by darkness, I close my eyes

and lean my head gingerly against the wall behind me. The chains rattle and my adrenaline spikes, fighting against the claustrophobic feeling it's evoking inside of me.

Lucy.

I latch onto the image of her in my mind like a masochist, I replay our last few moments together and I'm left with a bleeding hole in my chest. How her eyes glimmered, resplendent and intoxicating after our first kiss. Then, like a bloated corpse floating up from the watery depths, my mind conjures up the sickening difference of what her eyes must have looked like while she was getting… when they were doing…

Before she died.

I don't think I can survive this.

I don't think I *want* to survive this.

There are no positive outcomes to my kidnapping.

Even if I somehow get out of this alive.

I am still dead.

At least if they kill me, I won't have to live in a reality where she has died.

A world without Lucy is a world I don't care to exist in.

I've been trying to keep time with the dripping of the water that I can't seem to locate. As if it has the same steady cadence of seconds ticking by. After a few hundred drips, I've given up.

I drift off, my back still against the wall.

Eventually, I'm woken up by the lightbulb flickering on. I squint and watch the man who threw the bucket of water enter the room and head toward me. He pulls out a gun and jams it into my forehead. "Don't try anything stupid, asshole," he says while his other hand frees me from the shackle around my neck, but leaves the ones around my wrists and ankles.

He motions for me to stand and I struggle my way onto my feet with the help of the wall, the gun still pointed directly at me. He presses the weapon in between my shoulder blades and shoves me forward.

"Out, and take a left," he orders.

In the hallway, I try to take in as much information as possible, but the building—or wherever we are—is stripped of anything useful. I slowly shuffle past a few closed doors, then down another half-lit hallway until finally, the Gravedigger tells me to turn into the only open door to our right.

With a quick look around, I notice this room looks more sterile. There's a medical feel to it with its starchy white walls, stainless steel trays on counters lined with glass jars, and glaring fluorescent overhead lighting.

Lee is standing near, what looks like, a dentist's chair in the middle of the space, alongside another one of his lackeys.

"Strap him in," he barks, and for a split second I consider resisting, maybe even head-butting the one still pointing the gun at me.

I don't put up a fight, half hoping whatever they have planned will kill me anyway. He shoves me into the chair, hands and legs still bound, and I can't resist—I spit in the guy's face while he secures my chest to the chair. I give him a bloody grin, waiting for his reaction.

I see the rage explode on his face, the gun cocked and ready to shoot, but Lee barks, "Stand down, Derek."

Derek is shaking so badly, I swear I can hear his Glock rattling. So I smile even wider just to see what he'll do. He pistol-whips me over the temple and I fight hard to stay conscious, the edge of my vision growing dark.

"What the fuck did I just say," Lee growls between clenched teeth while he grabs him by the collar, spitting the words in his face. "Next time you disobey I'll use your own gun to blow your fucking brains out."

"Sorry boss," Derek blubbers.

Lee lets him go, his eyes still on him when he says, "Jacob, finish the job will you?"

My gaze jerks to the other man in the room who's been motionless until then. Must be Jacob. He shoves his palm into my face, pinning me to the headrest, nearly suffocating me in the process. Maybe it's a promise of what's to come because when he straps my forehead to the chair, I suddenly know without a shadow of a doubt what is coming next.

A cold wet towel is slapped over my entire face, covering my mouth, nose, and eyes. The freezing water that follows is not only a shock to the system, but sends an uncontrollable panic coursing through my body.

I'm drowning.

I try to stay rational. Repeating to myself that this will ultimately end, bound to last only a minute, maybe less, but my mouth is gaping open, swallowing water seeping through the wet cloth and I can't breathe.

I can't fucking breathe.

I lose control of my body, survival instinct making my head thrash but I can't move, the straps just digging deeper into my forehead and chest.

I don't know how long the first round of waterboarding lasts, but it's long enough for my mind to blank and my chest to tighten painfully.

The fluorescent lights blind me when the rag is lifted off my face, but I only have time to take a few ragged breaths before it's placed back on, the darkness suddenly feeling like nihility itself. A dark hole of nothingness where all my fears are staring back at me. I'm still clawing to keep myself rational but it's useless. The water is suffocating me, the air ripped out of my lungs.

I try to focus on something calming.

Lucy.

But even her name feels like a razor blade to the soul. My psyche turns into sand, sifting through the holes of my mind and I can't keep a hold of anything.

Especially her. Especially now.

By the third round, I've lost all sense of pride, my body is convinced it's dying and I'm desperate for some kind of respite. My muscles start to seize and I feel a warm wet sensation trickling down my legs. I have just enough where-withal to realize that I've pissed myself.

When the rag is pulled off me once again, I retch but nothing comes up. Gagging, chest heaving, I try to suck in as much air as possible before that damn fucking thing is back on me.

But it never comes.

The room is silent, save for my coughing and hurried breaths. Lee stands a few steps back smoking a cigarette. I lock eyes with him and he smiles. He takes a few steps toward the chair and stubs his butt on my forearm. I barely register the pain, my head still lightheaded from the lack of oxygen.

"Had enough?" he drawls.

This time I don't smile. I don't taunt. I don't pretend that what I just endured wasn't harrowing and fucking agonizing.

I just match his stare and say nothing.

I'm thrown back into the dark room not long after, the

shackle back around my neck. My clothes are wet and piss-soaked, the chill seeping into my bones, making my body shiver uncontrollably. Somehow I fall asleep, the exhaustion soul-deep. The shock my body took today—or was it tonight?—has rattled some old memories back to life. My dreams are filled with nothing but childlike fear so potent it oozes into the cracks of my mind, haunting me and festering any semblance of sanity I thought I still possessed.

36

Two days earlier

When I tentatively peer into the motel room, I only find emptiness.

I let out a relieved breath, but my adrenaline is still making my heart beat wildly in my chest. Inside, I latch the door shut, making sure to slide the chain at the top of the door as well. I march to the only window in here and draw the curtains closed, but do not turn on the lights, still unable to shake the feeling that someone has been trailing me.

The tears continue to spill down my cheeks, falling over my lips and I lick them away, ignoring them as best I can. Convinced Bastian would have some type of weapon hiding in his duffel bag, I riffle through it with the help of my phone flashlight, and finally, find a switchblade tucked in one of the side pockets. I flick it open, holding it much too tightly in my palm, and slide myself onto the bed. Sitting crisscrossed, back straight, in the middle of the mattress, I finally decide to make a call. Maybe Kenzie would be the better choice in this situation since he is relatively close by but he is not the number I dial.

"Loosey Goosey," Lenix sing-songs through the receiver when she picks up. "How is my favorite sister in the whole wide world?"

My words stick to the sides of my throat at the tone of her voice. So stark to how I am feeling in the darkness of a motel room, tears still staining my cheeks. I suddenly do not know what to say—or *how* to say it.

I do not know if the silence that follows is what makes Lenix drop her happy tone or maybe I sniffled but suddenly her voice holds an urgency I have not heard in over a year.

"Lucy? Lucy, are you there? What's wrong? Tell me what happened?"

I close my eyes, in an effort to compose myself, biting my wobbling lip. After a deep inhale, I find enough words to form a full sentence. "Bastian is gone," I manage to croak out.

I hear Lenix laugh in disbelief as if her first reaction is to dismiss the severity of what I just said. "What do you mean he's *gone*?" she says a little too harshly. I know my sister well enough to recognize that she is being defensive. The truth is scary, and she would rather be dismissive than have to think about me being alone in the middle of nowhere.

"We were at a carnival, and he—" my voice cracks, and I instinctively squeeze the knife I am holding before continuing, "and he just vanished, Lenix. I do not know what happened. He never came back from the bathroom... What if—what if something bad happened?"

At those last words spoken, reality crashes into me and I let out a loud sob, barely hearing Lenix shout for Connor on the other side of the call. They exchange a few urgent whispers, Connor raises his voice, and it almost sounds like they are struggling for the phone, but Lenix seems to eventually win. Her voice returns, softer as if trying to soothe a small child, and maybe if I was not so agitated it would grate me but instead, I welcome it.

"Lucy, where are you exactly? I'm coming to get you."

"But what about Bastian?" I rasp, followed by a few more sniffles and sobs.

"Connor will take care of it, he's coming with me. We're taking the plane. You just need to tell me where you are, okay?" she says soothingly.

I slowly nod although I know she cannot see me. I tell her the address of the motel and I overhear Connor in the background saying they will be there before morning. I can tell Lenix does not want to hang up, now knowing my current situation, but I tell her I will be fine for those few hours.

She makes me promise to keep my phone on at all times and tells me she loves me profusely. I seem to have once again lost the capability of speech. Holding back tears, I force a goodbye out of my strangled throat. As soon as I hang up, I burst into tears, rolling into a ball on the bed, facing the door, the knife still in my hand. I stare at the door, never moving from my fetal position for what feels like hours. I go through every possibility of what could have happened to Bastian. None of them are good.

My eyes droop from exhaustion but still, I stare into nothingness.

Because deep down, I know...

Only heartache can follow his disappearance.

Present

It has been more than forty-eight hours since I last saw Bastian. The last time I felt such a sense of profound displacement was when I ran away from Sacro Nuntio and left everything I knew behind. But how could I feel so untethered when what I am missing is a person and not a place? It startles me to realize how intense my feelings are, but I refuse to deny them either.

There is a knock at the door, and Lenix appears a few seconds later.

I am back in Colorado, in the same room I shared with Bastian at the Black Plague compound. The room makes my heart ache but still soothes me with memories I did not think I would miss so soon.

Lenix does not say a word as she enters. Walking in, she slides onto the bed beside me, taking me in her arms. She and Connor are staying in the room next to me, but she has spent most of her time in mine. I have not really been able to speak much on anything other than the essentials that could help Bastian be found. I know my sister must have picked up on what has been left unsaid, that maybe something deeper has happened between him and me, but to my surprise, she has not pried. I would have expected her to start with her overprotective sister act that she loves to put on, mostly spurred by her trying to make up for lost time.

Instead, she has given me space, but I know I should tell her sooner rather than later. And maybe it is because I am so used to managing my pain alone, keeping it hidden and out of sight, but there is still some discomfort with opening up and telling Lenix all that has happened. And most importantly how I am feeling about it.

I sigh deeper into her arms, my head resting on her shoulder, while trying to choose the right words for this conversation.

"It was not Bastian's idea," I say tentatively.

"What wasn't?" Lenix responds.

I let out another long sigh. "You know."

"Actually, Lucy, I *don't* know. You haven't said a word since I got here. Not to mention the fact that I've never seen Bastian with anyone romantically *ever*, so honestly? I'm having a hard time picturing any of this—or whatever the hell even happened between you two…"

I chew on my lip feeling slightly guilty. I do not even know how to start this, considering I would rather perish than admit to Lenix that we had some sort of sex deal—and everything that followed.

So I go for the closest thing to the truth.

"It was only meant to be a fling." My words hang heavy between us, and I can tell by Lenix's silence that she is biting her tongue. "We were having fun. I was even starting to see this whole new side of Bastian." I pull myself out of her embrace and push myself up with my arms to look at her head-on. "He was smiling, Lenix. Laughing even."

Her eyebrows shoot up. "Bastian. Laughing?" she says incredulously.

I nod my head a few times to drive in the point and continue, "This road trip was everything I dreamed of and *more*, I have never experienced such freedom, and Bastian, well he—" My voice cracks, my throat growing tight and I am suddenly fighting back tears.

I keep my gaze steady although my eyes are welling up with tears, and Lenix's face softens as if realizing the depth of what I am trying to say. It only makes me want to break-down, fall into hysterics, but I close my eyes for a few seconds and take a deep breath.

Finding Lenix's gaze again, I say, "Bastian was a large part of that. I know it has only been a little less than a month, but…" My eyes fall to our clasped hands, my voice small. "I have never felt like this before."

I do not know what else to say, especially when things with Bastian are already so convoluted to begin with. I hope that Lenix will not need more explanation than I have already given her, since I do not think I have anything more to give.

"Lucy…" Lenix says gently while pushing my chin up so I look at her. "Are you in love with Bastian?"

"No," I say far too quickly but then concede, "I mean… I do not know. What I feel for him is—is complicated, and we were just starting to…" I cannot finish my thought, the tears now spilling over, my bottom lip trembling. "I cannot lose him now," I say so meekly that I can hardly bear the sound of my own voice.

Lenix pulls me back into her arms as I silently cry into the crook of her neck. "Oh, babes… We're going to get him back. The boys are doing everything they can to find him," she says softly while caressing my hair, which only makes me cry harder. "And as for everything else… you'll figure it out. You just—" She pauses as if weighing her words and then finally finishes her sentence. "You just have to have faith."

I suddenly understand her hesitancy, a word I am not sure I have heard her say since we were young girls. And somehow her saying it, shakes a memory loose in my mind. I am too mentally exhausted to push it back down like I usually do, so I let it take up space, here, in the safety of my sister's arms.

I must have been twenty-one, already married for far too long, and still, not yet understanding that I could question what was happening to me—even if it was only in the safety of my mind. It was a morning like any other, the community had gathered for our daily sermon, my brother in front leading the prayers as always.

I was feeling particularly uneasy that day, Patrick had made me submit to him earlier that morning. It did not happen often, maybe once a month, but when it did—it was nothing but cold, painful, and humiliating. He never used any lubrication so I was often left bleeding most times.

I am not sure why that morning was any different, this had been happening for years. But as I sat in a front pew, barely able to even sit, something akin to rage seeped into the cracks of my soul. I listened to my brother speak of faith, of godliness, and servitude. I must have heard this sermon hundreds of times and even found comfort in the message it conveyed before.

On that day, it was as if I had gained a sixth sense, suddenly able to listen to everything left unsaid. To *hear* what was unspoken. How ridiculous it all sounded now. Especially when this growing feeling of wrongfulness was slowly replacing the faith I had been holding on to so tightly all my life. That day it was as if the very God my brother was preaching so fervently about, had pulled the veil from over my eyes to see the evil that had always existed around me in plain sight.

I thought my faith was merely fractured that day, but it took me leaving Sacro Nuntio to understand that I had in fact lost it entirely. I just never allowed myself to admit to it. It was an act of self-preservation. Because how could I have survived all that abuse without faith? How could I have kept hold of my sanity if I did not believe that I was good and worthy to be saved?

I held on to that belief even after leaving that place. Was it really God that saved me? Or was it my sister? Or the men who quite literally wore the word sin as a badge of honor every day? That word holds no ill meaning now when the most sinful men I know have shown me the most decency.

While burrowing deeper into Lenix's arms, needing to hear her heartbeat to remind myself she is here and not just a dream, I realize she is asking me to have a different kind of faith. A much more personal kind. One that I can touch, taste, and *see*. Faith in us. Faith in our ability to protect our own. Faith in family, the one you choose. Faith in Bastian and most importantly, myself.

Resting my head on her lap, I curl myself into a ball next to her. "Okay," I whisper, my eyes suddenly drooping with sleep. "I will."

37

BASTIAN

I've lost track of time. Not that it's of any use to me here. The room they've kept me in is so dark, my eyes can't even get accustomed to it. Trying to find any meaning from the darkness staring back at me is having a bizarre effect on my psyche. As if my brain is trying to make sense of such a lack of sensory inputs, making up things that aren't there. I'm barely fed, and given little to no water— my body aches and my mind is slipping.

And Lucy sits in the corner of the room, watching me. Never saying a word.

Or maybe it's all some misplaced hope that she's here with me.

But why would she be? I'm the reason she's dead.

The waterboarding continues, but I still refuse to give Lee the encryption key. He's been getting more aggravated the more I stay silent; at some point he'll be moving on to another kind of torture. The wait is the most agonizing part.

As if summoned, the metal door opens violently, and

Lee appears in the lit doorway like a fucking demon from hell. Turning on the light, he strolls in, hands in his jeans pockets, and an ugly grin on his face while Derek flanks him as usual. The light hurts my eyes, and while I slowly adjust to it, I realize he's not alone.

White coat. Holding a syringe. I can only assume he's the resident doctor… or some kind of overpaid corrupt vet. Who fucking knows.

"Boy do I have a treat for you," Lee says, slowly enunciating all the words to drive in the point.

My eyes snap to him, but I'm drawn immediately back to the syringe, adrenaline spiking along with the dread shooting down my spine. I know that whatever is inside is bound to soon be flowing through my veins.

"Can't wait to piss on your corpse," I growl.

It's the first reaction he's gotten out of me since our first encounter.

Lee's face lights up in delight.

"Interesting," he hums, motioning the doctor toward me. "Maybe I'll find your breaking point after all."

The chains continue to rattle, as always, while I try in vain to distance myself from the syringe. As if I have anywhere to run to in the first place. Derek kneels beside me, grabbing my arm and holding it out. I try to struggle, but it's no use. Even after a few failed attempts to locate a vein, the needle finds its home and the substance is slowly pushed into my system.

A familiar wave of euphoria overwhelms me almost instantaneously. A poison that feels like home. And so fucking conflicting, it hurts to even think. Like slipping into a warm bath, knowing I will soon drown in those same waters. The surrendering curse barely leaves my lips, as I mourn all the time spent fighting against this transcendent urge.

However, I can immediately tell that this dose is different from the ones I used to chase. I feel my heartbeat accelerate like a false sense of alertness, energy overtaking me, while I simultaneously feel my brain grow drowsy—my body sinking into a forced state of relaxation.

Before I lose myself entirely to the drugs, I realize they must have given me a combination of uppers and downers. Slowly, drowsily, it dawns on me that the drugs won't let me sleep. Whatever they gave me will keep me awake in this insufferable state of limbo, while my eyes see shadows in the dark.

I barely notice them leaving until the lights flick off. The same fear that's been stalking me since I've been thrown in here, reappears like an old friend. One that used to visit me almost daily when I was a child. It's only been minutes. Or has it?

All I know is that I can already feel the heightened agitation making my body vibrate and hum, confusion rattling in my brain

I'm under the covers when my father finds me. He drags me out by the hair, pushing me on my knees, my arms and hands flat on the bed. The terror of his belt whistling in the air is almost more painful than the strike itself. But the leather hits the thin skin on the back of my thighs, and I take it back. I take it all back. The pain is blinding and I cry out, hot tears spilling out immediately. I sob into the duvet which seems to only anger him more.

"I'm sorry," I cry loudly, choking on the words. But I don't know what I'm apologizing for. His anger is a poison I can never seem to

detect, a scorpion's tail always ready to strike. At age eleven, I've long since given up trying to understand him. His violence is my birthright.

I HEAR A WARM, soft laugh and I blink through the darkness.

"Lucy?" I rasp, and immediately the shame of even saying her name out loud in this void of a room hurts more than any beating my father ever gave me.

Where did the laugh come from?

I must have imagined it.

Wasn't I just eleven years old?

On my knees with welts on my thighs?

Nothing is making any sense.

"Lucy?" I whisper, my voice shaking in the dark.

"*Fuck!*" I slam my fist into the hard floor, chains rattling, fighting against the shackles.

Why do I keep saying her name?

I fall silent, listening to the erratic sound of my breathing, and remember—*how did I forget?*—the drugs.

They're fucking with me more than I ever thought possible.

How long has it been? How many hits have they given me?

I slam the back of my head into the wall behind me, squeezing my eyes shut.

This is bad.

I'm fucking losing it.

"*Not the cage!*" *I scream in protest. I'm ashamed that I can't stop the plea from leaving my lips. At thirteen years old, I should be used to it by now. I should know how to control my emotions. The last thing I want is to let my father see me like this.*

"Shut the fuck up, boy," my father spits out while he squeezes my arms so tightly I know it will leave bruises. We used to own a large Doberman named Killer, but one day he was just gone. My father never told me why. But the crate stayed, and somehow it became mine.

"Nothing but a filthy fucking animal since the day you were born. I'd kill myself too if I'd had to push you out of me," he mutters to himself while shoving me hard into the cage.

My mother died when I was only a few months old. My father found her hanging from the apple tree out back.

He blames me.

I can't remember a time when I didn't blame myself too.

The tears are hot on my cheeks. I let them fall, fear wrapping itself tightly around my throat, threatening to suffocate me if I don't start slowly counting my breaths.

I sit in a corner, my knees pulled up to my chest while he locks the cage with me in it. My bottom lip trembles, I bite it hard with my teeth trying not to make a sound. But every small click and groan of the door being locked is an agonizing reminder that I'll be stuck here for hours, maybe even days. I never know. I've long stopped trying to count the time I've spent trapped in here.

IF I TRUST what my brain is telling me, I'm still thirteen locked in that cage. But my eyes track the man in the white coat. Like an apparition, flickering in and out. He walks up to me, Derek right behind. Or maybe it's someone else. I can't remember the last time I slept. If it's been days or maybe hours. I wouldn't know. I watch both of them crouch near me and I'm barely there.

Or maybe I'm everywhere. All at once. Multiple time-lines stacked on top of each other, experiencing every shit thing to ever happen to me in the thirty-two years I've been alive. Beaten. Locked in a cage. Treated like a dog. Finding my girlfriend dead in bed. Shooting up.

Just like now. Whatever now is, or was. I can't be so sure anymore.

"No," I mumble, my eyes rolling, my head loose atop my neck.

But they don't listen.

My heart pumps the drugs deeper into my body, and for a hot blissful moment, I see Lucy. She's standing in a kitchen, smiling back at me, looking prettier than ever.

The faint smell of sawdust and fresh paint.

But this… this isn't the past. Is it? I don't recognize the kitchen. I try to look around as if I'm actually sharing time and space with Lucy.

Lucy.

Dead Lucy.

All my fault.

The room goes dark, left alone again.

My father's fist connects with my jaw. I tongue my cheek, tasting a coppery tang, and idly wonder if the taste of my own blood has become the most familiar of flavors in the sixteen years I've been alive. I'm now old enough—have endured enough—to know not to say a word or react while he takes his rage and insecurities out on me. It's for my own good, he's said innumerable times before.

I'm the son of a Sin Eater. He has a reputation to uphold.

I look at him now, aging but still strong. Dark hair, dark brows.

We look so alike, it sickens me.

While he continues to beat me, I decide tonight is the night.

The quarter moon is shining through the window when my father wakes up gasping for air, clawing at his neck. Rope wound tight around his throat. Found it in the shed. Maybe it's the same rope my mother used to hang herself with. Wishful thinking. Still makes me smile while I watch my father's mouth open and close like a dying fish out of water.

I don't say a word, while my father tries but fails to even say one. Adrenaline is rushing through my ears, I can barely hear a thing. Transfixed by my hands ending my father's life. Engrossed by his hands now rendered useless, powerless, his fingers weakened by the lack of oxygen to his brain and lungs. His lips turn blue, blood vessels bursting in the white of his eyes.

I'm giddy.

MY EYES BURN, the light's back on and I struggle to find the strength to pull my head up.

What does it matter anyway?

My eyes lift and I startle. The chains clatter on the floor as I pull myself into a crouch and instinctively try to get myself as far away from my father as possible. I blink trying to clear my vision but still my father remains.

"Are you finally smart enough to fear me, Lover Boy?" he drawls, and the very same fear he's describing grows thick in my throat.

"I killed you," I say confused, still huddling in the corner of the room, the clasp around my neck taut and pulling me back to where the chains are connected to the wall.

My father laughs, but it doesn't quite sound like his. I squint, trying to look closer at him but all I can see is his revolting face grinning at me.

What the fuck is happening?

"Only in your wildest dreams could you kill me," he responds, strolling up to me. "Ready to give me what I want? Or are you going to waste more of my time?"

Give him what he wants?

Numbers and lines of code flash in my mind.

An encryption key, I vaguely think. That's why I'm here.

It doesn't explain my dead father. Was he alive this whole time?

"I killed you," I repeat distractedly.

My father hums. "Maybe those drugs were a little too strong after all." He's holding a pocket knife in his hands and lazily waves it around while looking down at me, still crouching against the wall. "You've been our lab rat of sorts."

He crouches down, now eye to eye. His face seems to flicker, just like the doctor's before. Someone I recognize. Someone I hate. But then it steadies and my father is still here, staring at me with a wicked evil grin.

"I'm an impatient man, Lover Boy. You have twenty-four hours left before I feed you to the pigs. But for now?" He flicks the blade of the knife open. "Maybe a little bit of pain will jog your memory."

My head slams into the wall, my father's palm holding me by the chin, his fingers curling and digging into my cheeks. I can feel the cold blade slicing into the skin below my left eye before the pain even begins to register.

Why is he doing this?

I killed him.

How can he be torturing me?

I fucking killed him.

Nothing is making sense except the white-hot pain and the blood already pouring down my face and over my lips.

My blood. A nostalgic taste.

I'm trying my hardest to dissociate, to set my mind free —protect me from what's to come but something about these drugs is keeping me captive, forced to *feel* everything being done to me. I hold my father's manic gaze, his face flickering in and out. In and out.

Am I dreaming? Hallucinating?

But then the sight from my left eye goes black. I can feel the knife scrape over the bone of my eye socket and I must be screaming, I must be fucking screaming.

Surely, I'm in shock, because my mind begins to drift. In a desperate attempt to block out whatever my father is doing to my face, I focus on a list instead. But it's not the same list I made years ago. No, this one is different.

A new list.

A Ferris wheel. Cotton candy. A giant stuffed flamingo.

Now, I'm sure that I'm screaming. My father tells me to shut the fuck up.

A mic. An open stage. Red lipstick on perfect lips.

The knife digs deeper. I scream louder.

A place called Santa Claus. A dried-up well. And a wish that was made true.

The pain is so intense, I'm not sure I can even call it pain.

Then suddenly the hand is off of me, and I'm gasping for air, choking on my own blood still pouring down my face. My father is holding my left eye in his hand, looking triumphant.

But I've lost all sense of self.

I don't react. Everything about this feels too gruesome, too sickening to be real.

His face flickers again.

The room is so silent that I hear the *pop* of my eye when he drops it on the ground and crushes it with his heel.

I plead for my body to pass out, to lose consciousness so I can at least escape from this hell. But it never comes. I see only darkness. Then the door locks.

And all I have left to cling to is the harrowing knowledge that my eye is somewhere on the floor, while the taste of my own blood keeps me company.

38

"We've found him," Connor says, his tone vengeful but also celebratory. His black hair is disheveled, falling over dark eyes, bloodshot and wild. His suit looks crumpled, shirt sleeves pushed back and his collar unbuttoned, showing the countless tattoos on his body. He does not look like he has slept in the five days we have been here.

Lenix and I are coming back from a walk around the compound when he finds us outside.

My sister lets out a small shriek of excitement, and the relief I feel at the sound of his words propels me into Connor's arms. He hugs me back—reassuring and steadfast. Suddenly, I wonder if that is actually what it should feel like to have a brother. Then the anxiety, fears and the what-ifs take a hold of that relief and suffocate it.

"What if... what if he is already..." I whisper.

Connor's hands find my arms, pulling me away so he can look me in the eyes.

"We're getting him out of there. You hear me? That kid

can survive anything," he says assuredly. "He *has* survived everything."

I cannot stop the tears from spilling out of my eyes, but I still nod.

Faith. I need to have faith.

"I want to help," I say without much forethought. "I need to see that he is okay."

All I know is I must be of some kind of help. I cannot stay here and just wait while everyone else does the heavy lifting.

"No," Connor says flatly. He lets me go, turning on his heels toward the door.

My heart sinks.

"*Connor*," I hear Lenix say behind me. He whips around at the sound of her voice. "We're *both* helping and that's the end of it."

My eyebrows lift in surprise, thinking Lenix would have been adamant about me staying out of danger. But there is something in her expression that I recognize… of being in a similar situation not long ago, and knowing that somehow I need this too.

Both sets of eyes narrow as they stare back at each other, while Lenix slowly crosses her arms clearly unimpressed by Connor's intimidation, quietly standing her ground.

"If anything happens to you—" he says slowly.

"Don't you trust me?" Lenix interjects.

I can tell she has just won this little stand-off by the way Connor groans out loud, looking up at the sky, swiping his palm over his mustache. He mutters something to himself while pulling a metal case out of his coat pocket. He yanks a joint out of it and lights it before his gaze lands back on his wife.

"Fine," he says, then points to us both, two fingers still holding the joint in his hand. "You can help Kenzie with the diversion."

EIGHT HOURS LATER, we are driving up to a large rubber factory near Denver. If Kenzie had not shared the plan with us, I would immediately doubt how we would even find Bastian in such a place. According to a long-time informant, this place has been the Gravediggers' best-kept secret ever since the factory shut down over a decade ago. He also told Kenzie that they mostly use the north wing, leaving the rest abandoned. That is where we are heading.

It is the dead of night when Kenzie finally parks the black Sprinter van. Connor, Barker, and a few other men from the Black Plague have been here for a few hours staking out the place. They made sure the diversion could work and eliminated potential threats, like jamming the surveillance cameras that line the property—although I am not quite sure what that means or how it would work.

Kenzie pulls out his phone and sends out a few texts, the van silent as we wait for the okay. Lenix, who is sitting beside me, finds my hand and laces our fingers together. She squeezes my palm three times and gives me a quick knowing look.

"Alright lasses, you remember the plan?" Kenzie confirms, turning around to look at us both.

I am about to respond, having memorized every step when Lenix beats me to the punch, "Blow shit up," she deadpans.

Kenzie guffaws, sending her a wink, muttering something about how he now understands why Connor is so obsessed with her.

I realize I am smiling at their interaction, and drop it as soon as I am aware of what I am doing. The image of Bastian locked up somewhere in there, so close but still so unattainable, leaves me feeling ashamed that I can even smile at a time like this.

"Okay wait here," Kenzie says before silently climbing out of the car. Staying in the van was part of the deal we made with Connor. Kenzie would place the bombs and we would detonate them. I would have agreed to anything if only to have the chance to be here when Bastian is rescued.

What if he is dead?

I squeeze my eyes shut, trying not to let that thought etch itself in my mind like it, unfortunately, has for the past five days.

He is alive. He is alive. He is alive.

I repeat the words over and over while I watch Kenzie's silhouette stealthily crouch down near the parked cars leaving deadly crumbs as he goes. The cars are parked close enough to create a diversion, but far enough not to damage the integrity of the building.

I count my breaths—*one, two, three, four*—as I watch Kenzie jog back to the van. He starts the engine, putting it in reverse, taking us outside of the blast radius before giving us the okay. Lenix carefully places the detonator in my palm and I swallow hard. She gives me a small nod, and my heart takes a leap. I press the detonator without any lingering guilty conscience, determined to do my small part in saving Bastian.

The explosion is louder than I could have ever expected. The reverberation makes the van rock even from this distance. I let out a shocked gasp, my eyes glued to the large flames billowing out from the wrecked cars, one even having flipped onto its roof. We hear shouting, and then a slew of men run out to see what the commotion is about.

This time I do smile, knowing somewhere around the north end, Connor and the others are making their way into the building.

39

BASTIAN

A loud explosion above me.

Walls shaking.

Shouts outside the door.

Voices and footsteps getting fainter and fainter.

Silence.

I'm so far inside my mind that it takes me forever to even piece that together. Or maybe I never do. The last thing I do remember clearly is more drugs being forced into my veins.

White cloak. Needle in the skin. Locked door.

That same door now blasts open.

Or I think it does.

I don't bother to open my one good eye, my chin too heavy to lift up from my chest.

A few voices enter the room. One I recognize most of all.

"Jesus Christ," Connor hisses. "What the fuck did they do to him?"

His voice is disembodied. Nothing is real. Not even him. It can't be him.

I listen to Connor talk about chains—my chains—while I fall deeper into the dark abyss of my mind.

I take a long blink, and suddenly we're out in the hallway. Connor isn't just a voice anymore. His body holds me up, my arm around his shoulder while he keeps me standing, holding on to my waist. My head is still too heavy to lift, so I stare—painfully—at my feet, half walking, half dragged.

But then there's a shout and I force myself to look.

My father. No. Lee?

Lee is holding someone by the neck, close to his chest like a shield.

The face is vaguely familiar, his eyes locked on mine.

Barker?

I might have said his name out loud.

Connor's gun is louder.

The bullet rips through Barker's neck, the blood spraying against the wall with the impact.

He goes limp, falling to the ground at the same time as Lee.

Connor shot them both?

Connor shot them both.

But Lee is still alive, groaning loudly as Connor screams for me to hold on.

Just fucking hold on.

His gun fires one more round. This time the bullet finds Lee's head.

Silence. Heavy breathing. My feet dragging over two dead bodies.

I take one last slow blink and I'm outside, Connor's arms still holding onto me.

Then I'm laid flat on a car seat. An engine running. Voices shouting to *go, go, go*.

I'm chased by darkness, my consciousness in a losing battle with oblivion.

Then suddenly I know for certain that I am dying.

Because Lucy's here.

Her warm hands on my marred face.

Tear-soaked lips on my own.

I must be dying.

Because heaven tastes like Lucy.

40

The machine's steady beep reminds me that Bastian is alive. I have not slept in twenty-four hours. I cannot. I have been sitting here beside him, hoping he knows I am here. Will it even make a difference? Does it even matter? Every time I close my eyes, I am assaulted with the image of Bastian, bruised and bleeding. The terrifying realization that someone had done this to his face—his eye... The horrific vision of his empty eye socket. Barely conscious, laying limp in the back of the van while Connor screamed at Kenzie to get us to the nearest hospital.

When I can no longer bear those thoughts, I pull up the picture I took of him at the beginning of the trip. Of him leaning against the wall, smoking a cigarette. I stare at it for much too long, as if it holds the cure to all my pain and heartache.

He has been unconscious—or asleep, I am not sure which—since he came out of surgery six hours ago. His doctors say he had a lethal dose of barbiturates and amphetamines in his system. And if, as the doctors suspect, the drugs were somehow used as a form of torture, Bastian might suffer from long-term psychological damage but they will not know for sure until he wakes up. That plus the shock of losing an eye—they do not think he would have survived much longer if we had not gotten him out of there.

I have never felt this hopeless. Never felt such an all-consuming pain for someone else.

I was in shock when I first saw him. I am still in shock, I think.

Lenix is sleeping on Connor's lap on the sofa near the window. I do not think Connor has slept either. He has had the same haunted faraway look in his eyes since we got here, mostly silent, as if stuck in a memory while still anxiously monitoring his cousin's wellbeing. Then I remember that Lenix once told me that he found his best friend Byzantine in a similar state, years ago. My heart only aches more.

Kenzie has been in and out of the room. Never staying long. Always hovering near the bed but never really getting close to Bastian's inert body. Something tells me he is feeling guilty since it was Kenzie's favor that got him taken in the first place.

Good. He should feel guilty.

I know my anger should be directed at the Gravediggers. At the evil men who did this to Bastian, but Kenzie is an easy target for my turmoil right now. He has not been able to look me in the eyes since we got here and if I am being honest, I do not want him to.

Not now. Not when Bastian is still lost to me. Still so far away.

A small rustle pulls my attention back to the hospital bed. My tears are a steady stream while I watch Bastian struggle in his sleep. His eyebrows are knitted together, and I just hope he is not in too much pain. The now crushingly familiar feeling of hopelessness wraps itself around me like a too-hot blanket. He looks so frail like this. He has lost weight. Sallow skin and gaunt cheeks. A large bandage over his left eye covers most of the damage, but you can still see the red and sensitive skin on his cheek below poking through.

I do not know what else to do but wait. Anxiously, I wonder if I would even be the first person he would want to see when he wakes up. Maybe I have deluded myself into thinking he feels the same way I do, that this was not all just an elaborate deal to pass the time while on the road.

But then I remember our first kiss, the closeness and warmth I felt that night, and how perfectly *right* his lips felt kissing mine.

No. I did not make this all up.

Leaning closer to the bed, I find his hand and press my forehead against the back of it. It is colder than usual. It does not feel right, like he is not fully *here*, existing in his body. As if a large part of him is somewhere else, far away.

Far away from me.

Feeling like my thoughts are too tight in my skull, I breathe slowly in and out, my head still resting on his hand. My first instinct is still to pray, reach out to God, and ask for strength. But it does not feel right. Not anymore. Especially now. But then Bastian's steady voice comes back to me, from that day we sat in the abandoned church.

Prayer is just prayer.

I decide what it means.

Although the word prayer now makes me uncomfortable, the act feels too familiar to ignore. But today, I do not direct my thoughts to God. Instead, I whisper them into the scratchy hospital bed sheets and direct my words to Bastian, and hope he can hear them.

I pray that he can hear me, and how much I need him to be okay.

MY EYES FLUTTER OPEN, the early morning rays peeking through the half-closed blinds of the hospital window. It takes me a few seconds to realize I fell asleep, still resting close to Bastian's body. My head is facing the couch, Lenix and Connor missing from their usual spot. Then I feel a hand stroke my messy hair, and I freeze, my heart falling into my stomach—because that can only be one person.

Bastian is awake.

I lift up my head, the hand that was in my hair falling back on the bed as I find his seeking gaze. His expression seems perplexed, like making out an impossibility while staring back at me.

"Baby Blue," he rasps.

Those two words somehow hurt as much as they heal. I nod, the tears blurring my vision, unable to find even one single word to speak.

"But you're dead," he says slowly, still looking at me like he cannot believe what he is seeing.

My heartbeat triples. He said the same thing when we were in the van.

"Bastian, I am not—" Taking his hand in mine, I bring it up to my face, and press it against my wet cheek. "I am here. I have always been here."

His right eye slowly blinks like he is trying to process something, and I suddenly realize that he must not be completely lucid. *Maybe I should call a doctor.* But I do not move, frozen in place, staring at the man who is looking back at me like I am a ghost.

"I built you a house near the water…" he says, licking his chapped lips. "But you're dead." His voice cracks and my heart shatters along with it.

"Bastian, you—you are not making any sense," I say through choked tears.

He falls silent, and I do not think I can withstand anymore of this as I watch a single tear fall across his temple and onto the pillow below him. His throat bobs on a hard swallow and his hand slackens in mine, his eyelid slowly closing and I know I have lost him to whatever sedation the doctors have him on.

I do not move for what feels like an eternity, but an eternity watching him sleep, although painful and confusing, is better than an eternity without him.

It is not until the door opens and Lenix and Connor reappear that I look up. Even then it is hard to coax me away from Bastian. I am not sure what expression I am wearing but it is enough for Lenix to notice and ask me what happened.

I tell them he woke up, that he was speaking, but was not making any sense. Connor rushes out to get a doctor, and Lenix pulls me into her arms as I cry into her shoulder.

"He's fine," she soothes into my hair. "Everything will be just fine." But I can hear the sliver of doubt in her tone and I latch on to it, sinking far and deep alongside it, unable to see the end.

41

BASTIAN

"What are you doing here?" Connor barks as he walks into his study. I startle but pretend I didn't, realizing I've been staring at my uncle's portrait sitting over the fireplace for God knows how long. He and my father were twins. My gaze slides to my cousin, impeccably dressed in a navy three-piece suit.

"Meeting," I simply say, finally turning away from the portrait.

"I know that, but what are *you* doing here?" he replies while pouring himself a mezcal on the rocks. Gesturing toward me asking if I want one, I shake my head. "Shouldn't you be resting?"

"I'm fine," I grit out.

Still, my hand unconsciously lifts up to the eye patch I'm wearing and I snap it back down as soon as I realize the gesture. The left side of my face throbs, reminding me that I'm missing an eye. As if I can forget.

We've been back in Noxport for a little over a week and a half now. Connor flew us all back as soon as I was stable.

Stable but still suffering from withdrawals and not close to being lucid.

It took me days to piece reality back together. It's still a jumbled mess if I'm being perfectly honest. The most confusing part is still Lucy. My mind keeps believing she's dead and every day I have to go through the shock of remembering she's alive.

Especially those first few days at the hospital when I was so deep in my delusions that I couldn't even tell if I was alive or dead, but she was still the first thing I'd see when I opened my eyes—eye? *Fucking hell.*

I must have told her countless times that she was dead. And she'd just shake her head with a watery gaze and tell me she was here, that she was alive.

I never believed her.

I've been avoiding her calls ever since we got back. And every missed call is like a small cut to the skin, always bleeding, never healing.

Connor studies me from behind his glass while he slowly takes a sip. His slow appraisal is making my skin itch and I idly finger the small bottle of painkillers through the pocket of my jeans.

"What?" I say coldly.

He shrugs his shoulders, unbuttoning his suit jacket, and sits down behind his desk. He drums his fingers on the mahogany surface before he speaks. "Doctor says you should still be—"

"Doctor can fucking die for all I care," I say, ignoring his amused smirk at my little outburst. Sitting in the chair facing the desk, I add, "I've missed too much work already. Especially with that silly little road trip, you made me go on."

"Silly?" Connor says, quirking an eyebrow.

"What?" I bark, this close to walking out of this fucking room, desperately needing to numb my thoughts with a few more of the pills in my pocket.

"Nothing, except..." he trails off, taking a slow sip of mezcal before continuing, "According to Lucy, there was nothing silly about it."

His eyes narrow, most likely waiting for a reaction but I don't give him the satisfaction. Except I do, and regret my words immediately when I say, "I don't want to talk about her." I avoid eye contact and stare out the window behind him.

"What the hell were you thinking fucking Lenix's little sister in the first place?" he says incredulously and with a lot of bite.

My gaze snaps back to him. Anger burns like gasoline through my veins, but I keep my face flat. I know he's goading me, pushing me for a reaction, so I give him a slow blink and say, "It's not like that."

Connor's laugh is dry, his eyes moving about the room as if he can't believe what he's hearing. "It's not like that," he says, parroting my words back to me. "Look, I usually don't give a shit who you fuck Bastian, but you made it *my* fucking business when the person who's crying over you is my goddamn *sister-in-law*," he hisses.

The idea that Lucy has been crying because of me is enough for me to spiral even deeper into self-loathing. I've never felt like more of a piece of shit in my entire fucking life. But I say nothing, avoiding his stare.

"The only reason Lenix hasn't come for your balls yet is because... well—" he says, vaguely gesturing my way as if to say *well look at you*.

I stew in silence for a few seconds and finally say, "I'll handle it."

"You fucking do that," Connor mutters while his attention shifts to the door. I recognize Byzantine's steady footsteps without having to look.

He places a hand on my shoulder and my first instinct is to pull away but I don't. He's standing to my left, and since I've lost all peripheral vision from that side I don't even bother to look up.

"How are you doing, brother?" he asks and the genuine concern in his tone makes me want to light myself on fire.

"Fine," I say glacially.

Suddenly, I'm breaking out into a cold sweat, continuously tracing the curves of the bottle in my pocket with my thumb. I'd pull it out right here if it wasn't so obvious.

Eventually, the attention shifts away from me as more of Connor's men filter into the room. Gradually, I realize the conversation might have shifted but the attention is still on me as I catch most of them furtively glancing my way, to look at my eye—or the lack thereof.

I'm not sure what I feel then; shame, embarrassment. All I know is that I'd rather be dead than be this self-conscious. I white-knuckle my way through the meeting, barely paying attention—making my being here even more fucking useless. I leave as soon as I can, not bothering with any goodbyes.

In the car, my heart is beating wildly in my chest, my hands clammy and shaking as I finally open that pill bottle. I tell myself it's for the constant pain in my face. But I know better. The angel of temptation perched on my shoulder knows better, delighted as ever.

I shake three pills onto my palm, stare at my hand for a beat, then decide on five. I swallow them down dry, cringing at the acrid taste but nothing about that matters, as long as they dissolve fast and get to work. Unfortunately, there's enough time between now and when the numbing wave of warmth crests over my body for the all-consuming grip of shame to take hold.

I hate everything about this shit. Except for how it makes me feel.

How else am I supposed to process any of it, when most of the time I wonder if I'm still locked up in that dark fucking room, and this is just a hallucination. How can I know if any of it is real? How can I know for sure that I didn't just create an alternate reality, a psychotic break, where Lucy is alive? And that's not to mention the constant flood of flashbacks from my childhood that I can't seem to suppress or manage.

I squeeze my eye shut, hitting the back of my head on the headrest behind me, breathing hard through my nose while I grip the steering wheel with both hands.

"You need something stronger," the angel whispers in my ear, still sitting on my shoulder. *"Don't you miss it? You can't lie to me. I know you do."*

I ignore the voice—as soothing as it is—and start the car.

Fifteen minutes later, I'm back home, sitting on my couch, wringing my hands together. The pills have finally hit, I'm high but nowhere high enough for what mental hell I'm trying to escape. I swallow hard. From across the loft, I stare at the bottom drawer of my nightstand.

My knee bounces as I sit and stew. Finally, I spring up and cross the space. I open the drawer, push a few knick-knacks out of the way, and find the latch for the false bottom. Underneath, there's a metal tin box the size of a book. Pulling it out, I walk back to the couch and place it on the glass coffee table in front of me.

Biting my lip bloody, I stare at it, then finally open it.

Slowly, I take its contents out one by one. A blackened spoon. A white cotton ball. A syringe. A shoelace. And finally, an old beer cap. The few syringes, and whatever else is still left in the box, rattle around as I push it off to the side, surveying the layout I just made.

No one can quite understand the rush of this ritual more than an ex-junkie.

I haven't bought heroin in over fifteen years, and still, the very act of lining everything up makes my mouth water and my brain tingle. The sweet promise of obliviated bliss.

At first, I kept the box as proof that I could control the addiction, the spoils of my victory. But now I wonder if I always knew, deep down, that I would fail. That I'd always be this weak.

It doesn't take that much longer for me to pick up the phone and make the call.

42

The cement surrounding the pool burns the soles of my bare feet from the mid-afternoon sun as I reach Lenix's sunlounger. I've been visiting a lot more often than usual, unwilling to be left alone with my own thoughts.

She has a soft pink bikini on and I catch a glimpse of a surprised look behind her large sunglasses at the black one-piece swimsuit I've chosen to wear, but she says nothing. I realize that she's still used to seeing me covering up with a loose t-shirt and basketball shorts. It dawns on me how much the road trip, no matter how it ended, has overall been a blessing.

It certainly helped me to get out of my own way.

But now the most influential person is refusing to talk to me ever since we landed back in Noxport. I don't know what I did wrong.

Maybe all my worrying was for something, after all.

I didn't matter in the end—not like I thought I did.

I settle into the chair beside her, gathering my hair into a messy bun to stave off the heat.

She doesn't even wait half a second to jump right into it.

"Connor told me he saw Bastian at a meeting yesterday," Lenix mumbles while lighting a joint. "Have *you* talked to him?"

My heart squeezes painfully and I let out a long sigh. "I don't want to talk about it today," I answer a little too mournfully.

She hums, taking a drag, and says, "Sounds like day drinking to me."

I can't help but let out a small laugh, and nod. "Sounds about right," I say while gesturing for her to pass me the joint.

Her mouth falls in mock shock, pulling her sunglasses down her nose as if taking a better look at me. "Lucy Lincoln," she says slowly while still handing me the joint. "What have you done with my sister?"

I smile, pulling the smoke into my lungs and then exhaling. "I've smoked with you before," I reply playfully.

She lets out a small scoff. "Once. And only because I coerced you," she says with a laugh and then turns more thoughtful. "It's not just that though, you just—you just feel changed. More self-assured. Like you're not constantly second-guessing yourself like before." She pauses and looks at me more intently. "What *happened* on the road?"

The subject is veering a little too close to what I already established I was ignoring today but after a long beat I answer her anyway. "I think it was just time for me to find myself."

"And did you?" she asks while taking the joint back.

"I think so."

I know my smile is most likely morose but I hope it still conveys the accomplishment I feel.

She gives me a similar smile, squeezing my hand three times.

"I'm so proud of you," she says, her voice cracking. But then her demeanor changes before I even have time to answer, her mouth falling open on an excited inhale, eyebrows raising up from underneath her sunglasses. "We should go out dancing!" she says sitting upright. "Tonight— to celebrate. I can dress you up all cute and sexy and do your makeup." She gives her hands a few quick happy claps, and then adds, "I mean only if you want to."

I'd take any form of distraction right about now if it meant keeping my brooding thoughts at bay. Especially if it means spending time with my sister.

I smile wide, and nod. "I would love to."

HOURS LATER, the sun has set over Noxport and Lenix is leading me inside Vinyl, one of the many clubs the Sin Eaters own around the city. She looks impeccable in her leopard print heels and 20's inspired tasseled red dress, her black bob shining under the neon strobe lights.

Lenix lent me a black crushed velvet bodysuit paired with the shortest pair of frayed jean shorts I've ever dared to wear, and some cute platform sneakers. She even gave me a winged smokey eye and a nude lip to finish the look. I feel sexy. And for the first time, maybe ever, the attention I'm garnering doesn't affect me negatively.

The club's atmosphere is dark and moody, with large black booths lining the walls while the massive dance floor sits in the middle. Lenix weaves us through the crowd and then up the stairs to the VIP area, a table with a bottle of champagne on ice already waiting for us.

She lets out a pleased sigh while we sit. Reaching for the chilled bottle, she pours two glasses, handing me one.

"I thought we could dance up here," she says with a wide grin. "More room."

I take a sip, the bubbles going up my nose and making my eyes water. I clear my throat and survey the club from this vantage point. From here, the dance floor is right below us, full of writhing bodies and people enjoying the music. It crosses my mind that Lenix is still trying to shelter me, most likely worried I'd get overwhelmed with so many strangers encroaching on my personal space. I feel slightly irked at the thought, but she's also not wrong—I don't *always* have to jump into the deep end.

I smile back in earnest and nod. "Sounds lovely," I reply.

A few glasses of champagne later, we're both dancing to the music while Lenix shows me more and more provocative dance moves. When she gets distracted by the server at our table, I turn my attention to the floor below me.

I find Bastian in the crowd so easily. As if I didn't have to try, my eyes seeking him out in every room I happen to be in, no matter the improbability.

What is he even doing here?

Somehow his eyepatch only further accentuates how lethal he looks, the angry scar below his left eye still red and visible, his dyed blond hair pushed off his face, the dark roots noticeable even from here. My breath catches in my throat when I realize he's staring directly at me, his eyebrows pulled down, making him seem even more guarded and intimidating.

I turn around for only a second, moving to tell Lenix I won't be long. When I glance back to where I saw him standing—he's gone.

"*No*," I breathe out. Hurriedly, I mutter something about going to the bathroom, not waiting for a proper answer, and fly down the stairs. My heart is pounding in my throat as I try to find him in the crowd. I can't let him just leave. I can't.

I've pushed myself through the crowd trying to get to where I saw him last, my hair sticks to my nape, breathless and overheated, when a hand grabs me by the wrist. The loud music swallows up my shocked gasp as my front is pushed against the large speaker near the edge of the dance floor. My adrenaline surges as I struggle against the hard body pinning me flat until Bastian's voice finds my ear.

"Stop," he rasps. His hands grab my hips forcefully, grinding me against him. He doesn't let me answer, react or *do* anything while his palms travel up my body, heatedly kneading my breasts.

I should tell him to stop. Confront him. Make him *talk* to me but I do none of those things.

My body is ablaze, his every touch like another struck match. My head falls backward onto his right shoulder while his fingers greedily push inside the front of the body-suit, finding my peaked nipple and rolling it between his index and thumb. I unabashedly moan, my eyes closing with the sensation of his hands finally back on my skin.

I can only see the right side of his face, and I try to find his gaze but I am distracted by his other hand smoothing up my throat, circling my chin, and turning my head toward him.

Then the world stops. Quiet. Because his lips are on mine, desperate and hungry. I whimper into his mouth, his hips still pinning me to the speaker, the vibrations thudding along with my heart. I need more of him. Better access. As if reading my mind, he spins me around, my back landing hard against the flat surface behind me. He cradles my face with urgency, deepening the kiss, his tongue finding mine, possessive and reckless. I'm losing myself in the moment, eager for him, starving, while I palm his erection through his jeans, unbothered by the crowd surrounding us.

Bastian breaks the kiss, his teeth nipping at my earlobe.

"You're not dead," he says almost to himself, his lips trailing down my throat, and it's laced with such agonizing desperation that it impales me straight through the heart.

His words snap me back to reality. And I suddenly know with painful clarity that something is wrong. That even now, he's not being himself. He's lost and I'm not sure how to find him.

I stiffen under his touch, and I can tell he senses it because he tenses up too, stopping his heated kisses across my collarbone.

"Bastian don't—" I begin to plead, but he's gone before I can even react. His presence alone splits the crowd open and I watch him walk away while I try to catch my breath, my head spinning. Tears burn my eyes, but I don't run after him.

Back upstairs, Lenix barely notices I was gone, having made friends with the table beside us. I force a smile for the remainder of the night, and pretend nothing substantial happened between then and now. My mind nostalgically replays bits and pieces of the road trip, desperate to feel anything else but *this*.

43

BASTIAN

The cigarette I must have still been holding has time to burn through the fabric of my shirt, then my skin underneath, before I bother to wake up. For a time-warping second, I think I'm back in that room. *Maybe I still am*, is the parasitic thought that always follows. I jerk upright, patting my t-shirt as if I'm putting out a raging fire on my chest, the orange cinders of the cigarette flying, while I try to grab the dropped butt before I burn myself again.

Fuck.

Must have nodded off on the couch. There's an old rerun still playing on the television. My heart is pounding but my eyes are already drooping back closed, high as I ever could be on a random Tuesday morning. It's been a few days since I made that first call. Everything else that followed was like muscle memory. The first hit was so strong and made me so nauseous that I threw up. But I managed. Knowing what was waiting for me on the other side if I just powered through and got over that first time.

Sweet fucking nothing.

I consider finding my phone to see if Connor needs me, but my eyelids are so heavy, I can't seem to open them back up. My head falls back on the couch and I let myself slip into the warm dreamless void instead.

I'M JERKED BACK AWAKE AGAIN. It takes me a second to understand that the loud banging is coming from the front door. I smooth a hand over my tired face, looking around for my phone, noticing that the sun is setting through the windows. Must have slept all day.

The banging continues, and my irritation spikes.

"Hold the fuck on," I bark, wondering who the hell would even have the gall to show up here.

I check the cameras on my phone and my stomach sinks when I realize Lucy is the one making all that noise. I half consider pretending I'm not here but I just yelled out loud like a fucking idiot, and something tells me she won't be backing down this time.

"*Shit*," I mutter, surveying the living room table. I grab whatever I don't want her to see and throw it in a plastic bag, sticking it under the couch. I try to find a hoodie on my way to the door to hide the track marks on my arm but can't find one. I curse under my breath again, the banging grating harshly on my frayed nerves, and give up looking. I hope Lucy won't notice or if she does, won't be able to make any kind of accurate connection to where they might come from.

I slide the two bolts, one at the top and the other at the bottom, before swinging the door open. Seeing her here is like Hell disguised in a breathtaking paradise. A loose braid falls over her right shoulder, faded blue overalls and—I realize with a hard pang—my old band t-shirt.

I wish I would just fucking die already.

For a long beat, we just stare at each other, her tight fist still hanging in the air. Then, as if realizing it, she clears her throat and crosses her arms over her chest, the skin between her eyebrows creating a divot as she looks at me with hard intent.

"Let me in," she demands.

"Luce…" I say all too ready to deny her.

To deny myself.

"Don't *Luce* me," she answers angrily. Then falls silent, seeming to take me in with a long drag up and down of her gaze. "Are you sick? Contagious?"

Her question takes me by surprise and I sputter out a response without even really thinking about what she's asking. "No. Why would I be—"

She gives me a quick nod, her shoulder clipping mine as she pushes herself inside. Surveying the loft, she turns back to face me. I concede, closing the door and locking it. Her arms are still tucked tight over her chest, her glare unrelenting.

"So just a coward then," she says, her eyes growing teary. "Because those would be the only two reasons why you have been refusing to see me." Her voice cracks and I don't think I can bear much more of this but we've barely started this conversation.

I feel so tight in my own skin, I think I might just split open and bleed out on the floor in front of her. I don't immediately answer, instead heading to the kitchen first, fishing a beer out of the fridge and cracking it open, then lean against the kitchen island. I gesture to her, offering her one but she dejectedly shakes her head, declining.

"I'm not avoiding you, Lucy." I'm not sure why my first impulse is to gaslight her. Her angry expression morphs into one of hurt, the words seeming to affect her more than I meant them to and I'm immediately filled with regret.

"So it really did mean nothing to you…" she says so softly that I need to watch her lips for the words to properly make sense.

I wish I hadn't.

"I never said that," I reply quickly. Even I'm irritated with my fucking non-answers. I take a long swig of beer, trying to blur the edges of whatever shit existence I'm currently living in.

"So what *are* you saying?" she demands, raising her arms in exasperation. Then her demeanor falls quiet, still standing in the middle of the loft. I watch her lip quiver, a tear tracking down her cheek. "Talk to me, Bastian." Her voice is so small, and I'm the reason she feels that way.

Maybe the dark room was better than this after all.

"I don't want to hurt you, Luce. I just—" I'm growing flustered and agitated, the more I'm trying to find the right words. I take a deep breath in and rake my fingers through my unkempt hair. "I… I…"

I feel myself unraveling, holding on by a thread, the emotions and feelings, and just—just *all* of it fighting to burst out.

"What?" she says. "*Please*, Bastian—"

My resolve snaps.

"I thought you were fucking *dead*," I say forcefully, pushing myself off the island. "Do you understand what that means? I *mourned* you, Lucy… I spent days in that—in that." The words get caught in my throat, and I look down, trying to blink the memories of that place back down. "I don't think I can go through that again," I mutter.

I feel Lucy step closer to me. "Go through what?" she asks tentatively.

I find her gaze, her eyes swimming with tears. I chew on my lips before answering. "Losing you."

"But you never did," she answers hoarsely.

"One day I will."

She lets out a frustrated sigh. "Says who?" Followed by an equally frustrated shrug of her shoulders.

"Says *me*," I snap back, jamming my index finger into my chest. "Don't you get it?" I tell her, trying to ignore the tears now falling freely over her freckled cheeks. "Nothing this perfect will ever be meant for me."

She falls silent for a long quiet beat as if thinking. "You know… I did end up finding something to believe in." She pauses, wringing her hands together. "It's you, Bastian," she says. Her tone is hard, wiping the tears almost angrily off her face. "I believe in *you*."

Her words have the same effect as a hard blow in the gut and I nearly double over gasping for breath. Her words should feel soothing but instead, they wreak havoc and it only takes me a few seconds to ruin everything.

My laugh is dry. Cold. "You believe in me, Luce—a fucking junkie? That's your big reveal? Think about what you're saying next time," I say with a scoff, reeking of self-hatred.

I know I've caught her off-guard when her eyebrows scrunch together. "A what?"

"A drug addict," I say, slapping the crook of my left arm and regretting my knee-jerk reaction when Lucy's gaze falls on the track marks still visible there.

A heavy silence appears uninvited, settling between us while we both don't move, Lucy's eyes still on my arm.

Then, finally, she looks back up at me. I expect to find disgust, instead, I find acceptance.

I take a step back. She takes a step forward.

"I know what you're doing, Bastian," she mutters.

I shoot her a perplexed look, not sure if she means drugs or something else.

"My therapist calls it self-sabotage," she says, her face resolute. Her tone is so matter-of-fact, so innocent, and so *fucking* Lucy, that I suddenly want to weep at her feet. "You're trying to hurt my feelings so I leave you alone." She stomps forward and passes me, heading for one of the stools around the kitchen table. She sits, crossing her arms again. "I'm not going anywhere."

I blink. Not able to process anything she just said. We both fall silent and after a few seconds, she shoots me a defiant look as if to say *well?*

I stare at her, knowing she's goading me, unwilling to leave me alone, despite my best efforts to push her away.

I'm suddenly desperate to touch her.

To remind myself that she's real.

Alive.

I reach Lucy in three quick strides, grabbing her by the waist and lifting her up onto the island. There's a flash of hesitancy in her eyes but she must see the consuming need in mine, because she blinks and my name leaves her lips, breathless, her arms linking around my neck. I lean into her open thighs, catching her bottom lip with my teeth. Kissing her feels the same as the first time. Like remembering something I should have never forgotten.

My hands are just as desperate as my thoughts, fumbling over the straps of her overalls.

"Get this shit off," I say pointedly, half-crazed.

Her soft, effervescent giggle is like a balm to every wound I never knew still bled. She jumps down, and I barely let her do even that, aching to touch her as much as I possibly can. She unclasps the front and pulls them down, sliding the overalls over her hips. She's about to take the t-shirt off but I don't let her, the sight of her in it making my cock throb.

I practically throw her back on the island, far from gentle, and she takes it in stride, her legs circling my waist and pulling me close to her. She's serious now, and I detect the same fraught need as my own in her blown-out pupils.

I slide my hands up her thighs and when I feel a soft cotton fabric under my touch, I twist it around my fingers and then rip her panties clean off. I swallow the gasp I knew she'd make, my thumb tracing up her cunt, finding her already wet and ready.

Perfect. Cause I can't fucking wait.

"I need you, Luce," I groan, my hands now on my jeans, urgently pushing them down, freeing my cock. "I fucking need you so badly," I say, my voice cracking over every word. And, at this point, I don't care what I'm saying or how I'm sounding, as long as I can feel her warmth around me.

Lucy's hand finds my hard length, guiding me to her entrance, coating the tip with her wet desire as she slides my cock up and down her pussy. "Use me," she whimpers.

Hearing those two words sends me barreling over the edge, thrusting deep and to the hilt. I don't think I've ever heard Lucy moan so loud. Like a true addict, I'm still not satisfied. I pull up her shirt and suck her nipple into my mouth, laving my tongue over the hard peak while I fuck her hard on the countertop, needing her moans more than I need drugs in my veins.

My hands travel up her back, my fingers curling over

her shoulders, and with the grip I use her entire body as leverage to pump myself into her. The steady pace makes my piercing grind against her clit, her pussy clamping around me, and I can tell she's already close. My forehead falls against hers as our heated breaths mingle, both mindless with need. We don't utter a word, our bodies speaking a silent language that's much more vital.

And when I feel her legs squeeze around my hips, fingers gripping the hair at my nape, her lips finding my own with heated persistence, followed by a moan so fucking beautiful I barely even feel worthy of hearing it—I know I'll never be able to let her go again. Not when the feel of her coming around my cock is the very definition of transcendence.

"Let me be yours," I whisper heatedly near her ear, my lips trailing down her neck. "Tell me I can be yours." My tone is laced with far too many emotions for my liking but I'm not sure I care anymore. Not when my hips are still pumping hard into her, my cock throbbing, and aching for a release.

But not before she says it. I need to hear her say it.

"You were always meant to be mine, Bastian," she says with a choked sob. "Let me be yours too."

I come so hard, I nearly black out. My palm slams onto the counter for balance while I continue to pump my cum into her pussy. My thrusts slow as we both try to catch our breaths. My gaze finds hers, my heart beating wildly in my chest, silence floating like plumes of smoke around us.

Tentatively, Lucy's hand reaches up and touches my left cheek, and I jerk my head away, suddenly remembering what I must look like. I unceremoniously slide myself out of her, tugging my jeans back over my hips but don't zip them up. Before I even try to distance myself, her fingers dig deep into my forearm.

"Don't," she says, her eyes hard, but also brimming with sadness. "Do not ruin this."

I match her gaze, licking my lips and swallowing hard. "This doesn't fix anything," I finally say.

She gently takes my hand in hers and places it on her chest. I can feel her heartbeat underneath the skin and I'm not sure why it rattles me so much.

"I know," she says softly, leaning over to kiss me and I don't move, letting her warm lips press against mine. I breathe in her sweet scent, letting it ground me into the present moment. "Let's just start by spending the night together," she adds.

I can't ignore the subtle hope in her tone. Unwilling to deny her something so simple, I nod. Her face lights up with a smile, and my heart squeezes at the sight.

And for a few hours, everything is... fine. Even when I start feeling the effect of withdrawals. I try to ignore it as best I can—for now. Lucy convinces me to watch an old spaghetti western and I pretend to hate it. I'd spend an eternity watching bad cowboy movies if it meant having Lucy by my side.

44

My eyelids flit open. I'm disoriented until I hear the pained muttering beside me and realize I'm in Bastian's loft, and by the sounds of it he's trapped in a nightmare. I press my hand to his chest, his heart pounding against my palm, his skin clammy to the touch.

"*Bastian*," I whisper worriedly.

The sounds emanating from his person are starting to scare me, incapable of even imagining what kind of horror he's managed to trap himself in.

"Bastian," I say a little more urgently, shaking his shoulder, and then shaking him again. "Wake up."

My mind is still sleep-heavy, and I'm not sure what to do so I do the only thing that springs to mind. I fling the covers off his overheated body and crawl over, straddling him. Gently, I cradle his face with my hands and kiss him, trying to murmur some soothing words in case he wakes up while I'm saying them.

"*You're safe. I'm here.*"

You're safe, you're safe, you're safe.

I press my lips against his, between each spoken word, while my anxiety simmers, worried he won't wake up and he will be trapped in his mind forever.

"Wake up, Bastian." My voice is low and soft, kissing down his jaw and then back up to his lips. "Come back to me. You're safe."

Suddenly, Bastian takes a long, fraught inhale, sounding like a man waking up from the dead and I don't have time to react before his hand is clamped around my neck, cutting off my airway. Shocked, I choke out his name, but his grip never lessens, my fingers now clawing against the back of his hand, already feeling light-headed.

The moon illuminates his stony face, his one good eye is open but terrifyingly vacant and I realize with gut-wrenching panic that he is not lucid and if this continues, Bastian might end up killing me. A powerful mixture of survival instincts and the excruciating knowledge that Bastian would not survive finding me like this pulls me from my frozen state. I start to fight back with all the force I can conjure up.

I slap him across the face and beat my fists over and over against his bare chest while trying to pull myself from his grasp. I garble his name again, this time much louder while I slap him again and again. I'm growing faint, my eyesight bleeding darkness when finally, his fingers loosen against my neck and he lets go of me. I double over, still half-straddling him, wheezing in much-needed oxygen, retching, and coughing.

"*Lucy?*" The fear in Bastian's voice slices my chest open, my heart aching for him.

For me. For us.

And in between painful breaths, the tears start falling, my fitful breaths growing even more irregular as I begin to sob. I vaguely understand that it must be the shock of what just happened that has heightened my emotions like this but I cannot stop. Suddenly, I feel like I'm crying for much more than just this.

"Luce, talk to me. What happened?" His voice is soothing, but the bite of fear is still sharp in his tone. Sitting up, his arm encircles me and I melt into him despite my body's lingering resistance to being vulnerable around him. His plea for an answer becomes more desperate the more I can't find the words to explain it to him. His kisses are feathery and light all across my cheeks, drinking up my tears with his soft lips until I finally manage to calm down.

I would rather not tell him, protect him from his own demons but the bruises I know will bloom around my throat by morning will nonetheless tell the truth if I'm unable to.

So I tell him. He grows quiet and so still that he might as well have turned into the marble statue I used to compare him to. I feel him mentally withdraw as if his body is walking away from me, and I can't bear that either.

"Don't Bastian, *please*." Because I can already hear the words out of his mouth.

"That was—" He clears his throat. "That's unforgivable."

My body is suddenly bone tired but I manage to find the strength to pull myself out of his grasp, straddling him once again. My palms cup his face much gentler than the last time my hands were on him, but my voice is sharp when I speak, determined yet shaky. "You need help, Bastian... that's all." He avoids my gaze and irritation mixes in with the sorrow still coating my insides black. "Look at me when I speak to you," I scold him like a child, and the look he gives me is shockingly reminiscent of one—a lost boy with the depth of lifetimes of hurt in his gaze. "You will get through this," I say, my kiss just as soft as the words I'm speaking. "We will get through this."

I repeat the words over and over, through wet, desperate kisses and I'm not sure if the tears I'm tasting on my tongue are only mine. His hands are sliding up my back, fisting my shirt as our embrace deepens, our harrowing emotions clawing at each other, threatening to take over.

I break away, tugging my shirt off, my panties still torn and in shreds somewhere on the floor of his loft.

"I'm so sorry, Luce. I'm so fucking sorry," Bastian says despairingly, his fingers trailing delicately over my bruised throat.

"I'm not leaving," I tell him once again, spoken like a prayer. Fervently. Zealously.

My skin is suddenly just as overheated as his, my tongue finding his neck, licking my way up to his ear, sucking his lobe into my mouth, my core grinding hard on his rapidly hardening length and I wonder if having sex with Bastian will always feel like this. As if we might die if we deny ourselves. As if the cure for all this ache is feeling the rush of him slowly push himself inside of me—a craving so insatiable, it's almost unbearable.

It's just as unbearable now.

Bastian lifts his hips, pulling his boxers down and without another word, I'm sinking down on his cock. The sensation of him stretching me so full somehow mutes every other feeling, and suddenly I can breathe freely, my lungs full of life-giving air as I start rocking my hips back and forth. His piercing hits the perfect spot as always, while I mindlessly grind against him. Bastian groans loudly, his forehead falling on my heaving chest, his hands never stopping their caresses all over my body as if he still needs the constant reminder of my presence.

His gaze lifts up, eagerly seeking mine. The words left unspoken behind his loaded stare could fill a thousand books but he doesn't utter a single one. Instead, he kisses me with every fiber of his splintered soul and I return it with the same fervor.

My climax feels like uncovering a new religion, suddenly unaware of how I'll ever be the same again when I can put all my faith in something so potent—a feeling of peace so powerful that it's only created when Bastian is inside of me.

While I tumble over the edge of reality, he trails his tongue over my collarbone, pressing heated kisses to the skin where my shoulders and neck meet.

"You're so beautiful like this," he whispers urgently. "So perfect. So fucking mine," he continues, his lips on my skin, again and again. Softly. Lovingly.

I feel Bastian's own orgasm ripple through his body, tremors wracking his limbs as he holds me tightly, his mouth still ravenously seeking mine as we finally come down from whatever just happened between us.

And I honestly don't know if I even want to.

However, the soul-deep exhaustion returns and I fall into Bastian's arms. My heart pounds in my chest while my head rests heavily in the crook of his neck, breathing in his warm skin and hope I'm right—that we will get through this.

Without a word, Bastian pulls out, flipping us to our sides, and curling around me while drawing me as close as possible into his chest. He gently kisses my neck, goosebumps breaking out all over my body. I fall asleep not long after, his lips still peppering an unsung story across my skin.

45

BASTIAN

Leaving Byzantine's house, I drive just a few streets east and arrive at Connor's. The gate slowly yawns open, letting me into the long driveaway. Parking, I make my way up into the large mansion, past the marbled foyer, through the kitchen, and out the sliding doors to the back of the house. I find Connor doing laps in the pool and I sit down in one of the chairs while he finishes.

I'm on my phone catching up on work, when he finally gets out of the water, his red swim trunks stuck to his tattooed thighs. Slicking his wet hair back, he quickly dries himself off and sits beside me, popping his black shades on.

"Where's Lenix?" I ask, my gaze still on my phone.

"How should I know?" he answers gruffly.

I give him a blank stare, looking at him like he's an idiot.

"Bedroom." His smile is bright and arrogant, and a melancholic pang hits me in the chest. The question is on the tip of my tongue: How did you know it was love? But I swallow it back down, cringing at the thought of ever saying that out loud to Connor.

I wipe the sweat off my forehead and pretend it's only from the heat and not the withdrawals, my hand shaky as I do so. I took a handful of painkillers before I left the house to evade the brunt of it but I need to execute my plan soon before the worst catches up with me.

Which is why I'm here.

I don't beat around the bush. "I need to borrow the plane."

"Oh?" Connor says unbothered, stretching out on the chair. "What for?"

"I'm flying to Midnight Cove—tonight if possible."

"What's in Midnight Cove, other than Byzantine's cottage?" he says, slightly confused.

"That's where I'm heading… I just need a week or two, and then I'll be back for good."

Early this morning, while the sun was rising and Lucy was still tucked in my arms, I relented and told her about my relapse—and some details of my past along with it. Although still wracked with debilitating shame from waking up from a nightmare into what felt like another nightmare —Lucy's throat now colored with bruises—I told her things I'd never told anyone before. I agreed I needed help, most likely rehab, and some serious therapy according to Lucy. But I wanted to get clean on my own terms first and intended to do it alone. She flat-out refused. Demanding I let her come with me. I'm ashamed to admit, I didn't need much convincing.

Connor takes a beat, then asks, "Alone?"

I know what he's asking, but I take a second to answer. Squinting against the hot Californian sun, I swipe my hand over my face, wishing I'd brought my shades with me. "Lucy's coming with me."

He hums while lighting a joint, inhaling deeply, and then puffing it back out before speaking. "Do you have anything else to tell me?"

Shame collars my throat and squeezes. I know he's fishing for more information but I'm unsure what exactly. Lucy or—

"You think I wouldn't notice?" Connor says, his tone serious and hard.

I play dumb, trying to avoid reality as long as possible. "Notice what?"

His chuckle is dry while he takes another long drag. "Don't fuck with me, Bastian."

My swallow is hard as I break out in a cold sweat. "How did you find out?" I say slowly.

"Which time? When you disappeared for two weeks when you were eighteen? Or now that you've fucking relapsed."

I blink, not knowing what to say. "Why didn't you say anything back then?"

Connor shrugs. "I knew Kenzie had it under control. I didn't want to pry. You'd been through enough."

I know he's alluding to me killing my father. He helped me dispose of the body that same night. We never said a word about it again.

Connor slides his inquiring gaze to me, his expression grave. "Should I be worried?"

I shake my head. "I'll be fine."

"Good. 'Cause I'll kill you myself if you aren't," he says, placing the joint on the ashtray between us.

I stand up, ready to get the fuck out here.

"And Lucy?" Connor adds before I can leave.

I sigh. "What about Lucy?"

"Should *Lenix* be worried?"

Irritation spikes, but I answer anyway, "No." I turn, shoving my hands into my jeans pockets. "Thanks for the plane," I say over my shoulder, sliding the patio door open.

"You're welcome, fucker!" I hear Connor yell before I disappear into the house.

LATER THAT EVENING, we land in NorCal. My shakes are getting worse, and I'm starting to feel the nausea crawl up my throat. *Fuck*. Here we go.

I tell Lucy to drive the car waiting for us outside the regional airport and give her directions to the cottage. Forty-five minutes later, we turn into the driveway leading up to the small yellow-painted house with its wrap-around porch overlooking the water.

It's dark out but Lucy is still impressed, an awed look on her face as she steps out of the car. "How lovely," she says, her voice low and hushed as if trying not to bother the scenery around us.

Grabbing our bags, I say nothing, simply kissing Lucy on her warm cheek before leading us up to the front door. Inside, I head up the wooden stairs to the mezzanine where the master bedroom is located. Dropping our things, I walk back down and meet Lucy in the living room near the fireplace.

She seems lost in thought, chewing on her lips, then looks up at me. "You'll need some space, won't you? I can sleep on the couch until you feel better, I've been researching the symptoms and it says that—"

"Luce," I say, interrupting her while trying to sound

soothing. "There's a guest bedroom down the hall, I'll just stay in there for the first few days. You can stay upstairs."

Her eyes are watery while she studies me in silence. "Are you sure?"

"I'm sure," I tell her with a kiss on the lips. "I've done this before."

A tear rolls down her cheek but she tries to smile nonetheless, giving me a small nod.

"We're going to be fine," I whisper.

"We're going to be fine," she repeats softly.

46

I spend the next four days in a state of limbo. Bastian hasn't left the guest bedroom since that first night. He warned me it would be like this. But it's worse seeing it. I try not to spiral into calling reinforcements—a priest maybe... because if I didn't know any better, I'd say he spent these past few days exorcizing a demon.

Every few hours, I creep into the room just to make sure he's breathing. My heart breaks every time I see him like this, laying on his side most times, curled into himself with the sheets pushed off the bed, shivering but also burning up, barely conscious. I press cold, wet towels on his skin, and he sometimes lets out small hisses as if even this gentle contact hurts. I leave fresh water and food on the bedside table and resist the urge to crawl in next to him and wrestle against the demon in his stead.

I spend a lot of my time on the back porch, lost in thought. The cottage is perched on a small hill, and I find myself staring into the ocean for long periods of time, quietly lulled by the waves crashing below. Noxport has the ocean too, but it feels different in Midnight Cove. I could see myself living here. Remote but peaceful. I guess, by definition, the commune was remote too.

But peaceful? Far from it.

On the fifth day, Bastian starts to leave the bedroom, never for long but at least it's a start. We sit in silence outside while he smokes cigarettes and I pretend to read. Then he returns to his bed to sleep, but not before kissing me on the forehead first.

ON DAY TEN, while the morning sun still paints the sky a soft pink, I find Bastian already sitting on the back porch, writing in a small black leather-bound book. He looks better, all things considered, but the dark circle lining his right eye tells me all I need to know. That, and his gaunt-looking cheeks, knowing he's barely touched the plates of food I've been bringing him.

I settle beside him while he tucks the pen into the notebook and closes it.

Pulling my knees up to my chest, I lock my arms around my legs, keeping my gaze fixed on the ocean and the looming cliff in the distance, the shimmering horizon further ahead.

"How are you feeling?" I ask.

His eyebrows dip as if remembering something painful.

"I'll be okay," he says after a moment.

My heart sinks, knowing he's keeping the worst from me and I wonder if he will ever be capable of expressing his feelings. Be free of the need to keep everything locked inside.

I don't push. Instead, I change the subject.

"I love it here," I say with a smile just as the fresh morning breeze dances through my curls.

"Yeah?"

I nod and then look at him. "Yes. I think a house near the water would be a beautiful place to live, don't you think?"

Bastian peers over, studying me with a look that I can't decipher. "I can build you one, Baby Blue,"

I laugh, slightly confused. "Build me what?"

"A house near the water."

I drop the smile, my heart suddenly too big for my chest. "You—you'd build me a house?" I whisper, then, a little more cautiously, I add, "For us?"

He nods, settling back in his chair, his gaze a lot more intense than a few seconds ago. Grabbing my hand, he rubs it distractedly. He seems to mull something over before speaking again. "Would you believe me if I told you that I saw our future, Luce?"

I blink back at him a few times, wondering if I heard him right. "You—you saw… *our* future?"

He shrugs trying to look nonchalant but he's clearly nervous as he pulls out a cigarette and lights it. "I mean, who knows what I saw? It's just—" He drags his hand over his face. "There's just too many coincidences adding up to ignore it." Then Bastian tells me all about his last overdose when he was eighteen, the resulting itemized list, and how those same objects started to appear on the road trip. "That map you brought with you was the first thing," he says with a shy half-grin. "I ignored it, but then I saw you in that store trying on your baby blue cowboy hat and it felt like…" His gaze lands on the crashing waves for a beat, then back on me, his expression serious yet so open. "It felt like fate."

It shouldn't make sense, still, I'm left with this over-whelming sense of nostalgia. My tears well up, my bottom lip trembling while I continue to listen to Bastian speak.

"What I'm trying to say is that I think… this whole time I was being led here—to you." He sighs, looking out to the water, his cigarette still hanging loosely between two fingers, which he then stubs in the ashtray. Taking a hold of my hand again, his thumb caressing the top, he stares at our joined hands for a beat, then looks up, his gaze searching. "Luce… I think I loved you before I ever met you," he says so quietly I barely catch it.

My palm flattens over my mouth, a sob filtering through my fingers while I sit with what Bastian just confessed. He keeps his gaze steady, but I can detect uncertainty in his body language while he waits for me to compose myself long enough to speak.

"What did you just say?" I can't help the disbelief laced in my voice, half convincing myself that I just made it all up.

"I said I love you, Lucy," he says with a slight huff. I can tell that being this vulnerable is making him uncomfortable, so I unfurl from my position and step forward, falling into his lap. His arms circle my waist, pulling me closer to his chest as I bury my nose into the crook of his neck. Pulling back, I wait until his gaze meets mine before I speak.

"I love you too, Bastian." I feel his throat bob on a hard swallow, and I give him a watery smile. "How could I not?"

He shrugs. "A lot of reasons." His words don't sound self-deprecating, more factual than anything. I roll my eyes. And he gives me a sad half-grin.

"There's also a lot of reasons why I would, you know," I

answer a little playfully because I'm suddenly so tired of always being sad.

And it's as if Bastian picks up on it too, the mood shifting.

"Oh yeah?" he says, giving me a quick squeeze around the waist. "Like what?"

I smile, and hum, looking upwards, pretending to think. "Like you saying that you'll build me a house near the water," I say with a laugh.

Bastian smiles back, leaning over, and whispers, "I'll rebuild the entire world for you Baby Blue. Just the way you want it." His following kiss is so tender that I try my hardest not to let the tears fall again while my hands comb through his hair, then link around his neck.

It's that kiss that solidifies it for me—that knowing feeling that the worst is finally behind us. That everything *will* be okay. And that these words, filled with such trepidatious hope, no longer exist solely inside a half-hearted prayer. It's a tangible thing now. Floating all around us, like a cocoon keeping us safe. If only for a little while.

Because at least now, we have each other.

And it feels like home.

When we finally pull away, Bastian leads us back inside for breakfast. I find him a few minutes later, in the bathroom, staring at himself in the mirror, a distant look in his gaze. My heart sinks thinking it's because of his missing eye. But then he pushes his overgrown hair off his face, the roots even darker than the last time I noticed.

"What's wrong?" I find myself saying.

He shrugs, not answering right away. "I don't like who I look—I mean, how I look with dark hair." His gaze finds mine through the mirror. "Want to help me bleach it?"

This simple ask shouldn't affect me this much. But it

does. Something about being welcomed in such a domestic task makes tears prick the back of my eyes. I smile, nodding slowly, then circle my arms around his waist from the back and press my cheek against his warm skin. "Of course."

47

BASTIAN

One year later

I kept my promise.

I built Lucy a house near the water, a few miles down from Midnight Cove.

First, I went to rehab. Connor was adamant I'd go to the top facility in California, so I spent two months attending morning group therapy with depressed pop stars and socialites.

It was awful.

But it also helped a lot.

Lucy came to visit as much as she was allowed, which was once a week. Since I had so much time on my hands, I took the opportunity to read books on woodworking and carpentry. Because although I told Lucy I *would* build her a house, I didn't actually know how. I did plan to hire a contractor to oversee it, but I still wanted some kind of active involvement. Now that Lucy and I were officially together, I needed her to be as close as possible, *whenever* possible. And having two separate apartments in the city wasn't going to cut it. I started the process of getting permits and land as soon as I was out of that fucking place.

Ten months later, the bungalow is ready and we've moved in. My last surprise was to paint the front door baby blue. Lucy burst into tears when she first noticed it, and then jumped into my arms, kissing me like we were back in Texas, on top of a Ferris wheel.

That was over a week ago.

I'm making coffee when Lucy walks into the kitchen, what has become our routine a week into living here.

"Morning," she sings-songs, padding up to me and pressing a kiss between my shoulder blades. I add some sugar to her mug, before turning around and handing it to her.

"Morning, Baby Blue," I say with a smile, kissing her softly on the lips. "How'd you sleep?"

"Amazing," she says with a sleepy grin, taking a slow sip of her coffee. "I'll never tire of hearing the sound of the ocean as I fall asleep."

I'll never tire of you.

I let that thought float in my mind while I watch her settle into the breakfast nook, the large kitchen window overlooking the water. All she has on is my old band shirt, looking even more faded now that she sleeps in it every night. Still, a year later, I can't believe she's mine. I must have done something right in a past life to have Lucy love me in this one. I watch her in silence for a few seconds longer before pushing off the counter.

"I have something for you," I tell her with a wink. "Wait here."

I catch her curious look before I exit and head for my office down the hall. Finding the small box I hid there, I head back into the kitchen, feeling slightly nervous.

"For me?" Her face beams as she takes the cardboard box out of my hands.

I shrug, downplaying it. "A housewarming gift of sorts," I mutter as I stand awkwardly next to the table while she opens it. "It's stupid really."

"Don't say that," she says offhandedly but then her breath catches in her throat. "Bastian... is that... did you..." She can't seem to find the words, looking up at me teary-eyed.

"Well, if I knew it was going to make you cry like the door—"

Lucy cuts me off, standing up. "These are happy tears, you idiot," she sniffles while jumping into my arms, peppering me with kisses, followed by a gleeful squeal before jumping back down. "I love them," she says willfully.

She picks the box up and skips to the fridge. Finally, she starts pulling magnets out one by one, each of them representing a different city or town that we drove through during our road trip. I began collecting them even before we started our little sex deal. It was like a compulsion, any time I saw one I just had to buy it, not understanding why but *knowing* someday I'd give them to Lucy as a souvenir. I never expected for them to end up here—inside the house we share together.

But here we are.

Living inside a dream I could have never dared to conjure up in the first place.

Then it hits me.

Or maybe the inexplicable feeling could be better described as—*then something leaves me*. I think I was speaking but must have stopped mid-sentence, because Lucy's eyebrows dip in worry, stepping toward me.

"Are you okay?" she says.

I blink, shaking my head as if trying to snap out of it, and clear my throat before answering, "Yeah, I just…" But I let the thought trail off because the room feels like it's expanding around me, then an odd pulse, like the house is taking in a long inhale until finally, everything snaps back to normal. It's then I realize that I've been in this… this *moment* before.

The smell of fresh paint and sawdust.

"Bastian?" Lucy coaxes.

My gaze falls back to hers, realizing I must look like I've seen a ghost. Can I even call it a ghost when it's the future that's been haunting me this whole time?

"I think we've passed it," I say, knowing I must sound unintentionally vague.

As expected, Lucy questions me. "Past what?"

"The future I told you about."

"Oh," Lucy says, a little surprised, finally connecting the dots. She pauses, looking around, and then adds, "This is the last thing you saw?"

"I think so," I answer, pushing my hair off my forehead. "I mean, it's more a feeling at this point than anything."

She smiles, her gaze shifting back to me. "Maybe you've always been chasing this feeling, but you don't have to anymore," she says with a shrug as if talking about the weather.

"What feeling?"

Her smile is serene when she wraps her arms around my waist and kisses me. My hands cradle her face, deepening the kiss as her hair tickles my cheek. I'm not sure I even care about her answer when having her like this surpasses any expectation I could have had of us together. But then she pulls away, her smile still as wide and beautiful as before.

"Home."

EPILOGUE

BASTIAN

Six months later

My hands slide up Lucy's legs, her smooth skin warm under my palms, reaching the harness sitting on her hips. I adjust the straps tighter, my fingers trailing over the baby blue dildo resting just above her pussy before pressing a lingering kiss on each of her thighs. Kneeling, naked, on the plush carpet between her widened feet, I peer up at her with a loose grin.

The image of her like this is pure divinity.

Naked, aside from the strap-on, her light brown curls tumble over her shoulders, grazing the top of her peaked nipples, the rays of the setting sun through the bay windows making her glow golden.

There is such self-assurance in her stance, I'm left in awe.

How far she's come…

I don't think this was on her bucket list. Or maybe it was—because there was barely any hesitancy when I offered a few months ago—thinking it might help with her past. By the mischievous smile she flashed me, it was as if she had already considered it. Something tells me she must have stumbled onto a few videos while doing her *research*.

Her fingers push through my hair, her smile widening as she takes in the sight of me at her feet. She's been insatiable in her desire to see me like this, the power wholly in her hands as I let her use me as she pleases. I'd do anything to see her thrive.

What Lucy wants, Lucy gets.

Gently tugging me forward by the root of my hair, I keep my gaze on hers while my mouth falls open, my tongue dragging up the length of the dildo, before wrapping my lips around it. As I do so, I palm her ass with both hands and her soft moan drifts like the most delicious of melodies into my ears, my hardening cock jerking at the sound.

"You look so sweet sucking my dick," she says breathlessly.

Her words shoot directly to my balls, and I let out a muffled groan, the dildo still in my mouth. It takes me everything not to flip her onto her back and fuck her senseless.

Instead, with my hands still near her ass, I slide my thumb down her slit, pushing it into her hot wet cunt while I release the dildo from my mouth.

Her perfect lips fall agape, followed by a small whimper, her eyes darkening.

It only takes a few seconds for Lucy to compose herself, her hands resting on her hips, a smirk pulling her mouth up.

She gives me a small tsk. "On the bed," she says pointing to it. "On your knees, facing the headboard."

I can't help letting out a small chuckle as I stand up. There's just something about seeing her like this that makes me fucking *giddy*. Before doing as she says, I grab her by the nape and pull her into a smoldering kiss, her taste as addictive as the thousand times before. She melts into me as I swallow her pleased hum like a man starved. I release her with a tug of her bottom lip, and step onto the mattress, on my hands and knees, facing away from her.

I feel the bed dip, her hand smoothing up the length of my spine and then back down, both hands now groping my ass. When I feel her warm tongue licking me from taint to asshole, I let out a heated curse, my head falling between my shoulders with a groan, goosebumps breaking out all over my back and arms.

Then my ears pick up the tell-tale sounds of what's coming next. The sound of the drawer sliding open. The click of a bottle cap. The soft breaths of Lucy approaching. The thrill is close to the one I once chased with another drug altogether.

Her fingers dance up my spine while she leans against my right side, her mouth close to my ear. "Ready?" she murmurs, low and sultry. Not bothering to answer, I give her a heated glance instead, and her lips quirk up before she disappears back behind me.

I feel the cold trickle of the lube first, then the slow stretch and push of the vibrating plug. I take a deep breath, trying to relax my muscles through the resistance, pleasure then pulsing through my body when it's fully seated. Lucy's mouth wraps around my balls not long after, her back now on the bed underneath me, in between my bent knees. When her lips find my cock, my arms start to tremble, fighting against all the sensations threatening to push me over the edge before having even started.

"*Fuck, Lucy,*" I growl. "I need to taste you, I fucking need you."

Settling myself onto my back, Lucy climbs on top, her cunt hovering right above my face while she swallows my cock into her mouth once again. I forcibly push her down on me, her strap riding up, allowing my tongue to find her swollen clit while she moans around me, goosebumps exploding on my skin. I slide a finger, then another into her pussy, and fuck her while I suck on her clit, half-crazed off the taste of her desire.

I don't know how I'm going to last with her gagging around me, swallowing my cock down her throat while she grinds harder and harder on my face, heaven can't taste this fucking good.

After a few blissful minutes, she comes so sweetly. So brazenly.

And I'm left floating amongst the essence of her perfection.

Lucy barely takes a beat, flipping over to face me, that mischievous smile back on her beautiful lips. She slides up my chest, and I pull her up, my arms wrapping around her waist while she kisses me. "I can't wait to fuck you," she says against my lips.

I smirk, giving her ass a quick slap, and she lets out a small yelp, followed by a giggle.

"I want you inside me," I rasp.

Her hands fall to my thighs, pushing me open, bending my knees and letting my legs fall to the side—the anticipation heightening every small sensation. Slowly pulling out the plug, Lucy kneels in front of me, the baby blue dildo firmly between her palm as she applies lube to it, and then to me.

She lines herself up, her green eyes consumed by heat.

Licking her lips, her gaze fixed on mine, she slowly pushes herself inside, while her free hand strokes my cock in long languid strokes. The pleasure is full-body, engulfing, and rhapsodic.

Lucy is a vision I still don't believe I deserve. But I'm selfish and greedy and *starving* to drink her in large gulps, desperate to consume her just as she's consuming me.

Her hips thrust into me, every push adding to the fullness. I watch her. Lucy's eyes fixed on where we connect, her tongue idly trailing over her bottom lip, her chest heaving and I can tell the sight is turning her on which only makes it all the more pleasurable. "Just like that," I say coarsely, my hand gripping her thigh. "You can go deeper."

Her gaze is ablaze when it slides up to mine, her smile salacious as she does exactly that.

Eventually, she slows, and pulls out. "Turn around," she says.

Back on my knees, she pushes my face into the pillows, tugging my ass even higher, sliding the strap-on back in. "Hold on to your legs, spread yourself for me," she orders, and a shiver skitters down my spine, the tone of her voice scratching a part of my brain only she can reach. I do as she says, wrapping my arms around my thighs. The shift in position makes the dildo hit even deeper and I whimper.

Her hand softly caresses my back as if pleased with the sounds I'm making.

"You're so pretty like this," she says heatedly, her fingers still dancing down my back. Reaching around, her hand finds my throbbing, aching dick. "You're doing so well."

She hums deliciously, and laughs. It's wicked and so alluring, that it only takes a few more strokes of the dildo for my body to propel into mind-melting euphoria. It's intense, and drawn out—nothing I've experienced before

Lucy. But my cock is still hard, having not actually come yet and a few more strokes of Lucy's hand has the second orgasm barrel into me, coming all over the towel under us.

Out of breath, my body is ready to collapse when Lucy carefully pulls out, and I use the last of my strength to roll over.

Lucy watches me, a few curls sticking to her heated skin, an inquisitive smile on her pretty lips. "Did I do good?"

I sigh through a sated grin, tucking my arm behind my head. "You did amazing, Baby Blue."

With her hands idly caressing my thigh she tilts her head to the side as if studying me.

"What?" I ask.

She shakes her head and smiles even wider. And I don't think I've ever seen her this happy. "Nothing... I just love seeing you like this," she says softly.

"Like what?" I ask curiously.

"Free."

MORE FROM NAOMI LOUD

Don't miss out on the other stories in the "Was I Ever" series.

Sunny and Byzantine	Was I Ever Here
Lenix and Connor	Was I Ever Real

If you don't want to miss out on any future book announcements make sure to follow me on Instagram, TikTok & Facebook!

And if you loved Was I Ever Free, I'd be forever grateful if you could leave a positive review on Amazon. Your support is why indie authors can continue doing what we love. Thank you!

You can also join my newsletter to receive updates, teasers, giveaways and special deals.

www.naomiloud.com

ACKNOWLEDGMENTS

First, I would like to thank Meghan. You are the very pillar of my creativity and I can't imagine writing a book without your help. Are we in love??? Thank you, Summer, my author bestie, we sometimes share the same brain cell while writing our books and I wouldn't want it any other way.

Thank you to my readers, you are the reason I feel so seen, and you make my little Leo heart burst with joy and gratitude.

Thank you to my husband Aldo, for lending some of your personal history to Bastian. He wouldn't have been the multi-dimensional character without it. I love you forever and always.

Thank you to my alpha readers, Summer, Meghan, Bella, Maddy, Shaye, Isabella, and Jessy, as well as my beta readers, Janine, Dani, Kaylie, Kristie, and Laura. The book wouldn't be nearly as polished without all of your bullying so thank you, thank you, thank you.

Thank you to my proofreaders Salma, and Christana, to my graphic designer Mallory, and my sensitivity reader Lo. Thank you, Van, for gifting me the computer on which I became a published author, you are the kindest and sweetest and I will love you forever.

And most importantly, thank you to my editor Louise who inherently understands how my brain works and is always such a pleasure to work with.

Here's to many more books to come!! xox

ABOUT THE AUTHOR

Naomi Loud is an author of angsty dark romance. While her first love are words; spirituality and magic are the lenses through which she experiences the world and this heavily influences her writing. She lives in Montreal, Canada with her husband and three cats but secretly wishes she could live underwater.

Made in the USA
Columbia, SC
14 September 2023

22850590R00185